CASTAWAY ON THE ISLE OF DEVILS

Elisabeth Carson-Williams

Contents

PROLOGUE

"What's past is..."
~ Antonio,
The Tempest, Act 2, Scene 1

Chapter 1

Stratford, England, September 1610

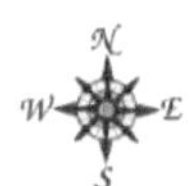

Silently sliding along the fire-warmed bench, Alice lay her head in Susanna's lap just as she had as a girl. She may be a young woman now, all of seventeen, but in this moment, she wished for nothing more than to escape into the comforts of childhood. She closed her eyes as her beloved cousin pulled a curl taut, an act so intimate she wanted to cry. How often had her mother done this and she'd swatted her hand away? Pulling the fabric of Susanna's skirt into her hand, she drew it to her nose and inhaled deeply. "Lavender. I didn't realize I missed it."

"I've placed some in your room, in the linens. Just like before," said Susanna Shakespeare Hall. She played with the tendrils of Alice's copper hair, still bright as though lit from within despite the sixteen-month absence. "I believed you were dead. I mourned for you. You and your mother." The crackling from the hearth punctuating her words, she sighed and said, "Well, let's just say there are herbs to help one sleep. And to calm the nerves during the day."

"Oh," mumbled Alice, sitting up. "I never considered you would miss me as much as I missed you. Our leaving was just *our* leaving. I'm sorry, truly I am. And I'm sorry for just reappearing on your doorstep after all this time. Returning here, to you and Uncle Willie, was all I could think about. It never occurred to me to send word."

"Shhh. You know what father says."

"*All's well that ends well,*" Alice mocked.

"I know you don't believe it, but you're a miracle. No word from you, from anyone, aboard the *Sea Venture* since May last year. Then, suddenly, here you are. All England believed you were dead—lost at sea or dashed upon the rocks of some deserted island."

"Except for me being dead, that's exactly what happened." Alice shrugged. "Instead, I'm right back where I started. Home in Stratford, whatever home means now. *The girl who survived,* as I'm to be known." She observed the fire, mumbling as though alone. "I wanted an adventure. I was so full of...of hubris. I was so, so—"

"Young. Young and indulged. Yes, your behavior verged on hedonism, a tendency you learned from your father. His only concerns social status and financial gain. He put all your lives in jeopardy. For that I won't forgive him."

"Don't speak of my father!" snapped Alice, pulling away. "You don't know anything about him. Or why we left. Besides, he's dead now. You shouldn't speak ill of the dead."

"Alice, you don't know he's dead. Not for a fact. And I know more than you realize. I've always known."

"I used to think I understood it all. But it turns out I knew nothing. And the few things I thought I knew? I was wrong. I got so much wrong. Thanks to my selfishness, my parents are dead. They're dead and it's my fault. That I do know." Alice stood to leave, but Susanna grabbed her arm and pulled her back onto the bench.

"But it isn't. You did not cause any of this."

"I want to believe you; I do. But walking through town, a town I grew up in? It's all foreign. As though my memory fails me. I don't recognize the life we used to have. My memories have lied to me. This isn't my home. That place wasn't my home. I have no home. Not anymore. And yes, it is all my fault."

"You're right: memories lie. They tell us what we want to hear. Want to feel guilty? Want to feel happy? Want to feel nostalgic? There's a memory for all of those. None of it is true and all of it is true. It's all perspective. And the change for you is growing up. Growing up means learning certain truths—uncomfortable truths. Things are always better as a child; the innocence shields us from realities. Now there's no hiding. But you are definitely wrong about not having a home. You do have a home. Will always have a home. With us. For as long as you need. Forever if necessary."

Susanna held Alice's face in her hands. Stroking the corners of the impish, almond-shaped eyes of the girl she'd known since birth, she promised, "And we'll always tell you the truth. Like it or not. You—we—just have to get through this tough bit."

Alice smiled at the sound of footsteps and off-key whistling in the hallway. Susanna nodded to the doorway, the whistling growing louder. "Father! Look who's finally awake."

"Ah, there she is! My little sprite," enthused William.

Alice straightened and stood up, welcoming the embrace of her beloved Uncle Willie. His warm arms providing scaffolding for her fragile emotions. Susanna was right—this felt like home.

"Uncle Willie," her voice broke.

"What's this about, little one?" he asked. He held her close, allowing her to feel the depth of her emotions, never chastising her for losing control, never hurrying her through them. Once the tears ebbed, she returned to the bench, Uncle Willie plopping between her and Susanna.

"You have no idea what I have witnessed." Alice bit the inside of her lip but offered no more.

"You've had adventures, my darling child. You've observed things people here only dream about. You've experienced the stuff of stories and myth," he gushed. "My dear, you were given a gift. A gift the likes of which I shall never have. To live in the New World! To travel across the ocean! To encounter the natives! Simply magical."

Alice wanted to believe she had been given a gift; that she had experienced something magical. To have his energy, his enthusiasm, his youthful, childlike exuberance for life. But alas, she didn't. Not anymore. She just felt so tired. And ungrateful. And resentful of his naïveté.

"It wasn't a gift. There was nothing magical about it. Not in the end. It was awful."

"'Not in the end.' You just said it yourself. Which means it was magical at some point." Uncle Willie took her hand in his. "Oh, my sweet child. It doesn't feel magical at the moment because you're too close to the event. However much you wish it never happened and run the other direction in every waking moment, it will find you. In dreams. In nightmares. It will haunt you the rest of your life. The past is prologue, which is precisely why now's the perfect time to write, when the emotion is raw, visceral. That's what makes a story interesting. You exorcise your demons."

"What if I'm the demon? I'm not proud of what I did," whispered Alice. "I don't want anyone to know just how wretched I am. How weak I am. How—"

"Human you are," he finished. "The only person who has to face the truth in all of this is you. And trust me, there are parts of ourselves none of us want to know. We all have demons. We are all demons. Which is why I love plays! Writing them. Performing them. It's also why people love watching them. It exorcises the demons, the parts of ourselves no one wants to address. You see, my dear, writing takes courage. The story is yours. You need simply turn the awful bits, the pain and horrors, into what seems fanciful, and voila! You have a story for all," Uncle Willie quipped, as though this were no great thing to accomplish, which, of course, to him—the Bard—it wasn't. "It's all about balance. So tell me: Did you experience glee? A moment of happiness or humor?"

Alice nodded.

"Well then, there you have it! Simply stir it all together. For balance. It's no matter if you embellish facts; there's no one in this country who can call you a liar. Only you saw what you saw. People don't concern themselves with facts. Most of these mutton-heads think the ocean is filled with serpents. So who's to say what you did on your journey? That scoundrel John Smith keeps writing, and people believe him. He even wrote about times he wasn't even in James Fort, and people believed him." Uncle Willie shook his head. "Now, the journal. You did keep the journal you were given for your journey, did you not?"

The question was rhetorical; and while she did not fancy lying to Uncle Willie, she didn't wish to disappoint either. Saying nothing, she averted her gaze.

"Did you at least make a few scribblings here and there? Just a few words and phrases perhaps? A sketch or two?" he asked.

Alice shook her head.

"Do you at least remember the main events?"

She nodded.

"Then you just fill in the rest. You're the magic." Uncle Willie winked. "People love a good story—it matters not that it's true. Just give them a story to remember. A story they can relate to. I guarantee you saw more than you realize. And as for the bad parts, it's your story. Share only what you want. But I can promise you this: England wants to hear what happened on the *Sea Venture*'s fateful journey. It sparks the imagination." He kissed her forehead. "It sparked my imagination. We'll speak of this later, when I'm not so harried and you have something to share. Perhaps I'll write a play about it!"

Winking, he left the two women in the sudden silence of the vacated room, a room ill-equipped to balance the void of his vivaciousness with the silent dust motes emanating from his wake in the sunlight.

⚓

Returning to her room, Alice stood in the doorway staring at the oak writing table at the opposite wall, the leather journal on top mocking her, reminding her of all she had seen, all she had experienced, all she had left unsaid. She walked slowly to the table, hesitant to touch the reminder, to open it, to confront her memories.

Sliding the chair from beneath the heavily oiled top, she hesitated. Closing her eyes, she focused on the once familiar sounds of her youth. A horse and cart passing on the street. The clip-clop of the hooves on hardened dirt. The chatter of house servants as they tended to their daily chores. If she concentrated, she could just make out the bleating of sheep in a nearby field. Much closer was the twittering of the wrens, nestled beneath the eaves of the roof outside her window. And that—what was that? Laughter. The laughter of children playing in the garden behind the house. These sounds, once so familiar, now sounded peculiar. These were not the sounds of the New World, of Bermuda or Jamestowne.

Slowly, Alice opened her eyes. She centered the journal in front of her, gently caressing the smooth leather, coaxing the pages to fill themselves with her stories, her memories. She fanned the pages, catching glimpses of names she wanted to remember. *Elizabeth. Thomas. Joanne. The Admiral.* Of incidents indelibly etched into her memory. *A wedding. Plates of freshly roasted pork. A noose.* Of things she grew to love. *Cahows. Sailing. Palmetto hearts.* Of things she grew to despise. *Storms. Strachey. Death.* An entity as real as any person she had met, Death had been her constant companion. Folding the journal to the middle, she pressed it flat against the table. Its empty, blank pages, cool beneath her fingertips, begging to be used. Forcing her to remember. Could she do it? Could she relive her life in the New World?

Her mother's voice came to her, calming her. As a young child, when she became overwhelmed and couldn't explain what was troubling her, her mother used magic to calm her. This particular magic didn't involve anything supernatural but could conjure memories nonetheless. She only need complete three simple tasks: close her eyes, take deep, chest-filling breaths, and go back to the beginning. Ever so carefully, her mother would coax her into examining details, small interactions, making each a vital part of the process. Thinking things through—start to finish—cleared the emotion from the narrative, helping to reveal the real story. Alice still considered the process magic and used it just as her mother had taught her.

Closing her eyes, Alice slowly, deliberately, controlled her breathing. Taking a breath in, counting to ten; exhaling until her lungs burned from the effort. "From the beginning." She spoke the words to the journal, her would-be co-conspirator, as she recounted her life of the past year, a life that had cheated Death at every turn.

Reaching for the quill, she placed a fingertip to the dull nib. Unwrapping it from the embroidered handkerchief, she exposed the paring knife. The finely embroidered handkerchief and the paring knife both gifts. Both linking her to another time, another place.

"Ow!" Alice winced, dropping the knife to the table. She'd nicked herself, the blade tip much sharper than she remembered. Scarcely a prick, but enough to elicit blood. As she watched the droplets fall onto the page, spreading along the line of fiber, she remembered Edward Samuel's head and the bloody shovel that ended his life. The first death of her adventure.

The first murder she witnessed.

"From the beginning," she whispered.

PART ONE

"More to know did never meddle with my thoughts"
~ Miranda,
The Tempest, Act 1, Scene 2

Chapter 2

Leaving London, 15 May 1609

"You checked your trunk before we left?" asked Maude Drinkard of her only child.

Alice nodded, watching as the laborers collected the passengers' belongings on the dock. Trunks heaped together. A desk. Some chairs. Cask upon cask of aqua vitae, or wine, or ale. Sacks of flour and oats.

"Once it's stowed away in wherever it is they keep belongings on a ship, you won't have access to it. It'll be months before you lay eyes on it again."

"Yes, Your Highness. And it's called the hold. Where our things will be kept is called the hold," corrected Alice smugly.

"I've asked you to call me Mother, or Mama, anything but—"

"And I still can't believe I only have one trunk. For everything I will need for the rest of my life. I know we're allowed six, which means I'm entitled to one more. Two each, father said so," argued Alice.

"You'll have one. We all have one. We're lucky to have that. The small chest will be with us in our quarters. The rest will be in the *hold*." She drew the word out to let her daughter know she'd been heard. Her Highness watched her daughter roll her eyes to the heavens. "We're all making sacrifices, Alice. Can you not, just this once, try to be more agreeable?" With a swish of skirts, her mother moved away from her toward the front of the ship. Preparing for a trip to the New World had left them all flustered and on edge. They were all ready to leave and begin their adventure. Their new life.

The necessities had been purchased and packed weeks ago—things such as Castile soap, combs, and a linen pouch filled with rosemary wood for a toothbrush. Her Highness had even insisted on packing alum and orrisroot to protect against any malodorous emissions, which if the rumors were true would certainly be the case in the hot and humid community of Jamestowne. Nothing in her trunk hadn't been used regularly her whole life. Nothing special to denote they were embarking on an adventure. Her Highness had even packed lavender in with the clothing, a nicety Alice liked but would never admit even though she despised her new clothing, all except the yellow dress.

Her Highness had taken a keen interest in Alice's garments for the trip, and insisted she have all new items, despite the cost and her father's rebukes. The Virginia Company had provided a clothing requirement list for the men, which Alice felt was of little use for the females making the journey, but Her Highness declared it to be a useful guideline nonetheless.

"It's the first time they've really encouraged women to be a part of such an opportunity. The first for families. I would think you'd be pleased there weren't rules for this," she explained. "You can't expect men to think of everything. They're far too busy with running a new settlement. I'm perfectly capable of determining what we need. With a little modification, we shall be as properly outfitted as the men."

After numerous outings to choose material and visit a seamstress, Alice had the appropriate wardrobe for travel. Tucked into her one personal trunk were one yellow satin dress, one pair of silk hose, a pair of silk gloves, two aprons—to protect her dresses—a muslin sleeping gown, a cloak, and one pair of sturdy leather shoes. Alice smiled at the yellow dress, the bright yellow gleaming against the deep brown of the mahogany trunk. She could still feel the delicate material slide between her fingers as she folded it, covering it in tissue paper to make sure it made the journey safely. Of all the garments she had been fitted for, this was the only one she insisted on, much to her mother's chagrin. Her mother had insisted on a formal gown, a gown Alice intrinsically understood to be her marriage dress, so she fought for it to be yellow, a color deemed unlucky for a wedding. But Alice would not be dissuaded. She forced her mother's hand with a deal: let this dress be yellow, and she would comply with the numerous fittings required for so impractical a garment, given they were going to a frontier settlement. Her Highness, dubious about the promise, agreed. She'd won that round, but lost on another front.

Alfred, the blacksmith's son. The blacksmith's son with the toothy grin that made her cheeks hot. The blue eyes that sparkled with mirth whenever she suggested they take the horses into the woods, away from her mother and prying eyes. The boy she had loved since her tenth year, the year her father gave her the palfrey, and a reason to visit the blacksmith's shop. If she had her way, she'd marry him. And he wouldn't care if she wore yellow.

Now, watching their trunks travel the length of the gangplank, Alice smiled, appreciating what was actually in her trunk. Carefully hidden in the folds of the new items were a few select items she deemed necessary: a too-short skirt and a threadbare blouse, the silver and coral teething stick her grandmother had given her as an infant, and Susanna and Uncle Willie's exquisite gifts: a calfskin leather journal with brass buckles to ensure her thoughts never escaped and a graphite pencil, a gift from a wealthy patron to the playwright who abhorred anything but quill and ink. *It's horrible for me*, he had insisted, *but perfect for a world-traveler such as yourself.* Susanna convinced her to take a sewing kit of pins, needles, thread, thimbles, and scissors, which she placed for safekeeping in her mother's jewelry box, a box Alice had stolen on a whim after being denied her second trunk. Hidden amongst the folds of the yellow dress, the box now contained all her worldly possessions. Feeling quite clever, Alice had locked the trunk and stored the key in the secret pouch sewn into the waistband of her skirt. She may only have one trunk, but it was hers and the key would remain with her.

Enjoying the start of her adventure, Alice initially failed to notice the man in the green britches, strutting about the dock as though he were in charge. As no one took any notice of him, not listening as he loudly complained and gave directions, she took him for a civil servant looking to improve his position, but when he almost knocked a man off the gangway, then proceeded to shout at him as though it were the laborer's fault and not the other way round, they all took notice. He was rude to the laborers, shouting for them to "Clear out" and "Pick that up" when he was clearly not in charge. His pinched face a permanent sneer, his nose so long and pointed he'd no choice but to peer over it.

"He seems a disagreeable lot," observed Her Highness.

Alice nodded; then she heard someone call to him.

"Mr. Strachey? Mr. William Strachey," came the voice, a soft tenor with the staccato pronunciation of someone raised with privilege.

"Ah, Mr. Gates," said Strachey, straightening his back. "Thomas. It's wonderful to make your acquaintance."

Gates grimaced at the impropriety of being addressed so casually by someone he'd just met. Alice eyed Strachey suspiciously, taking in his countenance: worn, scuffed shoes; a coat mended at the hem, the stitching visible as though done in a hurry; one mismatched button. This man's impertinence, combined with his shabby clothing, reeked of desperation. And to not address a knighted man by his title? That was not oversight; that was choice. A poorly calculated choice.

Bowing his head slightly, Strachey feigned decorum. "Forgive me, Sir Thomas Gates. I only meant to express my relief at finally finding you. I have some suggestions," he groveled, as he followed Gates onto the quarter deck.

Alice's gaze followed William Strachey, Uncle Willie's nemesis. Now she had a face to go with the name. And, unfortunately, she would be sharing a boat ride with him to Jamestowne.

William Strachey, a man with the same initials as her beloved Uncle Willie, had tried various schemes to get his own writing published. Strachey claimed, according to Susanna, to be responsible for a line in Willie's play *King Lear*, but Uncle Willie never acknowledged it. Uncle Willie and his friends often joked about the little man from Essex who wanted to overtake him as the court's favorite, to buy his way into the theatre, but little had come of it. Even his friendship with John Donne, a poet of some note, had not yielded a benefactor. His goal, if one were to believe rumor, was to overtake Uncle Willie as the best writer in England. His reputation, not rumor, was of a ne'er-do-well who postured more than produced. While his family at one time had money, and even a coat of arms to show for it, he was not of their ilk. No, his reputation for squandering money, while simultaneously refusing to do work, made him the butt of jokes. And here he was, a fellow traveler on the *Sea Venture*. Alice narrowed her eyes and screwed her mouth. Why was he here? What could possibly make him join an expedition? It was well known he was a man of limited means, so how did he buy his way into the Virginia Company? He clearly wasn't one of the laborers or servants who would work off their debt, so what was he playing at? Alice would keep a sharp eye on him, as she would anyone who'd bedeviled her beloved uncle. He'd already tried to pass his signature off as the Bard's, so he clearly could not be trusted. She would find out what this foppish man was planning. And as they were on the same vessel, it shouldn't be that hard to discern.

As Alice watched the sailors cast off from the dock, she felt the ship slip its moorings; momentarily unbalanced, she grabbed the edge of the gunwale. Her father grasped her elbow lightly to steady her, while Her Highness placed a hand on her shoulder. Their family of three watched in wonder as they began their slow descent down the Thames. Throngs of spectators emerged to cheer the fleet of ships bound for Jamestowne. All of them waving, shouting, some crying. Alice waved until her shoulders balked at the strain. These people, her people, understood her importance. Her presence in this fleet ensured her significance in the world. Her mission, the fleet's mission, to save James Fort for England, presented her with the grandest adventure imaginable, complete with a mission to save the world. Being the object of such an outpouring of support gave Alice a renewed purpose in their mission, their adventure. It made life with her mother more bearable.

Her Highness stood still, rooted in her spot, staring at some fixed point Alice was unable to discern. Her father lowered his voice. "I did as you requested: I've secured us passage on the flagship, with the best navigator in England, Captain Christopher Newport. He's made this journey six times; we couldn't be safer on the ocean." Still no response. "And the Governor is here with us. This is as good as it gets." His jaw tightened, the little muscles near his ears fluttering like butterflies.

Attempting to lighten her father's mood, Alice lowered her voice in imitation. "Damn it, Maude, the *Sea Venture* is a three-hundred-ton vessel specifically designed for the transport of one hundred and fifty people and supplies across the Atlantic to the settlement at Jamestowne. Unlike other vessels in the fleet, the armament has been placed on the main deck, allowing for extended cargo storage. Passengers will have enough room to ship anything they wish to take, while also allowing the Company to transport food and supplies to sustain a settlement population of five hundred for a year. Its design is for speed on the open ocean. The three bilges"—Alice glanced at her father as *bilge* was a word only recently added to her vocabulary—"make it unique to this type of transport, as—"

"Enough," huffed her father.

"Whatever do you mean, Papa?" she said, fluttering her lashes. "I was only—"

"Don't be impertinent, child," snapped Her Highness.

Her parents considered one another, then straightening their backs, wordlessly turned and walked away: her father returning to Gates and Strachey, her mother further along the deck.

A boy on the shore waved like a child possessed. His small arms raised above his head, he jumped up and down hoping to be noticed, the only person still standing on the shore of the Thames. The *Sea Venture* floated along the river, the water changing from a brown excrement-littered gash through London to a lighter brown as they entered the countryside.

Alice scrutinized the child on the shore; raising her hand to return the wave, she watched the grin spread across the child's face. She smiled back, waving until she could no longer see him, the last of the revelers celebrating the fleet long since dispersed.

Resting against the gunwale, Alice watched the other ships follow in their wake like cygnets on a pond, their ship the swan—larger, newer, the definition of beauty and grace. Alice watched London recede. All she had ever known, her home, her Alfred, Uncle Willie and Susanna, all part of the vanishing horizon.

For sixteen years she dreamed of trading her ordinary, scripted life for something spontaneously extraordinary. It was childish, she realized, but she imagined traveling with her father to a faraway land, where they'd meet exotic people, encounter unusual animals, experience a different climate, preferably one with more sun. Anything different than what she'd see from her bedroom window on any given day. She'd prayed for this. But now, standing on board, she could feel the sadness at what was left behind spreading through her body. Alfred foremost in her mind: his lopsided grin whenever she came near; the blush on his cheeks when she kissed him; his tears when she told him of their departure. The short walk to Susanna and Uncle Willie. No more afternoons spent with games or a story to chase away the gloom. Her grandmother, with curses for Her Highness, but hugs for her *dear, sweet Alice*. The last words her grandmother spoke as they left: "Leaving an old woman to fend for herself—you should be ashamed! If I never hear from any of you again, it will be too soon!" Then slamming the door before her mother could respond. Alice smiled; she'd miss the old termagant.

Unlike other travels, this one would allow no contact with any of her loved ones. If she were traveling to Italy or France, she could write, tell of her grand adventures, perhaps even send gifts, or, if fortune followed her, be allowed to visit on high holy days. But from the New World—from Jamestowne? None of it was possible. She would be cut off from all she'd known. It was exciting to think about being untethered from her boring, daily life, free to do as she pleased; it was a completely different thing to realize the cost of such freedom.

Hearing the gold bracelets as they clanged together, Alice felt Her Highness return to her. "You got your grand adventure; I hope you appreciate what a fortunate daughter you are," she hissed.

Alice trained her eyes on the water, never acknowledging she'd been spoken to. Perhaps if she didn't speak, or look at her, she would disappear. But she could hear it breathing, loud intakes of air, followed by grumbling exhalations. Then it continued to talk.

"I understand you didn't want me to come. I had little desire to make this sacrifice, but there was no choice. Family must always take precedence, especially for our children, however ungrateful."

"Ungrateful?" snorted Alice. "Why should I be grateful to you? You planned to marry me off to that...that...Mr. Cyrus! When you know I love Alfred! And all so you can have your trinkets, your gold bangles, your emerald brooches. You were willing to sell me to the highest bidder just so you can fill—" She stopped. She couldn't let her know about the jewelry box, not yet. "Just to buy more velvet gowns. And we both know why you came on this adventure—so you can ruin it for me and Papa, just like you ruin everything. You talk of family, of sacrifice, but what do you know of it?" Stalking away, Alice carefully balanced her steps with the gentle rocking of the ship as she moved to the ladder. Descending to the tween deck, her cheeks grew hot as she glanced once more at the maddingly unperturbed figure of her mother. She hated she couldn't stomp down the ladder, so she showed her displeasure the only way she could in a tight-lipped "Arrgh."

"You know nothing," whispered her mother, watching her only daughter slip beneath the deck.

Chapter 3

First Night On Board, May 1609

Night fell just as it had at home: without ceremony, without fanfare. Without Alfred. Alice expected life on a ship—a key element of her grand adventure—to be exciting, perhaps even enchanting. She had been here less than eight hours and she was already bored.

It started with their quarters, once an elegant idea, in reality a different prospect: thin wood tacked up to form a windowless enclosure more suited for animals than humans. A small bed attached to the wall. An even smaller pallet on the floor. A space, just big enough for their travel chest, between the bed and wall. The entire cabin barely bigger than a cupboard.

"I'll take the pallet," volunteered Alice as she watched bugs crawl on the surface of the straw-filled sack atop the bed frame. Crinkling her nose, she concluded she wouldn't be staying. Her real plan: to sleep in open quarters with some of the girls closer to her age. Servants, certainly, but should there really be a division of class on board a ship? She didn't think so. Besides, Uncle Willie and Susanna had encouraged her to meet all sorts people for a more fulfilling adventure. Uncle Willie claimed really interesting stories came from people who didn't adhere to social convention, from people not too ashamed to enjoy all the bawdiness life offered. Alice thought it sound advice, and had made her plan.

She spent the afternoon roaming the ship. Climbing up and down ladders between the decks, enjoying the views from the top deck, not returning to their quarters unless ordered. She was looking for the girls, for the open sleeping area they would inhabit. A complete waste of time: there were no other girls her age, servant or otherwise. In fact, there were very few women on board at all. Despite the Company encouraging families, their ship contained only four other women: the Goodwives Rolfe and Eason, Mistress Horton and her maidservant Miss Persons—the only other single woman on the ship besides herself. Alice nearly cried realizing the majority of time would be spent in close proximity to Her Highness.

That night, Alice lay awake on her pallet. Thank goodness her father had the foresight to commission a mattress for her, a down-and-wool-filled pillow of luxury tucked into the one trunk wedged into their quarters. It was small consolation for sharing the space with her exceedingly flatulent mother. With no windows the farts remained trapped within their dank wooden stall, the smell making her stomach lurch. First thing tomorrow, she would seek out a place away from this box of fetid air. She may have to spend nighttime in here, but she would be damned if all her days were spent like this. Her resolve was punctuated by another of her mother's farts, this one so powerful Alice swore she felt her hair move.

As she watched the lantern swing from the beam in time with the ship's swaying, Alice considered the argument from the night before. There had been terse words regarding the journey over the months of preparation, so why argue the night before departure? Why did her mother persist in vexing her father?

"The mattress was a nice gift," mocked her mother, "considering."

"Woman! You have no right to condemn me, not with what you've spent to outfit her. A satin dress indeed."

"We're representing the Virginia Company, are we not? We need to make sure we're not mistaken for others who may be traveling for nefarious reasons. Isn't that what you said?" she hissed, as she plopped onto the seat of the nearest chair, her bracelets clanging into the wooden armrest, the legs groaning under her weight.

"How dare you," her father growled. "If we're ever to be solvent, Jamestowne is our one opportunity."

"And what of Alice's marriage to Mr. Cyrus? What if we don't survive? Or worse, what if we fail and have to return?" asked her mother undeterred. "What then?"

"I will not have your dissent—not now. We were united when I struck this arrangement."

"We were never *united* in this arrangement! Need I remind you why we even need this arrangement? It was my money you gambled away; it's my money currently being used to house your mother. A woman who is certainly capable of remarrying, rather than saddling us with her upkeep." Tapping her rings against the hand rest, she continued to speak. "I appreciate the scheme; it may save us yet, but I fear for Alice. Robert, she's sixteen, nearly a woman. She doesn't need to be in the wilds of a new land, with God knows what dangers. And men—men who haven't seen women in quite some time. Some who've never been in the company of a lady. Can they be trusted? With a young woman present?"

"Don't you think I've considered that? Especially after Bertie—" He stopped. "No, I think it's worth the risk. Besides, you're unnecessarily focused on mere physical discomforts, what might or might not happen. We're perfectly safe. We're shareholders in the Virginia Company," he declared. "I don't think they'd encourage families to go if it weren't suitable for wives and daughters."

"Unless it's others like us," mumbled her mother. "Families who have no more options. With nothing left to lose but their lives."

Her father had stormed out the room, taking no notice of her. Now, in the dark fetid cabin of the ship, the phrase *no more options* refused to let her rest. What was really at stake for them? She had been relieved she wouldn't be marrying Mr. Cyrus—Father had seen to that, but now she worried they left because of a more ominous situation, a situation much more threatening than one complaining girl and an undesirable marriage.

Chapter 4

Plymouth, England, 20 May–1 June 1609

On the fifth day, they arrived in Plymouth, a port city. Alice had never visited a port city; it sounded quite exotic. She rose with the sun in anticipation. She dressed, carefully placing her belongings in the trunk before heading topside. As she opened the door, the rope handle scratching her hand, her father stirred.

"There's nothing to get excited about. It's just a place to load the remaining supplies and animals. And meet the new admiral," he mumbled, his voice still thick with sleep.

"I know. But I'd still like to see." She slid through to the narrow hallway before he could stop her.

Alice thought about the real reason she was excited: today she'd finally meet the girl from the *Blessing*, one of their companion ships. Each day at mid-morning, the girl waved to her. A wave so enthusiastic Alice feared the girl tumbling over the railing into the water. Even though there were to be nine ships in the fleet, she only ever saw the *Blessing*. Or, perhaps, she only noticed as there was always a flailing figure on deck poignantly gesturing to her. With any luck, they would have two weeks to get to know one another before the fleet left on the final leg for James Fort.

As the *Sea Venture* entered the harbor, Alice felt a surge of energy; she was downright giddy with anticipation. Her jovial spirit buoyed further by the harbor scene unfolding before her: ships of every description and size surrounded them; some with cannons still visible through port windows; others with port windows closed. Men yelling to one another between vessels or to others on the docks. There were flags from other countries, other kingdoms, the accents and foreign words humming pleasurably in her ears. Looking to the shore, she felt her heart soar as she had not expected such beauty. The lush green hillside looked like the luxurious velvet of a fine gown. She closed one eye, and her fingers followed the curves of the hill until dropping to the white cliffs that suddenly gave way to the sea below. It took her breath away.

Looking to the shore, she watched a crane load a lone stallion onto a waiting ship. The majestic creature shone like polished obsidian in the sun, held aloft in a canvas cradle, its legs protruding through holes in case he wanted to gallop on clouds. She knew horses could swim, so why not let them swim to the ship? Or gracefully prance up the gangplank? Held aloft in a sack, such a demeaning way for so majestic a creature to board a ship. Alfred would be astonished at the sight. *You must remember, for the journal.* She chided herself for tucking the gift away into her trunk.

Initially, two weeks loading sounded like a boring interlude to an otherwise exciting adventure; now, she hoped there would be enough time to explore the hills with her new friend and watch the cranes load animals. Alice was exuberant as they disembarked, so much so she didn't bother to shrug off the vice-grip Her Highness placed on her elbow as they navigated the crowded dock. The docks were teeming with people, a mixture of sailors, merchants, laborers, artisans, and families, some with servants, most without. Alice allowed herself to be guided, easier to look about as she pleased and not pay full attention to her steps. She bumped into a sailor carrying a cask, and Her Highness pulled her close, as though she were a priceless possession. Alice muttered an apology, the sailor merely cursing continued on his way, unabated by something as small and inconsequential as she. She heard the curses, and stifled a giggle as they continued toward their lodging, a local nunnery known to be clean and hospitable.

It wasn't uncommon for travelers to stay in places affiliated with religious orders, but she herself had never even entered one. She had heard of them, of course, but now foremost in her mind was the phrase Uncle Willie used: *Get thee to a nunnery.* He often joked women, especially undesirable ones, should get to a nunnery. Maybe Father planned to leave Her Highness here. Alice smiled at the image of her mother left behind as they sailed away to life in the New World.

But what if this didn't have anything to do with Her Highness? What if it was for *her*? What if this was the option instead of marrying Mr. Cyrus? She screwed her face and decided to be as noncompliant as possible. Perhaps if she was intolerable, she would be free to do as she liked; the nuns would reject her as incorrigible, and her father would have to take her to Jamestowne. But what if the rumors were true and nunneries really did have special rooms for girls and women who refused to behave? These rooms were inescapable, and permanent. Was this her mother's idea? To teach her a lesson? Only women stayed here. The men were at an inn. It would be easy to discard her here, while Her Highness traveled on to the New World and the riches that awaited them. And no one would even know she existed. They'd all believe she had simply vanished in the New World.

Alice's anger at her mother, at her mother's need to argue with her father, fueled her walk up the hill. She trailed behind Her Highness as they climbed the hill to the nunnery. Gone was the excitement of exploring the lush green vegetation, replaced by a nagging suspicion she didn't know the real reason for this journey or, at the very least, she had been fooled into thinking it was to be an adventure. She scanned her surroundings for a quick escape should she need one. She was quite certain, if need be, she could find her way back to Stratford and the home of Uncle Willie and Susanna. They would welcome her back.

Alice's concerns left her mind when she saw the girl standing at the doorway waving, bouncing excitedly on the balls of her feet. Alice recognized this—not the girl, she'd never met this girl—but the waving and bouncing. This was familiar. These same gestures greeted her each morning as she looked to the *Blessing*, a smaller ship that glided alongside them like a dog trails its master. Alice pushed past Her Highness and straight toward the girl. Laughing as though they were long-lost friends finally united, Alice announced, "It's you! The girl from the *Blessing*!"

"Aye, 'tis me," she exclaimed. "Joanne of the *Blessing*, at your service." She bowed deeply, then doubled over laughing. "I'm so glad to finally meet you. Father vowed I would meet new people. I love meeting new people, but there was only one other girl on our ship." She pointed to the girl behind her. "That's Jane. You never saw her—she never went on deck. Never even came on deck at all, did you? I'd remember. I'd have had someone to talk to. But no, she stayed below with some of the other women. Good thing she has me. Especially now on dry land. No need to stay with those old crones now. Get some fresh air. Enjoy the sunlight. She's nice enough, though. She doesn't talk much, but then I talk too much. But I've always talked too much. Mother has warned me it is a trait people find annoying, but I think she's just saying that because I'm usually only around her and she likes quiet. Ah, listen to me! Doing it again. What's your name?"

"Alice." She'd barely uttered her name when the girl started up again.

"Alice, that's a nice name. I've never met anyone with that name. So, you're my first friend named Alice. Congratulations! Oh, I do hope we'll be friends; we'll need female friends once we arrive. I was worried it would only be men—not even boys—and I would be bored with no one to talk to except Mother. She's awful to try to talk to. She's so serious. Well, not at the moment. At the moment she's furious with Father. That's him." She pointed to a man Alice had seen speaking with her father daily.

"Mr. Pearce? He's on the *Sea Venture*, with us. My father knows him."

"And therein lies the problem," confirmed Joanne. "We're assigned to the *Blessing*. Mother is so angry, she's now refusing to speak to him. But I think it's quite a stroke of luck. Mother is nowhere near as strict as Father; I'll be able to do as I please while on board." She smiled. "I can't believe how liberating it all is. You know, at one point I dreaded this trip. Having to leave all my friends behind. I wept for two whole days! I even used a curse word I'd hear my maidservant use! Then I discovered we would be on separate ships and I thought, now this could be fun." Joanne pulled the two girls into a circle, placing her arms round their shoulders. Making sure her mother wasn't within earshot, she whispered, "Mother has done nothing but weep since we left London. She didn't want to come at all, and she was seasick the entire first day we were aboard the *Blessing*—and we weren't even at sea! How does one get sick on a river? Is river sickness a thing? Anyway, it's fortunate for me. Father is on another ship and Mother is sick or crying all day every day, so I am free to meet people, the wrong sorts, of course, but that's what makes this so exciting. So, I—"

Alice cut her off, one had to if there were to be any other interaction.

"Are your parents with you?" Alice asked Jane.

"I'm being sent as I was requested," mumbled Jane.

"Excuse me?" asked Alice. "I don't understand—you were requested?" Alice's brows knitted, while Joanne stood mute, fixated on kicking a rock with the toe of her shoe.

"My parents are dead, and my uncle is my ward. He made a deal with a man, a friend of his already at James Fort. I am to marry him. My uncle claims this marriage will secure my future. We will all be rich. As the Virginia Company prospers, so shall we." Jane's words were flat, as though memorized from a pamphlet.

"Why didn't he just come to you? You could have a proper introduction and a wedding ceremony. Then he could go back and you could stay with your family," said Alice.

"He's under contract with the Virginia Company," Jane stated, as though this were common knowledge. "I was told I had to go to him. It's part of the deal."

Alice and Joanne stared at the orphan before them, as she casually explained her purpose.

"This supply is to help populate the fort. As his wife, until I give birth, I will be expected to help establish the fort. We all will. Nothing too complicated for a woman, just washing and cooking. Running our own homes. 'Tis quite an honor to run your own home as you see fit." Jane forced her mouth into what she must have conceived as a grin.

Looking at her, Alice guessed them to be approximately the same age, but there was no youthful exuberance. There was no girlish chattering like Joanne nor any innocence in the demands of domesticity. Instead, she presented the determined look of a young woman committed to obedience and survival. Alice thought of Uncle Willie and how he abhorred bad actors. She'd never really understood that until now; Jane was a bad actor. She may pretend to be stoic and resigned, but Alice felt her anger. The rage radiating beneath the surface, the same rage she'd harbored for years: the rage of always being beholden to someone else.

"We will prosper, ha!" Joanne snorted. "But you get a husband out of it. I'm excited for that." She rolled her eyes.

Jane just stared.

"You said we are all expected to help at the fort?" Alice shook her head. "And that this supply is to help populate the fort?" She pointed to herself and Joanne. "I am absolutely positive I am not here to help populate a fort." She contemplated Mr. Cyrus, what a forced marriage would feel like if her father hadn't secured them this passage, if she hadn't had a father who wanted her happy. Being left at the nunnery may not be such a horrible idea, in this circumstance. Not wanting to offend, she kept her opinion to herself, commending herself on her maturity and resolve.

"No, you're here to work. At least, for now. Encouraging families to travel together was a ruse, to keep the men happy."

Alice and Joanne exchanged a glance.

"Why did you think the Company pushed so hard to have women on this voyage? Why do you think there are so many families present?" Jane asked.

"To pay off gambling debts," muttered Alice.

"No, silly. To keep our fathers company. To keep families together. To ensure the men don't get lonely." Joanne rattled off the list without hesitation. "My mother says we are going to provide stability. She believes, as does the Company, if the men have their families, they will be more successful, and the more successful we are the more money we will make. Besides, I've never done *work*"—a word that prompted hand flailing—"I don't even know how to wash or cook! I can embroider; we all can. But work? I think you are mistaken. We are not *all* expected to help or populate. My father knows me; he knows Mother. He knows better than anyone we have no such skills. We're not laborers." She spit the word *laborers* out as one would a sour cherry.

Alice flinched. She didn't want to offend, as it was clear Jane did not have their advantages and was at the mercy of an uncle, but were they really expected to do work? And when would this work start? Immediately upon arrival? Or in the fall, say, for harvest? Certainly not every day. She could understand them being expected to help with events such as a wedding, but what else would require work? Was her father aware of this expectation? Was he too expected to work? She doubted he agreed with any of this. He would have told her, surely. What about her lessons? Alice decided to keep her mouth shut and start observing more. While it was nice to have two friends, Jane made her question how much any of them actually understood about Jamestowne or their mission.

The time in Plymouth went much quicker than Alice expected. While not every day could be spent with her new friends, most days she could at least catch up with them at supper, a mundane affair in the nunnery dining hall. Mutton, the local specialty, served with an ale spicier than she liked. The bread, however, was scrumptious, especially when paired with the hard-rind cheese from Cherbourg.

With only two full days remaining in Plymouth, *in England*, she reminded herself, Her Highness agreed to an afternoon stroll in the surrounding hillside. Goody Pearce, Joanne's mother, would also be with them. Her Highness and Goody Pearce made an interesting pairing; unlike the incessant talking of her daughter, Goody Pearce had little to say, and what she did say came out as scolding no matter to whom she spoke. Her Highness tried to engage her in conversation, about their lives, their interests, but after an hour the two women had ceased speaking, instead staring listlessly at the ships in the harbor. Sitting with her friends, Alice watched her mother; had she always been so alone?

"Are you even listening to me?" asked Joanne, pulling on Alice's sleeve. "I was just saying..."

Following her mother's gaze, Alice too stared at the ships in the harbor, focusing on the sounds of ships being loaded, her friend's voice consigned to the wind.

For two weeks, Alice had listened to Joanne prattle on and on about various and sundry topics from what they might do once they arrived in Jamestowne—making a fur coat from a bear—assigning names to her future children—Barnabus if it's a boy, Beatitude if it's a girl. Just childish dribble meant to while away the hours, but Jane never made any attempt to join in. While Joanne's incessant nattering rendered conversations decidedly one-sided, even when prompted, Jane offered nothing. In fact, Jane rarely spoke. Alice tried to engage her, but Jane spoke so softly Alice was never completely sure she had heard the full response. Perhaps once the sea voyage was completed, and they were settled in James Fort, she would become more sociable. But, like Her Highness, at the moment she appeared utterly alone. Ignoring the incessant chatter of Joanne, Alice took a new approach with Jane.

"We'll be with you, in James Fort. I mean, if you're afraid of your...of your..." She was unsure of what to call the man Jane was to meet and marry. Was he yet her fiancé? Was it too soon to say husband? She finally settled on a word: "Your man. When you meet your man, we can help you set up your house. You won't be completely alone; you'll have us."

Jane stared at the grass, saying nothing. Alice wasn't sure she had heard her, but then the soft voice emerged, answering in a whisper so light Alice had to lean in. "I'll be fine. But thank you."

Alice had never heard a thank you as sincere as the one uttered by the young woman in front of her and, for a brief moment, she saw the muscles in Jane's jaw unclench. She reached to touch her hand, to let her know the offer was sincere, but Jane flinched and jerked her hand away. The moment gone; the distrust back in place.

Placing her hands in her lap, Alice thanked God her life hadn't been like Jane's. She may have to contend with Her Highness, but at least she hadn't been forced to marry a stranger in a frontier settlement to survive. Alice thought about the other women in the nunnery: how many of them were in the same predicament as Jane?

Alice lay on the thin straw ticking the nuns called a mattress, wondering how best to spend her last day in England. The mattress scratched and pricked her backside as she tried to get comfortable. She fumed at Her Highness for having left their trunk, and her mattress, on board. She rubbed a spot on her thigh, convinced she was being eaten alive by bugs. Her mind churned through how they might have gained access to this small cell of a room. Unable to gnaw their way through the granite walls, might they have been brought by other travelers? Was she being eaten by foreign bugs? She lay still, listening for the soft rustling of their legs as they maneuvered inside the ticking. But instead, there was only the preternatural silence of being enclosed in stone. She felt the stones closing in, pushing on her chest, making breathing more difficult. Without a window, she could feel the air thinning around her. She closed her eyes, imagined herself back on the ship. The open air of the ship's deck. The sun on her skin. She felt her chest loosen.

Father had not lied about there being other girls, nor was she to stay at the nunnery permanently. All those concerns were for naught, and with one day left on dry land, her insides felt quivery for starting the final leg of their grand adventure. Not only were two girls her age traveling to Jamestowne, she actually liked them. Her fears of compatibility being quashed made the lonely voyage with only Her Highness tolerable. Only she, of the three, would be on the *Sea Venture*; they on the *Blessing* at least had each other. No matter. When they got to Jamestowne they would reunite. *Your merry band of three*, she could hear Uncle Willie exclaim in her mind. She and Joanne with their parents, and Jane with her new husband. With any luck, he would be a man Jane would come to love; at the very least, he could be tolerated and not unkind. She sighed deeply as she thought of Alfred; their love felt as natural as breathing. Too bad Jane didn't have that.

"Zounds," grumbled Her Highness, struggling to get comfortable.

Alice waited as she settled into position. Not hearing snoring, she figured her mother was still awake.

"Let's view the animals tomorrow," whispered Alice.

"Animals?"

"Yes. The animals are to be loaded tomorrow. I thought perhaps we could watch."

Her Highness didn't respond.

"We can watch from the hoe. You like that. I saw you smile while we were there."

"Aye, I did," conceded Her Highness.

"And I was thinking, perhaps Joanne or Jane could join us."

Alice heard the long exhale. "I'm not sure of Goody Pearce's plans for the morrow."

"She isn't very agreeable, is she? But it would be lovely to see Joanne and Jane one last time before we leave. It'll be months before we're together again. And there are no other girls on our ship."

"That is true."

"If we're lucky, Goody Pearce will be busy, and just the girls can join us. I don't think Joanne and her mother get on well, so I doubt if she'd mind staying behind. Oh, please say you'll ask. It would mean so much," she stated hopefully.

"Perhaps," said Her Highness.

"Thank you," whispered Alice. Closing her eyes, content with the prospect of a day spent walking the lush hills, she fantasized Alfred was with her, as she frequently did at night. She hugged herself tightly and imagined ending each day in his arms. As soon as she could return to England, this could be her reality. *Keep praying*, she told herself. *You'll be with him soon enough.*

Chapter 5

Last Day in Plymouth, England, 2 June 1609

Inhaling the salt air, Alice settled in to watch the harbor, her skin already pinking in the mid-morning sun. She watched the ships, their gentle rocking on the waves as the tide pulled out. Tomorrow, they too would pull out. While disappointed her friends couldn't join her for one last day in England, without Joanne's incessant chatter there was space to think. Here, in the solitude of the hills, Jane's words echoed in her mind: *we are expected to work.*

Sitting next to her on the ground, Her Highness moved closer to her daughter, their knees nearly touching. Alice watched the hurried activity of the harbor as people readied the ships for emigration. She ignored her mother for as long as possible, but had to acknowledge the handkerchief proffered. Taking the linen cloth, she opened it to find a narrow wedge of cheddar, the pale yellow of the cheese barely perceptible against the ivory of the linen. Looking more closely at the handkerchief, she noticed two distinct daffodils embroidered onto one corner, beneath them a sky-blue *M*.

"'Tis a sampler I made as a girl," said Her Highness. "I loved crewelwork in my younger years, before you or...well. I'd hoped I might do some on the ship, but there's not enough light in our cabin, and the deck is too windy. Perhaps another time."

Taking a nibble from the wedge, Alice studied the woman next to her. It was hard to imagine Her Highness as a girl, enjoying her crewelwork. Harder still was imagining Her Highness being told what to do and how to behave.

"It is thrilling, is it not?" continued Her Highness. "To see how many people are involved with running our small town of a ship."

Alice grunted.

"I know you're disappointed you're not with your friends, but there will be plenty of time for gossip and frivolity when we arrive in Jamestowne," she said quietly. "There'll be much more adventure and exploring to be done there."

Alice thought she heard a slight hitch in her voice, prompting her to look at Her Highness. *She's not very old*, she realized. *Some lines at the corners of her eyes, of course, but her skin is fair and unblemished. Her aquiline nose with a slight upturn and full lips give her a youthful profile. She's actually quite pretty*. Catching herself, she shrugged forward again.

Her mother, catching the look, smiled. "I know you'd prefer to be with them, no sense pretending otherwise. No matter how fascinating the animals may be, you're still stuck with me."

They stared at the crane hovering above a ship, an overripe sow nestled within the canvas hammock. Its squeals piercing the cry of gulls. Alice wondered why the *Sea Venture* wasn't transporting any animals. She reasoned as the men most essential to James Fort's survival were on board, best not to have them stinking of shit when they arrived at their new post. That would make a bad first impression. But it was funny to think about. Nodding to her thoughts, she realized her mother had continued talking.

"I did speak with Goody Pearce. You may visit with Joanne tonight. After supper."

"I'd prefer to meet this afternoon, not after supper."

"We don't always get what we want, now, do we? Be grateful you have any time with Joanne at all. If I were you, I would take what I could get and say thank you." Her Highness sniffed.

"I know that," Alice sniped. "I also know you and Father lied to me. This isn't an adventure. I'm expected to work."

"What? Who told you that?"

"You knew. You knew before we left. You can't fool me. I knew you had another motive for us coming. I just couldn't determine its nature. Until now. Then Jane told us everything," stated Alice.

"Jane?"

"The orphan? The only other girl you have seen me with for two weeks besides Joanne? The girl you yourself have spent time with? Doesn't matter. I'm right and I want you to know I know the truth." Alice stared into the hard blue eyes of her mother. "Is this how you plan to keep me away from Alfred?"

"Oh, my child! For your own sake, let Alfred go. But as for working, I know of no such thing," said Her Highness, glancing away quickly. "As far as what your father shared about the journey, I honestly don't know more than you. I know when we get to Jamestowne, we will have to build a house, but I doubt seriously if we have to do it ourselves. We've brought tradesmen. No, I expect our life will not be so different from our life in Stratford, save for the heat and the savages, so I've heard." Biting her lip, she turned from Alice.

"And? What else?" asked Alice undeterred.

"'Tis nothing," said Her Highness.

"Tell me. I'm on this journey too, and I'm not a child anymore. I know you are keeping secrets from me, and if we're to be crammed into that sty of a cabin for months, the least you can do is tell me the truth. I think I deserve to know what the real reason is for our adventure." Alice's gaze returned to the dock. A crane hoisted horses into the air before depositing them onto a ship.

"Aye, I told your father you should know," confessed Her Highness. "I told him you were no longer a girl. And you're right, you do deserve to know. But your father felt it a sure way to increase our fortunes. Give us a foot in two worlds. Would..." she hesitated "...erase all our debt."

"Our debt? Are we poor?" Alice had eavesdropped on her parents' earlier conversation but wanted confirmation her mother had been less than truthful. She hesitated to call her a liar just yet.

"No, no. Just a tad...impecunious...at the moment. But this is all perfectly safe. Your father would never put us in any real danger. I'm sure of it." But her voice did not convey total assurance. "I have heard rumors, probably the same ones you've heard. But I've not given them any credence. I am confident your father hasn't put our lives in danger," she reiterated, as though trying to convince herself.

Alice had heard the rumors, of course—all England had! The food shortages; the attacks on the fort; the men who left the fort never to return, their fate only a speculation. Alice had tried to determine why they were to be part of the Third Supply, and why the first two hadn't been enough if this was such a successful venture. It seemed odd, the explanation her father had given, but she did trust him and if he confirmed it safe, then it was safe. And they certainly were not poor! They had paid their way in full. They weren't laborers or artisans, or maids or servants. They were now shareholders in the Virginia Company. As though surfacing from a great depth, Alice straightened.

"Where are Elsie and Mooney? Why didn't they come with us?" she asked.

Never meeting her eyes, Her Highness said in monotone, "They are staying with the house. With your grandmother." Her jaw tightened.

"Is she the reason we are having this *grand adventure*?" The words no longer held their magic; they scratched her throat in their escape, and the bile rose with their utterance.

Her mother—Her Highness—a woman who had the reputation of being both haughty and frugal, merely trained her eyes on the shore, never uttering one protestation.

Alice recognized her father's debts had forced them on this adventure, but she wanted Her Highness to admit the real reason for the debts: her mother's behavior toward the locals and servants. They had to be compensated for her insularity. Ultimately, she was the reason they were now on the way to Jamestowne. It was her fault, and Alice wanted to hear her say it. To hear her take responsibility for once in her life. To admit if it weren't for her, their life would be happy; her father would be happy.

"So, we are to have no help," Alice reiterated.

Alice considered Mistress Horton, the old widow on board. She had brought her servant, Elizabeth. She had seen two other families from the fleet around town, also with their servants. She had never been without Elsie. She would miss her quick smile and sunny optimism more than she'd miss her assistance with daily tasks. Alice now had more questions, more concerns, but the swell of activity and loudening voices on the dock ended any further discussion, not that her mother would divulge anything. There would be more than enough time to talk crossing the Atlantic. Her Highness may be unwilling to share now, but six weeks, or longer, on a ship with no one else to talk to should loosen her tongue.

The shouting from the dock grew in intensity. Standing toe-to-toe were two men, and buzzing around the sides was Strachey, pretending to defuse the situation, but intentionally flaming the embers.

As much as her mother vexed her, Alice did share her predilection for petty confrontations. Sensing one about to erupt, Alice carefully tucked the handkerchief and cheese into her pouch, and the two women moved quickly to the scene, too riveting to not view first-hand.

⚓

At first, Alice was disappointed. This latest fight only involved the usual players: Sir Thomas Gates and Strachey. Despite the fact Gates had joined the fleet to much fanfare and groveling on behalf of the Company gentlemen, her father included, Alice thought the craggy-faced man with an unusually large, bulbous nose to be perpetually angry. In the five days they'd spent on the *Sea Venture* since leaving London, Alice had never seen him smile. As the newly chosen governor for the fort, and a military man, she supposed he expected immediate compliance with his hastily barked commands. For people like her? He was an annoyance.

"I, and I alone, am in charge of the soldiers and people," reiterated Gates boisterously.

The other man, Admiral George Somers, just smiled, no teeth, just a grin. He did not yell; he didn't have to—the fleet belonged to him. "I have no doubt when we land in Jamestowne, you will rule as you see fit. Here? My fleet. My orders. The men"—he gestured to the sailors still working to ready for the journey, albeit at a decidedly slower pace so as to eavesdrop inconspicuously on the conversation—"will follow my lead. That is to be the division of authority while we travel. Is that your understanding, Newport?"

Standing to the Admiral's right was the one-armed pirate turned naval captain. Alice judged the trio. Newport didn't look to be nearly as old as the two men arguing, but in spite of his lack of appendages and his clandestine past, Alice found him rugged and handsome. "Yes, sir, Admiral. That is my understanding. And if I might be so bold, I'm to be in charge of all while on board the *Sea Venture*."

"And you are?" interjected Strachey.

"You bloody well know who I am. We've been on the same ship since London, you damn fool!"

"I'm making sure we are all clear as to position." Strachey smiled, a leering snarl Alice felt meant nothing but malice toward the recipient.

"Newport—Vice-Admiral Newport, as you well know." Thumping his finger on the journal in which Strachey was forever writing, he said, "Put that in your little journal so you don't forget. Ye little bastard."

"Ah, there it is. Vice-Admiral. But you have no standing, no real position, as I understand it," quipped Strachey. "Not given the fact the *Sea Venture* will transport Governor Gates. Oh, and Admiral Somers, of course."

"I'm the captain of this bloody ship. Do you wish to survive the voyage?"

Strachey snorted. "Of course. That is a given."

"It is not a given," Newport asserted. "Nothing is ever a given when making trans-Atlantic trips. But I am the only man aboard who has made three *successful* voyages to Virginia already. I have captured Spanish treasure ships; hell, I even gave the King a live alligator!"

"You are a pirate," stated Strachey.

"And an exceedingly wealthy one at that," Newport stated. Leaning in as though divulging a secret, but speaking loud enough for all to hear, he said, "I dare say I have more money than you will ever dream of. Now or in the future. And, unlike you, I have a position and a title." He winked, then swaggered off to assist with a rigging.

Strachey's mouth drew to a tight line. The men around him chuckled, including Gates and Somers. Alice's father, however, just stood there with his arms folded.

"Thomas, you and I have known each other for far too long to mince words. You know where my loyalties lie, so just stay out of my way while on board," Somers said. "It will be fine as long as you do. And keep him well away from me and my men," he added, pointing to Strachey. "I would hate for him to have an accident." He chuckled as he walked away. He whistled, and a large dog appeared at his side.

Alice smiled. She loved it when adults acted like petulant children. She especially liked Strachey being taken down a peg by a one-armed pirate. Oh, how she wished Uncle Willie had witnessed this! She wasn't too keen on Sir Thomas, but her father had spoken highly of him. Instead, she felt an immediate kinship with the Admiral. Throughout the entire exchange, he never seemed upset, just amused. And he had a dog. Men with dogs could be trusted. Giggling at the absurdity of the incident, she glanced at Her Highness. She most definitely was *not* giggling. Her lips drawn in, jaw tightened, she glared at her husband with a ferocity so strong Alice expected him to burst into flames on the spot.

"That was funny, was it not?" asked Alice.

"It was not," she replied, never making eye contact with Alice.

"But it's interesting, don't you think? We're aboard the flagship. Everyone would love to be here with us, on the best ship with three leaders. And yet? They fume like children. But with Father in their midst, even if they do argue, I think we'll be safe. I think this bodes well for our adventure."

Leaving the docks, Alice spotted the Admiral in conversation with her father. She knew she shouldn't eavesdrop, but after recent revelations, and whatever secrets her mother was keeping, she decided it was in her best interest. Sneaking away from her mother was no problem, but there would be hell to pay if she were caught. Weighing her options, Alice determined knowledge trumped punishment.

Sidling behind the Admiral, Alice was caught off-guard by the dog. His head resembled a velvet-covered boulder—a huge solid mass covered in a soft veneer of black fur. His markings were unusual for a mastiff: a black velvet sky speckled with golden stars ran together to form their own constellations. His nose a black dot in the midst of the stars, underlined by a drooling smile with dark black lips. His paws larger than her hands. As he shifted at his master's side, Alice saw the muscle ripple just beneath the skin. Even sitting, his head rested comfortably on his master's thigh. Alice felt certain if he were to stand on his hind legs, he'd dwarf her. And yet? She was mesmerized by the colossal beast. In spite of his size, and his obvious power, she felt no fear. His soulful eyes met hers; she grinned. His tongue fell out of his black-lined lips and he smiled back. She knew not to step forward, for he was not hers, so she stood, feeling as though she'd been seen for the first time since boarding the *Sea Venture*.

As the two men lowered their voices into the conversation she'd so desperately wanted to hear, she watched the dog. In the distance, Strachey was still prattling on, she and the dog in silent agreement he was a fool.

Laughter broke her reverie; the Admiral turned to leave and her father saw her. Without her mother. Without a chaperone. In the one place she'd been prohibited from visiting. The Admiral watched her. Her mind searched for some excuse, some rationale for being there, at that moment, at the precise spot, and came up blank. But when she looked up, her father was gone; he hadn't noticed her after all.

"Put your hand out," the Admiral commanded. "Let him sniff you."

Without hesitation, Alice did as instructed. The beast sniffed, then gave her knuckles a gentle lick. Alice giggled, then quickly regained her composure.

"He likes you," chuckled the Admiral.

"May I…" she faltered. "May I pet him?"

"Of course, why do you think we're doing this?"

"Hello, boy." She felt the dog's fur; she'd been right—it did feel like velvet. The dog's mouth lolled open in contentment. "How are you today? Do you like sailing?" she asked the beast. "Will he be on the *Sea Venture* with us?"

"Of course, he's the ship's mascot. His name is Chance."

"Chance. That's a nice name." Alice continued petting the dog, cooing to it as she did so. "I like that we have this *chance* to meet."

"Ah—a clever lass. 'Tis why I named him Chance. He can be any chance I may need." The Admiral smiled. "In this case, for this voyage, he is Best Chance."

"Best Chance?"

"We are the settlement's best chance for survival. I purchased this ship, and two others, with my own money, so this is my chance."

Alice cut in, "So if he's with us, we have a good chance of—"

"Alice!" The voice strained and curt, much more so than usual, prompted Alice to stiffen. She knew that voice. That was Mother's angry voice. The real angry voice, not the simply annoyed voice. She'd be whipped for sure. She slid closer to the dog, cowering behind his massive haunches.

"Is this your daughter?" asked the Admiral.

"Yes, sir. I'm most sorry. She just got away. We won't trouble you any further."

"No need for apologies, she is a delight!" The Admiral beamed; Alice and Chance took on a similar quizzical look. "And Chance here quite fancies her."

"Well," her mother stammered, "I'm glad to know she isn't bothering you."

"On the contrary, she's quite clever. Picked right up on the ole beast's name."

Mother shot Alice a look that asked, *what have you done?* But she remained quiet and waited for the Admiral to continue. As for her, she'd be explaining a lot once they returned to the nunnery. She'd seen that look before, and it had cost her a month's worth of visits to Susanna's and five lashes. This time? It would probably cost her more time in the cabin with Her Highness. Or being thrown overboard.

"I'd like to employ her, with your permission of course."

"Employ her?"

"Employ me?"

They spoke at the same time, the responses eliciting a chuckle from the Admiral.

"Yes. I would like her to sit with Chance, play with him, perhaps even feed him, at least once a day for the duration of this journey. If that meets with your approval, of course."

"I'd love to!" Alice squealed, and immediately felt her mother's hand tightly grip her shoulder, thumbs driving into the flesh. "I mean, may I, Your High—Mother?" Saying the word *mother* made her mouth sour.

"If the Admiral requests it, then how can I refuse?" Her grimace registered her displeasure. Then turning to her daughter, her words clipped: "But you must promise to listen, and do exactly as instructed." *Instructed* was hissed out, the gravitas of her errant behavior clear in its tone.

"I promise." Alice tried to sound both contrite and grateful. How serendipitous! To play with Chance, *and* it would require her to be free of the cabin. Regardless of her mother's punishment for disobeying her, she would at least have one opportunity every day to be free of their cabin. She now had a reason to roam. Understanding there would be a talk later, and not wanting to lose this opportunity, she meekly thanked both adults, but especially her mother. With the deal made, and an appointed time for her to retrieve Chance the following day, Alice and her mother returned to their lodging.

PART TWO

"A brave vessel"
~ Miranda,
The Tempest, Act 1, Scene 2

Chapter 6

Saint James's Day, 24 July 1609

Alice gingerly rubbed the chemise across her forearm. It didn't hurt, exactly, but felt hot and tender to the touch. She pressed a finger into the skin. The white imprint quickly turning peach then deepening to pink as the burnt skin reappeared. There'd be no thorough sloughing today. Every morning, she was to vigorously rub her skin with a chemise; with no other means to bathe, a rough rub was to suffice. But it was no good for sunburnt skin.

She could hear her mother now if she were to find out the state of her arms. *I warned you. They warned you. Keep your sleeves down no matter how hot you are. Stay out of the sun. It will make you sick. But you knew better. Running off with that foul dog. That's what you get for not listening.* Alice quickly pulled her sleeves to her wrist. Feeling her face, she found no blisters or blemishes. A miracle. Just a touch of tenderness on her nose and cheekbones.

At the start of their journey, the sailors had graciously erected a tarpaulin for the six female passengers. They could sit above deck and get fresh air without blemishing their skin too badly. Even the sailors limited their time in the sun, working in shifts. Alice, however, chose to find her own spot to sit, away from the others. Unfortunately, sitting toward the bow of a ship headed west with the constant glare of sun off the water had been a very poor decision, a very poor decision indeed. *'Tis but a moment, and this too shall pass*, she heard Uncle Willie say. Yes, this momentary discomfort was well worth the freedom she gained.

Hearing her mother stir, Alice rushed through the remainder of her ablutions, dressed, and stole through the door into the hallway. Moving quickly, mindful of the tiller that ran the length of the tween deck, she passed the other makeshift cabins with their tenuous wooden scraps posing as walls, privacy now merely an illusion. Gently maneuvering her body between the maze of hammocks filling the area nearest the ladder, Alice glanced back toward the sound of her mother retching into the bucket, again. Seemed they each had their daily routine.

Alice did worry, a little, that the seasickness was taking a toll on her mother. If she didn't think about how her mother had tried to marry her off, she could almost feel sorry for her. Her mother had tried, twice, to go topside and get fresh air, the best remedy for seasickness, but the ladder proved to be too much. They'd been on board nearly six weeks and she still complained of feeling sideways and the world spinning inside her head. What made Alice feel sideways and nauseous was staying in an eight-by-eight cabin with no windows, which stank of vomit and shit and sweat, that only got more putrid as the sweltering days grew longer.

Alice stopped at the base of the ladder. Unlike the stairs in her house, the ship's ladder had no angle, just a straight vertical climb through a scupper hole with a heavy wooden grate that, unless secured, would crush her fingers or dent her skull. Even though it was only eight rungs in length, and she had the strength to push the wooden grate open, she still found she had to focus on each task before she could start the climb. Alice ran her hands down the front of her skirt to make sure they were dry. The smooth wood allowed no purchase for clammy hands. She pulled herself up, rung by rung, feeling the sway of the ship by mid-point. Clutching herself to the rungs, she closed her eyes and took a deep breath. So maybe she did feel a tad sideways, but she would never tell her mother this. Feeling a tug at her hem, she opened her eyes to see the Admiral's cook, Thomas, standing below her.

"Are you alright, miss? You need some help?"

Staring into his blue eyes, Alice felt her legs give way. "No," she whispered. "I'm fine."

"Are you sure, miss?" he asked, but she had already climbed topside, to freedom.

"Yes, I'm sure," she said, unable to look at him. What was it about him that reminded her of Alfred? She had to remind herself every time she saw him: He's not Alfred. He's *Thomas.* Maybe it was the blue eyes or the earnest way each of them offered help when they sensed her distress. Perhaps it was their gentle, caring nature. Or, more likely, she just missed her Alfred and saw him in the male faces surrounding her.

Alice carefully stepped over the threshold, mindful to not trip lest she be pitched overboard. She had claimed the corner to the left of the doorway as her own shortly after boarding, "larboard of the forecastle" according to the sailors. All Alice cared about was having enough room for her and Chance to sit, and that her mother, should she miraculously make it out of their quarters, not find her. Alice pulled her legs tightly to her as the beast lumbered to her side and lay down.

"Lovely day, isn't it? No sun to burn us and a nice, steady wind to cool us. And you know why?" Alice asked Chance, rubbing his ears. "Because it's Saint James's Day, the patron saint of travelers." She focused on the horizon. "I suppose it's a good sign, eh? We're traveling on the saint's day. Wonder if patron saints can provide something other than grey gruel with bits of salted pork for a meal?" She ruffled the dog's mane, lost in thought. "The sailors were wrong, weren't they? Those ill-winds in Falmouth weren't a bad omen. We're almost there. Captain Newport thinks we're no more than six or seven days out. So what if it's cloudy? Saint James will bless our travel, just as he has thus far. We'll be at our new home—in new lives—in a week. I wonder what adventure awaits us." Closing her eyes, she relished the breeze caressing her face. The rain started gentle at first, a drip here and there, that quickened with the wind. Within minutes, it became sharp and hard, stung her face as though needles were pricking her cheeks.

The sailors, now shouting and rushing about, furling the sails, interrupted Chance's nap. He suddenly leaped to his feet and away to his master, the loudest voice of all.

"Where's that infernal girl?" barked the Admiral. "Make sure she's in her quarters; I'll not be looking for her arse in the storm."

Alice stood, intent on remaining on deck, but a hand grabbed her. "You best get below," he ordered, his blue eyes stalling any protest. "Best not vex him." Thomas guided her to the ladder, but she missed the rung, the ship rolled, and she fell to the floor below. Hurrying down behind her, Thomas gently helped her to her feet. "Go on," he said, pushing her toward their quarters before returning topside. Alice walked unsteadily to her room as the ship pitched sideways again.

Chapter 7

The Storm, 25–27 July 1609

The prickly rain of the day before had metamorphosed into a storm overnight. Unlike the misty rain of home, the kind that invites deep sleep and calm dreams, this produced nightmares. The ship pitched so sharply Alice was forced from her mattress as though someone had picked up one side and jerked it, rolling her off, her shin cracking into the corner of their chest. Rubbing her shin, she glanced around. The ship pitched again in the opposite direction and Alice tumbled toward her prostrate mother. She must look like a marionette at the hands of someone with missing fingers, unable to move smoothly because the strings were jumbled. From beyond the door of their cabin men were calling out in a manner fraught with tension and curse words—more curse words than usual. Having been in their company since the fifteenth of May, she rarely paid attention, but today's expletives included a few she hadn't heard before. These words did not sound like light-hearted ribbing. No, these words were from people deeply unsettled—alarmed, in fact. What on earth could alarm a sailor? A fire? Alice sniffed. Nothing burning. The next wave picked the ship up and slammed it into the water like a toy. Flung to a new location, Alice listened to the sailors in the hallway let loose with a new barrage of curses. Then all was still, briefly. In the silence, the ship slowly started to roll to one side, then quickly picked up momentum. Items on the floor began sliding from the suddenly violent movements of the ship atop the waves. *Are we still atop the waves? Are we in the waves?* Alice could not figure out their position in relation to the ocean, and it made her head swim and spin.

Attempting to stand was futile. Moving to her knees, Alice was dashed into a wall so hard she saw sparkles. Changing clothes today would prove impossible, so she gave up trying. *Thwack!* She was flattened as another wave roiled the ship. Looking to her mother, Alice wanted to cry. Her Highness now sat cradling the bucket in her arms, her body covered in her own filth. Her stomach and bowels unloosed by the violent motions of the ship rendered the bucket a mere prop; she was a pitiful sight indeed.

"I'll find Father," Alice offered, as she crawled to the door. Reaching for the rope handle, she became aware of a noise, a constant, riotous hum she could feel in the base of her skull. Loud *thwacks* reverberated throughout the quarters as the ocean smashed against the outer wall. The noise was completely disconcerting: why was she hearing the ocean on their wall? They should be above the waterline. Looking about the tiny cabin, Alice noticed the walls were glistening. Not a lot, but as she ran her hand in the space between the boards, in the space that should have been sealed, there were tiny water droplets starting to appear. But how? The ship was watertight! Alice surveyed the ceiling, and while it was damp there was nothing dripping down the walls.

"It's not the whole wall, just the seams!" She may have been a land-lubber, but even she recognized the significance of a leaking wall on a ship.

Standing, she planted her feet to either side in a stance allowing her to absorb the motion in her knees. But just when she got the motion and her knees to coordinate, the ship lurched in the opposite direction and she fell, her kneecaps cracking against the floor. "Ow!" Rubbing her knees, she flopped back and began putting the pieces together. The ship was rocking more than usual, but they were on the open ocean far from land. Until today, she was certain she had gained her sea legs, as she'd had no problem moving between the decks or the various quarters since coming aboard. But these current movements? They weren't all just to-and-fro, side-to-side, there was the occasional feeling of going uphill, then suddenly dropping straight down. These movements were much more violent than any they'd experienced thus far. She thought about the water droplets on the wall. She felt the din of wind through her whole body. It was a cacophony of sound. No, something was definitely different today. *I'll just go ask*, she resolved. *I'll just hold on to the wall. Stay on one side of the tiller and go to the ladder. I've fallen down the hole once; it's not too bad. It must be better topside: more open space, less things to fall into. I'll find Father. Or the Admiral. They'll know what's happening. They'll know what to do with Mother.* The problems began as soon as she opened the door.

Streaming water roared down the hallway, enough to reach her ankles. It hadn't covered the tiller, so she could use that to navigate to the ladder. Placing her foot alongside the wooden beam, she followed its trajectory, slowly moving toward the front of the ship. Finally reaching the ladder, she realized she had a bigger hurdle: water poured through the grate of the scupper hole with the ferocity of a waterfall. She stood below, attempting to assess how she could maneuver through the torrents lashing her, but above was only darkness. No sun, scant light; dark, angry clouds surrounded them. And rain. Driving, relentless, destructive rain. Biting her lips, she tucked her head and started to climb the ladder. She struggled against the water to reach each rung. The noise from topside encouraging her to keep climbing; someone there would help her mother. The howling wind drowned out all but one discernible voice: the Admiral, who, lashing himself on the poop deck, continued to bark commands as though he could command the storm as he did his men. The sailors too had lashed themselves to anything solid enough to save them from being swept overboard. She felt the ship climbing a hill. Balanced atop the ladder, she felt herself being pulled backward. Threading her arms through the rungs, she watched through the holes in the grate as the bowsprit became visible, pointing them to heaven, then watched a wave break over all, pushing grown men aside as if they were dust. The giant wave roiled beneath them. Just as it had pointed them toward the heavens, it now pointed them toward hell. Water streamed over her as she clutched to the only solid base in her midst. She shut her eyes and remained still, knowing the next wave would surely kill them all.

Alice felt someone tugging at her arms. She looked to the sailor trying to pry her from the safety of the ladder.

"Get on now. Go back to your area, ye can't stay here," he yelled.

Alice shook her head *no*, scrunched her eyes shut against the water pouring over her head, and tightened her grip.

"I'm not asking ye, princess. Get back to your cabin. It's dangerous—now MOVE!"

Alice, regaining her composure, unlocked her arms and quickly scrambled toward the deck, the complete opposite direction of where she'd been ordered to go. As she breached the deck, the Admiral's voice boomed.

"What the hell is she doing up here? Get her down below—NOW!"

Alice smiled, sure the Admiral had mistaken her for someone else, another girl, one who hadn't been entrusted to care for his beloved Chance. He would never yell at her.

"NOW, I said, or I'll whip ye myself for insubordination!" he bellowed.

"Ye heard him—get down!" Grabbing her roughly by the arm, the sailor attempted to toss Alice back to the scupper hole, but he needn't have bothered: the next wave pitched them both through the opening to the hard wood below. Her elbow ached sharply from the fall, but she smiled as she watched the sailor lose his footing and stumble into the wall. Her laughter was short-lived as she heard the Admiral yelling once again, and this time her father was the recipient. Where was his humor now? Before, he had seemed so nice, so cordial and polite; even when needled by Strachey, he never once rose to a fight. But now? Maybe this was how storms were handled on ships: just tie the Admiral to a post and let him yell until all returned to normal.

"Get. To. Your. Quarters. NOW!" The sailor's voice was different now—harsher, more desperate.

Alice crinkled her nose, reluctant to do as she was told. Defiant, she stood, turned toward their quarters, and was promptly dashed to the floor with the next wave. Refusing to give the sailor the satisfaction of seeing her bested, even by nature, she attempted to stand. Unable to stand upright for more than a few steps, she clung to every surface as she made her way to the narrow hall. As the ship continued to pitch, each movement more violent than the last, Alice was tossed between the walls of the hallway as though in a game of catch, her shins and calves thrashed repeatedly into the tiller. Spying the entrance to their quarters, Alice could think of nothing more than to lie on her mattress and take a nap. Confident when she awoke, all would be normal. She would be able to go on deck with Chance and pretend to fly over the ocean. A simple pleasure, an act that just yesterday bordered on monotonous, was now all she craved. But as she struggled toward the room, her legs aching and her back now spasming from the fall, the dizziness began. By the time she reached the door, her stomach lurched. She reached the room, and the bucket, just in time to greet last night's supper.

Alice threw up, taking turns at the bucket with Her Highness, over the course of the day. At some point, there was nothing left, except dry heaves. But as Uncle Willie liked to say, *this too shall pass*. It used to make her laugh; now, it just made her wistful for a simpler time when there seemed to be laughter at every turn. And this great storm, still tormenting the ship, had occurred on Saint James's Day. It now appeared to Alice the patron saint of travel had wandered off and left them to fend for themselves against a storm and an ocean that wanted them dead.

Alice lay motionless, watching the lantern sway with the storm. She felt dizzy watching the motion of the lantern, but no longer sickly. It took a moment to gain her bearings as she was in bed with her mother. This hadn't happened since she came down with the pox, just before her ninth birthday, and once after the death of her brother. The crone's arm draped protectively around her midsection; Alice carefully slid from beneath the embrace. The ship was still being tossed haphazardly by the waves, but she needed to search for her father. And Chance. She could still hear the shouts of the sailors, but not the Admiral. As she placed her feet over the side of the bed, they were immediately soaked. The water now above her ankles. She noted the walls, which had earlier merely glistened, now sprouting tiny pinprick holes threatening to burst at any moment.

Alice turned to rouse her mother; they had to leave. This room wasn't safe, not anymore. As she shook her, her mother barely roused. It would be impossible for her mother to leave the room. She had been sick since leaving Plymouth. She had thrown up every morning, and sometimes during the day too. She ate, but meagerly, and nothing appeared to stay where it was supposed to. Alice examined the face of the unconscious woman beside her: the sunken eyes, the paleness of the skin accentuating her frailty. Her breaths were shallow, but consistent. A tiny fleck of spittle was caked at the corner of her mouth. In spite of herself, Alice gently wiped it away, then stroked the hair from her mother's forehead. Her skin smooth and soft, no lines save laugh lines. No crow's feet like Susanna. Alice thought this odd, but was then thrown backward off the bed with the next wave. Fully soaked, there was no way to get dry, they'd packed no full change of clothes for the ship. She needed to find her father and get help.

Struggling to her feet, she reconsidered and returned to her knees, crawling to the door. Tugging it open was an arduous task made all the harder by the fact there was now water on both sides. Alice made a space to fit through, sliding into the hall, searching for the tiller with both hands. She wasn't sure how to proceed. There was still water coming from topside—a lot of water—and the hallway now had items floating in it. Small items to be sure, but floating nonetheless. Incessant yelling interrupted her observations. It was a woman. Miss Persons, Mistress Horton's maid. Something about their room. Flooded. Her mistress being inconsolable. Nowhere to go. It was hard to hear her over the howling wind and thrashing waves ceaselessly battering them. Alice had no desire, or time, to hear her complaints as they were the same problems everyone was having, but she saw the desperation and fear in Miss Persons' eyes. Without saying a word, Alice grabbed her, found Mistress Horton, and ushered them into the cabin with Her Highness.

"We're all flooded," Alice yelled. "Stay here. I'll get help."

With the women safely stowed, for now, Alice left to find her father.

The nice thing about an emergency is no one pays attention to young girls wandering around; the bad thing about an emergency is no one pays attention to young girls wandering around. As she crept deeper into the belly of the ship, she realized she had never climbed into the hold. She had always remained topside, oblivious to the maze of rooms and belongings stored under her feet. There was little light here. An occasional lantern, swaying on a hook, was all she had to guide her steps. Having never encountered any of it without water made the search even more difficult. It seemed the deeper she went, the narrower the areas for walking and the higher the water level. The beauty of floating items was they could be pushed aside; the terror of floating items was they obscured walkways, causing Alice to stumble and fall. With several falls she swore she was on rocks, her knees now raw and skinned from breaking the falls. She made her way to where she believed she heard men yelling, only to discover it was the sound of water, now pervasive in every nook and cranny of the ship, even in the part that should have been under water and thus quiet. But it was not calmer as she had expected. Like the upper decks, they too were being dashed around, and had taken on significantly more water. It was to her waist here! The only reason she was able to stand at all was she was buoyed by the water, just as the items floating with her.

Alice finally located the bilge room, a room housing a device that supposedly made this ship safer for trans-Atlantic travel. She didn't grasp how it worked completely, but she understood it was supposed to drain water from the ship and, unlike other ships, the *Sea Venture* had two, making it the safest ship in the fleet. But it did not appear to be helping with any water now. There were several men working the pump manually, her father amongst them. She tried yelling, to get his attention, but to no avail. She moved closer, in hopes he would hear her, but she was pushed back into the wall. Standing to the side, she watched the men fervently work. Stripped to the waist and sweaty, they were taking turns working the pump. She had never seen her father do a minute's worth of manual labor, and the desperation on his face alarmed her more than the water spouting from the wall of their cabin. The men were dripping wet, shirtless and filthy, intent on contributing to their survival—all except Strachey. He just stood there, slack-jawed, gaping eyes. She could see his mouth working but could not hear any sound. No one paid him any mind; he had been pushed aside much as she had. Were the situation not so dire, she would have laughed. She noticed the men were pulling something from the pump mechanism. It looked like...bread! Of course! As it coagulated, it gummed up the mechanism to the point of ruination.

"That's it!" she yelled. She found the storeroom much quicker than she had her father, and the bread just there for the taking as the sailors had left the flooding room to help save their ship. Alice grabbed the closest loaves, filling her skirt with as much bread as she could carry. Fighting against the water, she struggled with every step to return to their quarters. Her thighs burning, her knees throbbing, she smiled as she forced her way up the flooded hallway.

Returning to the room, Alice undraped her skirt and let the loaves fall to the mattress. Smiling, she threw one to Miss Persons as she sloshed her way to the now dripping wall.

"Tear off bits and stuff them in the holes," Alice instructed. She demonstrated on one of the threatening holes. "See? They'll swell and fill in the gaps."

"But it's bread," protested Miss Persons.

"Do you want to die?" asked Alice. "Just do it! Or go back to your own quarters. I care not what you choose, but I'll not die, not like this!" She hastily began pinching off bits of the loaf and cramming it into any spot it would fit. Begrudgingly, Miss Persons followed suit. Before long, Mistress Horton joined the action. There were many more leaks than there had been before her first foray out, so she developed another plan. Carefully tearing the bread into strips, she laid them out longways along the caulking. With any luck these strips would swell and stick as the pieces had in the bilge, and they'd have secured the wall. Only time would tell and, from what she could discern, it wasn't on their side.

With all the bread gone, the three women regarded their handiwork. It looked a mess, to be sure, but did seem to be holding. The task complete, Alice tasked the two women with watching over Her Highness while she went to see where she could be of further assistance to the Admiral. In spite of his yelling, and her subsequent banishment to her room, she knew she had a role to play in saving the passengers.

Looking from the door of their cabin, Alice realized going topside was no longer an option: too much water falling much too fast for her to navigate her way up the ladder. The walkways were flooded, but if she held the walls, she could move into the ship. There had been two other women present—not all were fortunate enough to have cabins or rooms; perhaps she could convince them to come to their quarters. It would be crowded, but at least they would be on a higher deck with other women, a logic that was starting to make sense the longer the storm wore on. After what she had seen in the bilge room, she conceded anyone left below was in danger of becoming trapped, of drowning.

They were *soaked to the bone*, as Susanna liked to say. The women sat on the floor of the flooded cabin, their skirts caked in filth floating at their sides. They were exhausted. It had been three days, all told, and none had the energy to complain. Or to move. Or to care. They were just relieved to have survived the storm. As the ship gradually stopped tossing and pitching, and they found they could sit upright for longer and longer periods of time, the women eyed one another with hopeful suspicion. Foolishly, on the second day, they were lulled into thinking the worst of the storm had occurred. For a brief time—hours, or more likely minutes—the ship was still. They briefly rejoiced on their luck, on their tenacity for enduring the storm, for surviving. Then BOOM! The ship reverberated from the impact. Convinced the walls would now give way to the ocean, the women clung to one another in a futile attempt to save themselves. Still piecing together what may have happened, Alice heard the sailors' shouts as they relayed the message throughout the ship: rogue wave. Followed by the dreaded word *more*.

The waves and rain returned with a vengeance, draping them all in a shroud of water, choking out the day, making each passing minute an agonizing struggle to maintain hope. Not even the men were immune to despair now. The true believers prayed ceaselessly; those with less patience for the Almighty's trials cursed. By the third day, passengers and sailors alike were curiously quiet. Alice found this to be more unnerving than the riotous energy unleashed by the storm. Was this another of nature's tricks? Alice braced for another rogue wave. Hugging her knees to her chest, she recited the Lord's Prayer. If death was imminent, she may as well have

God's name in her mouth as she went.

Too exhausted to rest, Alice continued to listen to every sound. The creaking of the ship's walls; the hiss of water pouring through holes below the waterline; the sloshing of feet trying to maneuver through the flooded deck. Above her, Alice heard the sailors shouting once more. Not the fragmented, frantic yelps heard throughout the storm, but clearly articulated words and phrases. Their tone still tense, but gone was the desperation of the past three days. Perhaps they really had survived the storm. Allowing herself hope, however small, Alice moved to the door, finally able to stand upright without being knocked over.

The warm water around her calves, a not altogether unpleasant experience as compared to the chill of rain showers back in Stratford-upon-Avon, proved deeply unsettling when she realized it also contained all the waste material from every person staying in their quarters. Light emanated around the door frame. The light hurt her eyes; she squinted as she attempted to coax the waterlogged door to open. Pulling the rope handle with both hands, she rocked back onto her heels. She glanced back into the room, but none of the women heeded her call for assistance. Determined, Alice turned her attention to the door. She continued to tug, straining with each pull, forcing the door open a bit more with each effort. At last the door gave way, and her father, shoulder down ready to push again, stood before her.

"Oh, Papa—you're alive!" she cried, then hugged him round the waist. Still sodden, his linen shirt hung limply on his torso, the sleeves filthy and ripped; his woolen britches, once stylish and fashionable, now resembling those of someone who mucks out horse stalls. He smelled a bit like them too. He allowed her the embrace, his own arms slowly moving to return the affection, but too weak to pull her any closer. He kissed the top of her head, then moved past her and into their cabin. Secure in knowing her father would care for her mother, Alice fled topside.

Alice willed her legs to move to the ladder, each rung seemingly further to reach than the previous. She needed to check on her friend, to look to the deck of the *Blessing* and wave, to ensure the one last piece of this nightmare had ended and they would all be safe in Jamestowne shortly. If Joanne was fine, in spite of the destruction surrounding her, she might be able to sleep.

Shading her eyes from the glare, she crouched into her spot, watching as sailors took up various positions around each deck. Each now searching the horizon for...for what exactly? She could hear the Admiral's voice still barking commands, so there was little chance he would yell at her, specifically, again. Finding her chance, she moved to the gunwale, to wave to her friend, but there was nothing. She staggered across the ship to the poop deck and looked behind. Nothing. Standing in the center of the poop deck she took in the vicinity of the *Sea Venture*. There was nothing anywhere. The other ships weren't with them. Of the two pinnaces they'd towed, only one remained. They were alone. The only surviving ship.

Alice stared at where the *Blessing* had glided beside them in weeks past, at where her friend had waved each morning. Slowly lowering herself to the deck, she placed her head against the gunwale and stared through tears into the vast nothingness of the Atlantic, until she, like the *Sea Venture*, drifted aimlessly on the waves.

Chapter 8

On Board the *Sea Venture*, 27–28 July 1609

When Alice awoke, all was dark. She felt her guts clench as she feared the storm had returned just as it had after the brief respite a few days ago. She still felt the rolling and pitching of the vessel in her muscles, a sensation she expected to continue for the rest of her natural life. Convinced she'd never see daylight again, that she would die on this ship, lost to the sea just as Joanne and Jane were, she felt herself rising to a panic. She waited to feel shards of rain pierce her skin, hear the incessant howling of wind so forceful it made her ears ring, but was instead greeted with quiet. Complete stillness. The silence induced a level of fear she'd never known before the storm. Slowly opening her eyes, she could make out bodies littering the deck around her. People were lying everywhere. Some were propped against the gunwales, while others were fully prostrate over the deck. Were they dead? Alice willed herself to listen, to see how many were alive, and was met with soft, sonorous breathing blending with the sound of the ocean waves. The passengers from below deck were now strewn about topside. She wasn't alone. It was then she noticed not all were asleep. There were men standing near her, quietly talking amongst themselves.

"Father," Alice whispered to the male voices. Her body ached as though she'd been the ball in a game of tennis, tears welling from the sheer effort to move. She ached from her head to her toes. She remembered the pain reliever Susanna taught her to grind. Willow bark. She struggled to determine which trunk contained the precious elixir: The one in their quarters? Or the one in the hold? She hoped it wasn't one of the items deemed frivolous by Her Highness and consigned to be left. She stretched her arms and legs; everything hurt. Even her fingertips were raw! Struggling to an upright position, she was greeted with a wet lick across her chin. It took her a moment to realize it was Chance. Wiping the slobber off her face, she hugged her canine companion, ruffling the fur on his neck as she welcomed his presence by burying her nose into his mane.

Alice found herself at the feet of four men: her father, Gates, Strachey, and the Admiral. They were talking about the storm, unaware or uncaring about the girl right next to them. From their conversation, Alice learned the storm—the *hurricano*, the Admiral called it—had lasted a total of three days. And while there had been significant flooding below deck, and most of their provisions had been lost, miraculously no one died. Alice was both relieved and surprised at this fact given the state of the bodies on deck. The Admiral praised the work of the men.

"Well, sir, it should come as no surprise to you. It would appear your men are well trained—they handled the catastrophe as blithely as a mere rain shower. Honestly, I am impressed at their capacity and endurance for such strenuousness," quipped Gates, a well-known naysayer of sailors, himself being a soldier, until his life depended on them.

"Well, of course they are; who do you think trained them? And furthermore, these men were hand-selected—by me—for this mission." The Admiral paused as he regained his composure. "No, I was referring to the Company men, the land-lubbers. It has been my experience they aren't accustomed to manual labor, generally speaking, much less trained for a life at sea. Nevertheless, these men, and one tenacious little girl, worked unceasingly to protect the ship and all aboard her. Yes, I expected there to be great moaning and gnashing of the teeth the longer the storm raged on, or even a scurrying between posts as assignments were made. But for the most part, that was not the case. Of course, there is always one." He glared at Strachey, briefly, but enough for the offender to know it was he to whom the comment was aimed, his guilt admitted in an ill-timed nervous laugh. Then just as quickly, the Admiral slapped him on the back, knocking him forward ever so slightly.

Alice snickered, then quickly stifled the noise in the dog's side. Chance leaned into her in agreement.

"I assume you shall be recording this all, eh, Strachey?" asked Gates in a vain attempt to redeem the man.

"Yes, of course. I am hoping to capture the hopelessness, anxiety, and heroism exhibited during a moment of dire straits. I'm thinking about—"

"Thank you," replied Gates, dismissing the man with a wave of his hand.

Confident his efforts had been noted, Strachey nodded, continuing to stand with the group.

"You're excused," said Gates.

Strachey's mouth twitched as he struggled for what to say next, but even he knew he was no longer welcome, so he awkwardly bowed to the other two men and took his leave. When he was out of earshot, the discussion resumed.

"Did he work at all?" asked the Admiral.

"I believe he did work at a bilge. Once or twice," responded Gates. "He did produce calculations as to how much water we moved out of the ship."

"*As* it was being moved, I assume, not *after* the fact," stated the Admiral. Gates did not respond. "Calculations," harrumphed the Admiral.

Alice shifted. She had seen Strachey in the bilge room and knew, for a fact, he had done nothing. Her father had been there too. She waited for him to speak, to correct Gates, but he stood mute. She willed him to support the Admiral's assumption, let him know his assessment of the man had been spot-on. But he remained silent.

"What about that daughter of yours?" prompted the Admiral.

Alice perked up at the mention of her name, especially since he'd threatened to thrash her himself for her insubordination.

"You must be quite proud of her," continued the Admiral.

"Sir?" responded her father. He sounded as surprised as she.

Admiral Somers moved closer to Alice and Chance, dropping his hand to stroke the beast's ears. She could smell the sea-soaked leather of his boots—a sweet, musky odor reminiscent of moments stolen in the stables with Alfred.

"The lass. She helped with stopping the leaks. Newport tells me she was extraordinarily efficient at finding small holes and stuffing bread into the crevices. Methodical in her process of detecting leaks, and even had the other women helping her. She even went so far as to move the women from below to your cabin. All of her own initiative. Clever girl, that one," exclaimed the Admiral.

Alice watched her father, his face unreadable. She'd hoped he might praise her, acknowledge her hard work, her good deeds, her cleverness. Nothing. Not even a smile.

"What of those leaks, sir?" interrupted Gates. "This is a new ship, one designed specifically for trans-Atlantic voyages. The *Sea Venture* was billed as the safest ship on the sea. How could something like this have happened?"

"Aye, you're right there," acknowledged the Admiral. "And you're still alive, aren't ya? If I had to guess, I'd say the oakum didn't fully set. Without proper curing, it doesn't matter how much is between the boards—it is just a matter of time before leaks appear. I always expect some leaks. Even if we were simply to have sailed to Jamestowne as planned, with no storms or bad weather, there would have been some leaks. But with a hurricano? I'm surprised we haven't sunk. Still may, if truth be told."

While mildly alarmed at the Admiral's pronouncement they may still sink, Alice remained transfixed watching her father. She watched as his eyes drooped, his head lolling forward onto his oily, filth-encrusted shirt. She had never seen him this exhausted, this filthy, this human. Alice felt sorry for her father, but still she wondered why he hadn't spoken on her behalf when he had a chance. She glared at Gates. Could it be Gates was just using this opportunity to question the Admiral, a man he had openly feuded with before they'd even set sail? Or was it her father's own rejection of anything he interpreted as a hollow platitude? And he had, in the past, dismissed praises of his fiery, stubborn daughter. Perhaps this was a hollow platitude, and she just didn't recognize it as it came from the Admiral. She didn't think so, but she couldn't be sure. She'd do better. She'd earn his praise if it was the last thing she ever did.

Alice dozed, her head resting on Chance's shoulder. So warm and sturdy, it was hard not to feel safe with him by her side. The Admiral sat on the other side of Chance, his hand resting on the dog's boulder-sized head.

"Ah, finally awake," he said.

She nodded but did not reply.

"I know you think me unkind for yelling at you, but I was afraid for your safety."

"I understand. You knew of the storm and the danger; I just didn't want to stay below, alone with my mother. I do tend to follow my own mind. I apologize, sir."

"But there's more to why I was concerned," admitted the Admiral. "See, I used to have a daughter, Sarah. She was a lot like you: headstrong, defiant of her mother's wishes. She even looked a little like you. And she loved to sail." He smiled. "So, you see, I didn't mean to alarm you. I merely wanted to ensure your safety. I couldn't save her, but I could save you."

Alice nodded. She understood how parents reacted to a child's death; she'd witnessed her own parents after Bertie's passing. And while her own brother's passing had rendered her invisible for a time, in this instance she replaced another's daughter. Both felt equally odd, yet familiar.

The Admiral stood and offered her his hand. "Come, I want to show you something."

Alice took his hand. For a man used to running entire fleets, a man willing to lash himself to the deck of a ship during a hurricano, his hands were no bigger than her father's. They were strong, but otherwise quite average. She placed her hand, the one now blistered, red, and raw, into his. She allowed him to pull her to standing, noting a commotion amongst the sailors.

Admiral Somers pointed to a small burst of fire bouncing between the masts. It jumped to-and-fro, leaving a glowing trail as it moved.

"See that?" his voice boomed.

Alice nodded.

"It's called Saint Elmo's Fire."

"It's beautiful. Like a little ball of fire, sputtering flames. I like the purpleness of it." Alice smiled, looking to the Admiral, but his attention was now with the crowd gathered to watch the phenomenon.

"For those of you unfamiliar with the sight," the Admiral continued, "please allow me to explain. Named after Saint Erasmus of Formia, this is a good sign." He clapped his hands and laughed. "The patron saint of sailors has seen fit to bless us with a good omen, men! It is clear, with this sign, Saint Erasmus does not intend for us to perish on this, our brave vessel. We have been given a sign that all will be well. All will be well!"

Some men clapped; others cheered—none overly exuberant as they were all in want of sleep and food. But Alice was delighted.

Alice listened as the men decided who would stay awake and who would rest, for how long, and then the shift would change. She watched as the men made the decisions for themselves, then promptly headed below deck for rest, or to their posts for duty. They were so well trained none had to wait for instructions. Was this what the Admiral was praising when he complimented her initiative? She felt a warm glow of pride.

One sailor didn't respond to the Admiral's good news. He stood to the side and clicked his tongue, shaking his head. "What about the water? There's a lot of water still in the hold and tween deck. We can't travel with this weight—it'll drag us under. And it's still coming in," he stated matter-of-factly.

"It should be manageable," dismissed Admiral Somers.

"It ain't," said the sailor.

"Newport, go with him below. See what the devil he's talking about," he ordered.

Nodding, Newport followed the sailor below deck. Everyone else watched as the flames of Saint Elmo's Fire lazily sputtered and burned itself out. The dazzling array of blues and purples leaving color trails in their wake.

Alice watched Newport's return. Rubbing the back of his neck, he leaned in and spoke to the Admiral in low tones. Alice watched as Admiral Somers's jaw dropped. Turning from Newport he walked to the gunwale, placed both hands on it, and stared at the sky. Then resting his chin on his chest, he seemed to deflate.

Alice slipped away from the old seafarer. She wanted her father. As usual, he was communing with Gates, Strachey hovering at his side. She tried to get his attention, but he never looked her way.

Alice passed groups of men as she returned to their cabin. Flasks passed from hand to hand, and they mumbled and cursed as the alcohol loosed their lips. "Worst storm I e'r did see." "We gave it our all, we did." She found it strange that even the sailors were surprised they survived. But then she heard a much more ominous proclamation, one she didn't expect: "Saint Elmo couldn't give two shites about us. He'll leave us 'ere to die." Then they drank even more. Unnerved, Alice quickened her pace.

"Why must I always awake to yelling?" Alice tried to sit, but every joint and muscle screamed in protest. Running a hand down her legs, she could feel the raised bruises along her shin, inflamed souvenirs of days spent battling the elements.

"All hands on deck! All hands on deck!"

"No more, please. No more," Alice cried as she once again detected the frenetic activity outside their cabin door.

"Mercy on us!" The repeated plea echoed from man to man.

"Farewell, my brother. Farewell," came the call of another.

Groaning, Alice slowly slid from the bed into the fetid water now at her knees.

"I just want to see dry land again," whispered her mother. "Please, God, just let me die on dry land." She repeated this prayer as though in delirium.

Alice listened as her mother begged God for dry land and death. After a few minutes, she'd had enough. "Don't you think we'd all like dry land? Do you honestly believe you're the only person on the entire ship who's soaked?"

Her Highness's eyes flew open, her reverie broken.

"We all make choices—isn't that what you like to say? It's your choice to lie here. It's your choice where you die. It could be here; it could be on dry land. It's your choice. But so far you have done nothing but stay in this bed, expecting everyone to care for you. Just like at home. You lie about and have life happen to you. Well, not me. I'm going on deck. I plan on living." Placing a hand on her mother's arm, Alice reiterated, "This is your choice."

Alice stepped into the hallway, immediately pushed aside by sailors rushing by, sailors rushing to get to the sunlight. Sunlight? Her heart leaped a little as she spied a clear blue sky through the scudder hole. Racing up the ladder, she slipped twice on the rungs in her eagerness to once again feel the glorious warmth of sunlight on her face. She closed her eyes in anticipation, but quickly opened them as she realized the sailors were not rejoicing as she believed. She could smell the fear. She could hear Admiral Somers bellowing orders. She could see Strachey dithering around Gates, chattering nervously. But the bellowing. Why were they still bellowing? They clearly were out of the storm; Saint Elmo had delivered them a sign; they were safe now, weren't they?

Turning slowly to watch the Admiral, Alice caught the chain of buckets emerging from below deck. The sailors had formed a bucket brigade to haul water from below. She may have been a land-lubber, but she comprehended what was happening: they were sinking. In spite of Saint Elmo and his good omen, in spite of her prayers to deliver them to clearer skies, they were still going to sink. Here, in the ocean. Alone. With no hope of rescue. Like Joanne and Jane and all the rest of the fleet.

Alice watched the Admiral, never taking her eyes off him. His eyes were trained on something, something visible to him alone. She sensed no urgency in his countenance, simply focused determination. His men trusted him, and took to performing chores as ordered—no questions asked. He was their Saint Elmo, and they would follow his lead. He was her Saint Elmo and Saint James combined, and with the Admiral at the helm, Alice felt sure she would survive.

PART THREE

"Hell is empty, and all the devils are here!"
~ Ariel,
The Tempest, Act 1, Scene 2

Chapter 9

Landing on the Isle of Devils, 28 July 1609

Alice remained in her spot; Chance alert by her side. The Admiral pointed to a spot on the horizon; the sailor atop the mid-mast confirmed his finding.

Land-ho! The words ricocheted amongst the sailors on deck as they scrambled to new positions to make ready for landing. The sailors, moving with the speed and deliberation of a dance, were focusing ahead on the land, on Jamestowne. Alice sighed with relief they had finally arrived. Dry land. Food. Civilization. And, if her prayers were answered, Joanne and Jane, delivered safe and sound from the storm.

It was exciting knowing they were within sight of Jamestowne, the journey finally concluded. She could relax. She had survived a hurricano; that was adventure enough for this voyage. Catching a glimpse of the horizon, Alice saw nothing. No fort like she had been told there would be. *Shouldn't I see people? There should be nearly five hundred—a small city. People; a fort; movement; something!* Her mind screamed for answers.

Alice watched with mounting horror as the rocks appeared. First they were dots, then clearly identifiable boulders placed in the ocean, blocking their way to salvation. The *Sea Venture* never slowed. They were headed for rocks at full speed! Alice scanned for something to grab onto. Spying rope, she wrapped it round her wrist as she'd seen the sailors do when they encountered large waves.

"Prepare," commanded Admiral Somers.

"Aye, aye," came the chorus.

Each man at his station, Admiral Somers barked commands. Strachey regarded Gates before peppering the Admiral with questions. *Does that fool Strachey really believe he knows as much as the Admiral about sailing a ship?* Alice was appalled at his arrogance and audacity. But the Admiral wasn't. He ignored him—eyes never leaving the horizon, his men never ceasing work—he never gave the two interlopers so much as a second glance.

With the rocks rapidly approaching, death appeared imminent. Grabbing Chance by the scruff, Alice buried her head in his neck, and braced for impact. *What a fitting conclusion to my life. If this were a play, Uncle Willie would savor the irony of the heroine surviving a tempest only to die because of rocks.* Pulling Chance closer, she whispered into his warm fur, "Why did I insist we have an adventure?"

There was no sudden jolt. No crash tore the ship asunder. Just the high-pitched scraping of rocks along the bottom of the vessel, moving up the sides as the ship slid between them. The rocks tore into the wood; the sounds of planks breached by the violent motion gave her goosebumps. The women below deck were now keening, begging God to end this torture. Alice did no such thing. She was fairly certain he had deserted them for this leg of the journey. He saved them from the torture of drowning at sea; that should be enough. Alice unwrapped her wrist and let go of Chance. The scraping sound, coupled with the unsettling sensation of the ship vibrating, gave her the sense the *Sea Venture* had begun humming. Her buttocks and legs tingled. *We were so close. How pathetic to die now while our ship hums us a tune as it murders us.*

But they didn't die; in fact, nothing happened. Admiral Somers merely ran the ship between the two protruding rocks, wedging them there as if in a cradle. The only person any worse for wear was Strachey: knocked off his feet because he refused to heed the Admiral's warnings to brace himself. Tremendously satisfying to watch.

Alice continued to sit, expecting the ship to lurch, fall to one side and spill them into the water, like a box emptying its contents. When that didn't happen, she stood, her legs still thrumming. Then she saw what the Admiral had spied, why he had risked running between rocks—an island. Birds swooped on them in earnest; a warm breeze ruffled her hair; and the sailors began running.

"Abandon ship," they shouted.

"To shore," commanded the Admiral.

"Aye, aye," the sailors replied.

"Ah, Alice," the voice boomed. "Go to your parents. We're going ashore." Chance nudged her with his head as though stressing his master's words.

"Are we there? Are we finally in Jamestowne?" she asked.

The Admiral chuckled. "No. We're on the Isle of Devils. Now, go! That's an order!"

Alice raced down the ladder, along the still waterlogged hallway, into their cabin to deliver the news.

The darkness of the cabin after the glaring brightness of the sun made seeing difficult. Her Highness sat on the corner of the bed, feet dangling in the fetid water. Her father scoured their tiny room for belongings to return to the trunk.

"We're on the Isle of Devils. We're to leave the ship immediately." No one responded. "The Admiral asked me to tell you."

Her father continued his bustling about the cabin; Her Highness remained seated.

"Don't forget this..." Reaching into the water, she seized her mattress. Her beautiful down-stuffed mattress now a wet heap, covered with excrement and vomit. Under the guise of helping, she jostled her father aside to place it in the trunk.

"Child, it's too wet." He sighed, not stopping to scold her for her impudence, but dismissively hurling the article into the swirling muck on the floor.

"It'll dry."

Her father did not respond.

"What shall I sleep on?"

Grabbing her by the shoulders, he shook her hard enough to make her teeth rattle. "Child—stop!" Releasing her, he continued snatching any article within arms' reach and tossing it into the trunk.

Her Highness stroked her arm. "You'll have a mattress, I promise."

Alice jerked her arm away. Bending to the floor, she snatched the mattress from the swill and carried it to the door. The water increased the weight, making movement through the narrow door a Herculean task. Once in the hallway, she realized she would never get it topside on her own.

"Here, let me." Her Highness took one end and together they carried it to the ladder, unsure how to scale it to daylight and refuge.

"I'll tend to this," a sailor quietly assured her. "Ye need to hasten along. The Admiral, he'll be impatient to get you all to safety. Best ye do what he says."

"How will you know who it belongs to?" asked Alice.

"Of the hundred and fifty people on this ship, there's only one girl." He smiled earnestly as he deftly removed the mattress from their hands.

Alice watched as he took away her last vestige of home, and to the queue of dazed, exhausted passengers awaiting their final escape from the *Sea Venture*.

They, her father, Her Highness, and herself, crawled over the sides of the pinnace onto warm sand. It felt light, as though it would not support her weight. It shifted, and Alice's legs were unable to right themselves. She fell to the earth like apples from a tree. She felt a strong arm on her elbow as she was pulled to standing. Once her father dusted her off, he helped Her Highness walk to more solid ground.

"Are you alright, my dear?" asked a woman.

Alice nodded, looking around their new environs. The trio stood silently. Surrounded by water, it was a land like no other. There were groves of trees to either side of the beach; the azure water clear enough to see to the bottom; and hundreds of birds. But what impressed her was the breeze. Its warmth mixed with an initial crisp tang gradually dissipating into a floral scent. When inhaled deeply, it left a slightly salty taste in her mouth.

"It's enchanting," she whispered. Looking to her father, she asked, "Why is it called the Isle of Devils, Papa?"

"Ships rarely escape the reefs and those who've gone ashore were never heard from again," he muttered, immediately taking his leave for the group of Company men already assembling at the far end of the beach. In spite of the fact none of the men had any training in nautical affairs or surviving a shipwreck or living on a deserted island, they all jockeyed to supervise the unloading of supplies. Alice shook her head and followed her mother to the group of women they now called friends.

For the first time in seven weeks, they were on dry land, and it was as if she'd never walked upright. It felt weird to not feel constant movement, the swaying back and forth of the waves. Alice felt herself swaying involuntarily, but staggered step-by-step until she reached the small group of castaways they'd befriended on the journey. Goodwife Rolfe and Mistress Horton seemed to enjoy the company of Her Highness, only God knew why. She wondered why Mistress Horton's maid would agree to travel with such a demanding woman so far removed from her home. Mistress Horton didn't strike her as the adventurous type, nor did she seem equipped to life in a frontier settlement. Yet, here she was. Goody Rolfe was now with child, a miracle that had occurred before the storm. She had shared this secret with the women when they quartered in the cabin. Another woman, Goody Eason, shared she too was with child. Typically, Alice did not find these types of pronouncements as inspiring as other women, and now less so. She observed the little group: an old woman; two pregnant women; a maid; and Her Highness. In spite of her misgivings, Alice felt they were now bonded as they had survived not only a horrific hurricano but also a shipwreck. Their bond made stronger as they had quartered together throughout the storm at Alice's behest. Alice smiled. This was her doing, this creation of her very own merry band of women. She hadn't intended this; she was merely trying to find companions for Her Highness so she could go her own way while on board. But then the storm struck, and it became much more. Certainly her heroics during the storm would demonstrate her independence. Certainly she would be feted for her cleverness. *And I survived a shipwreck*. Her self-congratulatory musing was interrupted by the men. Voices were being raised and Strachey, as usual, was part of it.

"Oh my, not again," grumbled Mistress Horton. "Must he always sow discontent? I'll wager it's the same argument started in Plymouth."

"We survive a storm. We're on dry land, finally. You'd think there'd be some gratitude. Some humility. But no," said Goody Rolfe, "they go right back to quarreling. These men—they'll be the death of us all."

The women nodded their heads in agreement.

"Although," offered Mistress Horton, "our new governor, Gates, correct? He seems a practical man. It's that rascal Strachey who goaded him into this argument from the start. He's the one who's kept it alive for all these weeks. Were it not for his meddling, I think Gates and the Admiral could work out an amicable arrangement."

Alice moved away from the women. While she agreed with Mistress Horton that Strachey had provoked Gates and the Admiral, she was curious to learn what this latest spat entailed.

"Sir Thomas, if I may," stated Strachey to Gates, the pitch of his voice rising with excitement. "You were to be governor upon arrival; I think it matters not where arrival occurs."

"He was to be governor upon arrival in Jamestowne. We are clearly not in Jamestowne, ergo he is not in charge," replied an onlooker.

"The Admiral," stated someone else. "He got us safely ashore, and he was to be the commander while we were at sea, or at least until we arrived at Jamestowne. Arrival is not the issue. Jamestowne is the issue."

Narrowing his eyes, Strachey struck back. "You don't understand the issue. The issue is Admiral Somers was to command while we were at sea. We are not at sea anymore, in case you hadn't noticed."

Several men chuckled; most did not.

"But we're not at Jamestowne either," shouted a man from the back.

Alice watched Gates. He listened to each man respectfully. Never interrupting, never arguing. When it was clear both he and Somers had support for command, he finally spoke. "I think," declared Gates, his voice measured and steady, "we need to focus on the task at hand: helping the sailors unload our belongings as they are brought ashore and creating a campsite. I will speak to Somers once the ship has been cleared, but we need to establish sleeping quarters and secure food if we are to survive." And with that, he set about organizing the men. Alice noticed her merry band of women were standing with her, each developing her own scheme for survival.

Within a matter of hours, a campsite had been established a mile from the beach. The castaways were then assigned to work details: one group was to collect palmetto fronds; one group to collect wood; one to build fires; and one to find food.

Alice's father, even less inclined than most to tax himself with physical labor, joined the group establishing the camp layout. He, in particular, would determine where the sleeping quarters would be built—the perfect activity for a man who eschewed physical labor while capitalizing on his ability to visualize. Alice watched as her father, Strachey, and Gates moved about in the designated area, determining the role of each area in their makeshift community, selecting where each of the five families would sleep versus where the laborers and artisans would reside, determining the communal areas such as kitchen and privy should be central to both as this area needed to be shared. Admiral Somers, along with Captain Newport, had already claimed another area, away from the land-lubbers. It was quite apparent to Alice there would be two communities on this island, and each with their own leader. Strachey had managed to divide the castaways into us and them quite efficiently.

"He's a snake. Your father best keep his guard up, or he'll be taken down. Mark my words," remarked Mistress Horton.

Alice, along with Mistress Horton and her maid, were ordered to collect palmetto fronds. She moved into the vegetation, watching the enormous fronds slam onto the ground. Looking to the men wielding cutlasses, she conjured how to get an assignment requiring such a blade. Hacking fronds seemed more fun than simply gathering them from the ground. Reluctantly, she reached for a frond. She expected them to be sharp, to cut her arms as they were extremely large and inflexible. But they did nothing of the sort. They were heavier than she imagined possible for a leaf, but manageable. It was a boring task; however, it didn't involve imminent death and kept her well away from her mother. It would suffice. For the moment.

Watching the men hack away at the plants, she admired the gleam of the blades in the sunlight. After days of near darkness, swallowed in the belly of the ship surrounded by water both outside and inside the vessel, this felt like a dream. The sun was almost too bright, and Alice squinted against the flashes of light made by the cutlasses' blades. But the air was divine. The smell of excrement and sour sea water replaced by a light ocean breeze smelling of cedar. Standing on an outcropping of rocks, she could watch the activity below. Further to her right, she noticed the ocean for the first time since landing. Unlike the Thames, with its mud-colored water and aroma of dead fish, this water was clear enough to see fish swimming amongst the rocks. It felt like Eden.

Returning to camp, her arms loaded with palmetto fronds, she caught the fragrance of smoke, a smell she now realized had been missing from the ship since the storm. The cooking area was already a hive of activity, but she smelled no food, and her stomach churned in hunger. She had not eaten today. Had she eaten yesterday? Alice realized she had not eaten since the storm first arrived. Three days? Four days? No wonder she felt ravenous.

"Yoo-hoo, over here." Alice knew that high-pitched screech all too well.

Ignoring her mother's call, she pretended to be absorbed in locating a place to deposit the fronds. Official camp duty was the perfect excuse to attend to her own schedule. She was one of a team, a community, and as such would no longer be at her mother's beck and call. The chorus of "your mother is calling" and "no, no let me take that" and "you scamper on to your mother" dashed any hopes of her independence. With so many witnesses, she had no choice but to follow her mother to their designated area.

"I hope it's alright," said Her Highness.

Alice looked to where she pointed: a bed of fronds laid out in array with her mattress atop it. It resembled a lily pad for sleeping humans. She smiled, crossed to it, and lay down without protest.

"It's dry," she said. Placing her nose to the surface, she inhaled. "It doesn't stink anymore."

"Aye. That nice sailor rinsed it in the harbor, then laid it upon the rocks to dry. I didn't expect such niceties from them. Surprisingly thoughtful." Her mother smiled. "No stench. None at all. Sunlight works wonders, and the sunlight here is oddly invigorating. It's as though misfortune on the ship never happened. And us on the Isle of Devils experiencing angels."

"Aye, invigorating. Definitely more pleasant than the ship," agreed Alice.

"And that sailor was able to salvage our bed from the hold. Can you believe it? That's our frame. The ropes seem no worse for the wear."

Alice scrutinized the mattress atop the ropes. The ticking stained. The seams pulling apart. Straw breaching the corner. Her mother caught her gaze.

"It's from the cabin. The sailors made sure every woman should be as comfortable as possible. Given the circumstances. We can make a mattress with feathers. Eventually. At least now I have our blankets to lay over it. Improvement, yes?"

Alice watched Her Highness wipe her cheek. She appeared to have aged ten years since leaving Plymouth.

Chapter 10

New Home, New Beginning, 3 August 1609

Alice followed the scent of frying fish from the newly designated family area to the communal cook site. Carefully measured hewed posts seemed to grow from the ground along the narrow path. As the copse of trees receded, the posts proliferated. It was hard to picture these framed-up outbuildings as abodes for people. But it was all they had. In a mere four days, the Company men, along with Gates and Somers, had prevailed upon the laborers' sense of duty and decorum to build shelters for the women, who, according to the men, were delicate and needed protection from the elements as soon as possible. Which was ironic since the men, her father included, had no qualms about assigning the women manual labor tasks to be performed each day, if the camp were to run successfully. Work they themselves wouldn't, and couldn't, do. Alice didn't care. It gave her more time to herself and away from Her Highness.

Alice glanced to the harbor. The sailors were still unloading the *Sea Venture*, the once gallant hull now reliant on two rocks to stay upright. They tirelessly rowed between beach and ship, each load hastily thrown to the shore, then back to the ship. Alice watched in awe. How did they find the courage to go back into the water? She still dreamed the water surrounded her, swore she could feel it touch her fingertips while she slept, felt it dripping on her face before she rose each morning. Last night had been the worst: she dreamed she was in total darkness with water rising all around her. She felt it first at her waist, then her chest, neck, but awoke everyone in their area screaming before it reached her mouth. Her mother had placed a cool, wet rag to her forehead to calm her, but the sensation never left and she was unable to fall back asleep. So she rose with the sun and gathered firewood for the kitchen.

"At first I didn't like the idea of having fish for breakfast, but this is delicious," said Alice, joining her mother at a table. "I saw the Admiral and some of his men out on the water when I delivered the firewood. To hear the Admiral tell it, there's more than enough to feed us for a lifetime here. We shan't starve."

"I volunteered you to continue gathering fronds. The men are hoping to finish the roofs as quickly as possible, so hurry along," said Her Highness.

"I just sat down," muttered Alice, pulling a bone from her mouth.

"Yes, I noticed. But we all have jobs to do. At the moment, gathering firewood and fronds is yours." Rubbing her neck, Her Highness continued, "If they finish the roofs quickly, then maybe we'll have walls within the week. It's the closest thing to a home we'll have. For a while, at least. I deserve privacy. Is that too much to ask?"

Privacy would be impossible while they resided here. Each home, as Her Highness called it, was an open area. Theirs was spacious compared to the ship's cabin, but still smaller than her bedroom at home, the smallest room in their house by far. And with no walls, all their time when not performing duties would be spent together.

"So we are to stay here. What about us continuing to Jamestowne? Why take the time to build if we are to leave? And when are we leaving? How are we leaving?"

"Shush, child! You ask too many questions. You'll know in due time, like the rest of us. For now, do as you're told. Fronds. Collect all you can."

Alice nodded and took her leave. Returning her plate to the kitchen area, she noticed a crunching below her feet. Looking down, she realized she'd strayed into the refuse pile. She jumped to the side of the picked-clean carcasses. Then, intrigued, crouched down, fingering the translucent bones from devoured fish.

"Th-they are d-d-delicious," said Miss Persons, depositing more bones onto the pile. "I c-c-cooked th-them. T-T-Thomas helped. H-he's teaching m-m-me."

Alice stood. Before her was the woman who'd assisted with salvaging a leaky ship; the woman who'd asked no questions but diligently stuffed bread into crevices as instructed. She was tall, much taller than Alice. And thin, but strong. Her reddened cheeks were accentuated by auburn tendrils now falling loose from her mob-cap. And while her warm brown eyes were alight with excitement, her soft voice and stutter kept her from interacting too much with those she didn't know. Alice had seen her in animated conversation with Mistress Horton but reserved in the presence of others.

"You're Mistress Horton's maidservant," said Alice. "Miss Persons."

"I am," the woman acknowledged. "Please, call me Elizabeth."

"You are a woman of many talents," declared Alice. "Cooking and tending to your mistress. Saving ships."

"I'm n-n-not. T-T-Thomas is teaching me." She smiled. "He's very kind."

"It's his blue eyes, is what it is," announced Mistress Horton. She laughed heartily. "If I were her age, that look would stir me...to do a lot of things."

Elizabeth smiled as she returned to her duties.

"This is a strange situation, is it not?" said Mistress Horton. "Got us in here cooking and cleaning, and they're *meeting. Making plans.* Standing around wasting air, if ye ask me." She harrumphed. "The Admiral though, he's a hard worker. He's been fishing since daybreak, and he fished all evening 'til he couldn't see the fish no more. Trying to make sure we're fed. Gates and his pet weasel Strachey? Nothing. Assigning duties. *We're gentlemen, not laborers. We brought along those sorts for this very reason,*" she mocked. "Well, it's not my job either!"

Alice stared at the pile of fishbones, unsure of what to do, what to say. Remembering she was to collect fronds, she turned to go, careful not to make eye contact with the stout woman.

"Oh dear. I'm afraid I've let my mouth get the best of me. I'm sorry; I know your father is one of them. Please, I meant no offense. I'm out of sorts. I understand their position. Truly I do." Sweat dripping down her temples, Mistress Horton seemed concerned.

"Don't worry; I shan't speak to my family about what you've said," vowed Alice. "Like on the ship, we'll keep this between us three."

"You know what else we should keep between us three? I think my

Elizabeth may be volunteering to cook more." She winked at Alice. "Thomas is a handsome fella. She could do worse than the Admiral's personal cook for private lessons."

Elizabeth blushed as she smiled.

"I never properly thanked either of you," said Alice. "I appreciate the help with my mother while we were on board."

"'Twas nothing," said Elizabeth. "If not for your quick thinking with the bread, we'd have drowned." She returned to stirring the wood coals, careful to make sure the embers were evenly distributed.

"And for putting us in your cabin," added Mistress Horton. "Tending to your mother was a small price to pay for saving us."

Alice smiled. Small price to pay for being allowed to stay away. Saving them was merely coincidental; using the bread as oakum was another excuse to stay out of the room. She had only ever acted with one goal: avoiding Her Highness. But no one ever need know that. "You're welcome."

"Since we're all being grateful, you need to thank your mother for your breakfast. She's the one laid claim to the last fish for you as you're the last to eat this morning. If not for her, you'd be hungry." Mistress Horton smiled at her. "But that's a mother for ye."

Alice nodded politely.

"Aahhh," cried Elizabeth, clutching her hand.

Alice rushed to her side. Gently taking her hand in her own, she inspected the now swelling blister, the red circle marring ivory skin dotted with pale freckles, the dirty nails punctuating soft fingertips. *She's never done hard labor in her life*, Alice realized. She pulled Elizabeth to the tub of water, plunging her hand beneath the surface.

"We need to cool the burn," Alice explained.

Elizabeth and Mistress Horton watched Alice as she concentrated.

"I've brought a salve with me that will help with the healing," announced Alice. "Come with me."

"B-b-but I'm to stay here," said Elizabeth. "We're to—"

"Shush and do as she says," said Mistress Horton. "I can handle the work here. Go with her, then help her collect fronds."

"But we were told."

"Never ye mind what we were told. You're still working. And it's imperative we have roofs. I'll explain your absence if anyone questions it. You are, after all, my responsibility," Mistress Horton stated matter-of-factly.

As they walked toward her quarters, Alice remembered how she'd learned to make salve. How Susanna and her husband, Dr. Hall, had graciously let her stay with them after Bertie's death. On nights her father's drinking threatened violence, when sleep and peace were nowhere to be found, Susanna would welcome her into their home. She'd tut over her like a mother duck, and Dr. Hall would let her assist him in the apothecary since she could read and write, a skill his loving wife never mastered. Susanna had a keen mind: from memory she could recite measurements of herbs, explain the desired effect, or recalculate a recipe for a specific diagnosis. But she couldn't convey this onto paper. So Alice did it for her.

Alice retrieved the rosemary ointment from her trunk, held safely inside the jewelry box she'd stolen from her mother. Along with a few other herbs, she'd guarded this treasure from the past. She never dreamed her time with Dr. Hall would aid her on this grand adventure, and yet she'd packed tinctures and balms like trinkets.

She rubbed the salve over the blister, careful not to pop it. She wrapped Elizabeth's hand with a strip of muslin.

"Be careful not to bump the blister, or to pop it. You can unwrap it at night, while you sleep, but be careful in the cooking area. Perhaps stay away from the fire. I'll check on it each morn, apply fresh salve, until it's healed." Carefully, she tucked her salve and medicines back into the box, sliding the stolen box under clothes so it wouldn't be discovered by her mother.

"Thank you."

Alice nodded. "The fronds. We're already off to a late start."

Alice initially thought using leaves for a roof a ridiculous idea, but palmetto fronds were thick, easily stitched together, and durable. She hated to admit, but they would work nicely to cover their dwelling. And collecting fronds was safer for Elizabeth too, no chance of setting herself on fire or blistering her hands further. She was fortunate to have brought salve, but who knew how long it would last if someone was burned daily.

"The camp is full of rumors," blurted Elizabeth.

"Is it?" asked Alice. "I'd not paid attention." And she hadn't. Even if she'd known where the gossip was to be found, she'd been so busy fetching odds and ends for Her Highness she'd not had the opportunity to participate.

"One is about you," offered Elizabeth.

Alice remained quiet.

"Do you care to know?"

Alice shrugged, bristling to know why anyone would talk about her.

"Well," began Elizabeth, as though she'd been granted permission. "Your name came up as the girl who saved the women. What with the bread and moving us all into your cabin."

"That's not really a rumor. Plenty of people saw me. And there are five of you to vouch for me."

"Aye, but Thomas knows your name, knows what you did; all the sailors do. That was some quick thinking, and they don't think highly of passengers. But they do you. Then he mentioned you are acquainted with the Bard. That's the rumor."

"That's hardly worthy of gossip," dismissed Alice.

"Oh, but it is. It's not every day I meet someone who might know William Shakespeare himself. Me, I don't know anyone famous."

The two continued collecting fronds, while Alice mulled over why anyone would ever think her worthy of gossip and speculation. As the sun slid closer to the horizon, the piles of fronds grew. Dumping the last of hers onto a pile so high the leaves nicked her shins, Alice declared them done for the day.

Depositing her portion onto another pile, now sliding to the ground under its own weight, Elizabeth apologized. "I didn't mean to overstep; I know better than to engage in gossip. I just thought if we're alone, doing chores together, perhaps we could get to know one another. I was just making conversation; that's all. I meant no offense."

"It's true. Mostly. I do call him Uncle Willie; he insisted, even though he's not really my uncle. I'm close to his daughter, Susanna. We lie and tell people we're cousins, which makes sense given I call her father Uncle Willie. And while we're not related, I consider them family. So, yes. I am well acquainted with the Bard, even though it's Susanna and her husband that I know better." Under her breath, she murmured, "I miss them terribly."

"Shall I help you again tomorrow?" asked Elizabeth.

"I would like that," said Alice.

Rubbing the taut skin of her stomach as it screamed for attention, Alice walked to the cooking area. She could hear arguing, but the men had done nothing else since they'd arrived. As had happened with regularity on the ship, Strachey was at the center of the commotion, alongside Gates, Newport, and her father. The Admiral, with Chance by his side, was standing apart, smiling as he watched Strachey spin up into the latest calamity du jour. Scarcely within earshot, Her Highness intervened, pulling her roughly to the nearest table and into a seat.

"Here's your portion," she muttered, absentmindedly shoving a plate of fish in front of Alice.

The crisped skin now had Alice's undivided attention, while her mother stared nervously at the men, especially her husband. Fingering the crunchy skin of the fish between her fingers, Alice watched as the oil slowly coated the fleshy meat. Bending closer to her plate, she devoured her portion in record time. Much to her chagrin, she discovered she was, in fact, still hungry. The simple plate of fish had merely served as an appetizer. She surveyed the area: the cook fires, Mistress Horton rinsing cookware, and Elizabeth scandalously close to Thomas. *Mistress Horton is correct.* She snickered.

Her Highness moved closer to her, the men's voices raising exponentially with her mounting hunger.

"Father is angry," said Alice.

"Aye, he is indeed."

Alice inventoried all the things that made her father angry when at home in Stratford—taxes, employees, business deals gone bad—none of which were present here and now. Puzzling why he should be so angry in a place where none of the usual problems existed. Alice watched her mother's face for clues as the men raged on.

"They're arguing over who's to be our leader, our governor, while we're here," the woman whispered.

"While?" asked Alice. "I thought this our new home. Otherwise, why are we wasting so much time on building a village? And the answer is Gates. When we left, we knew he was to be the Lieutenant Governor, at least until De La Warr joins us. Everybody knows that." She smiled, repeating what she'd overheard her father declaring.

"Well, one would think so, but not everyone is of the same mind. Not everyone here is in the Company. There are soldiers and sailors and laborers."

"And artisans," added Alice.

"Yes. We have all sorts of people. But those two, Gates and Somers, have been arguing since before we left Plymouth. Mr. Strachey has pointed out, rightly I may add, the ultimate authority lies with Gates, the acting governor as appointed by the Virginia Company."

"Exactly," said Alice. It was all information her father pontificated on in their quarters, both on the ship and here. "So, I don't understand. Why are they arguing exactly?"

"Apparently there is some confusion about where he is to be governor. He is to be governor of Jamestowne. We're not in Jamestowne. And while we were at sea, Admiral Somers was to be the authority. There was no provision made for an in-between situation where we are neither at Jamestowne nor at sea. There are no directions for succession on a deserted isle. That's why no one knows who's to be in charge."

"We really have landed on the Isle of Devils," whispered Alice.

They watched as the men continued to argue, with Strachey pushing a bony finger into Newport's chest, and Gates half-heartedly trying to restrain him. Her father, clinching his fist, over and over, but not saying a word, flashed from one to the other in the group. Alice couldn't gauge who was winning, but each contingency believed it them.

"Why can't they share responsibilities?" asked Alice.

Her Highness tsk-ed. "That's not how governing works, Alice. Someone has to be in charge. Someone has to be the final authority. In case we peri—" She choked off the words too hideous to contemplate. "In case there is to be blame, someone has to take responsibility. Someone will have to be held accountable."

"It's only one hundred and fifty of us. Not a lot to govern. If Gates is in writing, follow him," Alice grumbled, having lost interest in the whole debacle.

"Things are never as easy as they appear. The sailors follow the Admiral. They were never to stay in Jamestowne; they're merely transport. The soldiers are loyal to Gates alone. Strachey and men like your father? They're Company men, supporting Gates because he was selected by the directors in London before we left. And that lot?" She tilted her chin toward the cook fires, laborers and artisans now entering the area for their meals. "I have no idea how they'll respond, regardless of who's in charge. They have more in common with the sailors but are under contract with the Company. And there are more of them than us. No, I don't trust them. They're not our sort."

"Our sort?" hissed Alice. "Was it *our sort* who helped care for you on the ship? Was it *our sort* that helped me wash and rinse your clothes so you didn't stay covered in your own filth during our journey? *That sort* brought you food. *That sort* checked on you, checked on me, to make sure we were as comfortable as possible. *That sort*"—she paused—"deserves your gratitude. Thomas and Elizabeth—*they're that sort*. And they've been nothing but kind to you."

"Oh, Alice, my poor naïve girl. It's their job. They know their place, and they merely did their jobs. Let me caution you: don't mistake servitude for friendship."

Glancing to the kitchen fires, Alice watched as Elizabeth gingerly stoked the flames, careful to keep her injured hand well away from danger. For the second time today, she longed to talk to Uncle Willie, the one person who didn't care about sorting people. He cared for nothing more than to know them as they stood. No pretense. Alice loved listening to his stories of life in London, beggars and courtiers, workmen and merchants—made no difference to him. He never judged them for what they did; instead he listened for what he called their human-ness. *Sometimes it's hard to hear, but we all possess it,* he'd told her. Looking at the angry men, the hungry laborers, her arrogant mother, and poor Elizabeth diligently toiling away at a job she'd never trained for, she tried to hear the human-ness. Apparently, it too had deserted the island.

That evening, while the human-ness may have been mute, her mother wasn't. The men never came to any conclusion; they drifted away, bickering into the growing twilight.

"You're to pick fronds tomorrow," announced Her Highness.

"I know. Kindling and firewood in the morning, then fronds in the afternoon."

"Since your fingers are already stained and you'll already be there, I need you to pick extra berries for bibey. That makes more sense than me or Mistress Horton leaving our duties to go."

Alice loved eating the palmetto berries; the tangy sweetness enhanced by the warmth of the sun made them impossible to resist. Others, namely the adults, swore by their curative properties, as Mistress Horton called it. While it could give one diarrhea, it did cure the flux. But the appeal of the berries to the adults lay in something more sinister: its effect on the brain once fermented. It took three and a half days for someone to discover the berries could be fermented into an elixir more potent than the strongest ale in England. An accident, at first, that became a staple drink for most in the camp. Alice had seen the effects first-hand, as her mother, never one to indulge previously, now imbibed enough each afternoon to render herself downright giddy at father's yelling, a nightly event. The madder he became, the louder he yelled; the louder he yelled, the more she laughed; the more she laughed, the louder she farted; the more she farted, the louder he yelled. She'd seen her father, on more than one occasion, deep in his cups, but he never degenerated into giggling fits, and he certainly didn't fart with such glee. In another place, in another time, it might have been amusing. Looking to her mother's hands, she saw the telltale glass of bibey.

"I guess we need more berries. For medicinal reasons," stated Alice. Her Highness nodded, her lips stained the color of berries.

Chapter 11

New Home, Old Habits, 12 August 1609

One evening, having made the circuitous route from her quarters to the sailors' camp and back again, Alice found her father to be more than slightly inebriated from bibey. Unlike the whisky he drank at home, this particular beverage loosened his tongue.

"Father, why do people call this the Devil's Isle? It's so nice here. It seems unlikely the Devil would live here."

"It's deserted," answered her father. "God has forsaken this land."

"How do you know God has forsaken this land?"

"Look around—there are no people! No one is here—the Spanish tried and the Portuguese tried, but no one could stay. God has deemed this isle unfit for humans."

"But it's so beautiful," observed Alice. "And there is so much food. Fresher and more abundant than any we've had at home, and so much more than we could have expected in Jamestowne."

"Could have? I think you mean can expect. And we don't know that for sure. This place is deserted. Imagine how much more will be at Jamestowne, with people already working. Jobs clearly defined. Houses already built. Crops established. You and your mother will have a much easier time of it there."

Was he delusional? Alice was shocked at her father's lack of awareness. Perhaps he had imbibed much more than she initially suspected. Did he actually believe Jamestowne would be better than this? The odds were not in their favor when they left England; they were, after all, the last supply. The last chance the Virginia Company had of staying in the New World.

"But if God, in his divine wisdom, delivered us to this land of plenty and didn't allow any of us to die along the way…" She hesitated, hoping her father would pick up the thread of her meaning. She waited; he did not respond. "Maybe this is where he meant for us to be. None of the other ships are here, and we were on the safest, sturdiest vessel. I think maybe—"

"You think nothing," he erupted, suddenly standing. "Gates is in the midst of devising a plan to save us from here."

"Save us from what? Each other? We have no enemies here; it's just us! And we have no boat. Not anymore. The one pinnace we did have is now gone with Mr. Ravens." She'd never spoken to her father like this, but if his bibey state of mind was anything like his whisky state of mind, he wouldn't remember much in the morning.

"Yes, Ravens and six men were dispatched to Virginia to secure help. But that isn't the entirety of the plan. Gates is building us a boat—laid the keel the day Ravens and his men left, in fact. Between the help Ravens will secure and this new pinnace, we have more than enough to be thankful for. Thanks to Gates, we now have two methods to continue on and leave this God-forsaken island. Now, go to sleep." He stormed off into the night to join other Company men for a few more rounds of bibey.

"Must you always be so contrary?" asked her mother. "You know how he gets when he's been drinking."

Alice sat on her mattress. Unlike her father, Alice didn't cheer for Ravens and his crew when they set out in search of help. Quite frankly, she liked it here: plenty of food and freedom, exactly what she wanted. But then again, she wasn't in charge—of the community or her own life. What she liked or didn't like mattered not one whit, least of all to her father.

"However, I think you may be correct. I too have wondered at God's master plan for delivering us to this island. While your father is correct—we should be in Jamestowne—I do think divine providence guided us here instead. If we were to start a new settlement in Jamestowne, why would starting a new settlement here be so different? I agree; the odds are more in our favor here than there."

In spite of herself, Alice nodded in agreement. "I know we aren't to question God's plan, but we are safe and fed. If we're His flock, we are well tended in this place. Maybe this was His plan all along and He forgot to inform the Virginia Company. Perhaps the men and God have different plans."

Her mother chuckled softly. "Someday your impertinence may cost you dearly, but in this case perhaps you are right."

Alice lay back, enjoying the tapestry of stars for a ceiling, the roof not yet completed. Counting stars, she drifted off to sleep to the sound of waves crashing on the shore.

⚓

Waves crushing her, pushing her into darkness as wood mangled every part of her body. Drowning torrents of water stealing away her breaths as she struggled to swim up, her chest burning for want of air. She swam up, the scudder hole just out of reach. She almost touched it with her fingertips, but she slipped backward. She tried again. Again. Her chest tight from the effort. And no breath. Her fingers, bleeding and raw, slipped from the rungs, the water tinted pink with her blood. She needed air. She opened her mouth...

Screaming. Alice never died in her dream, a fact she reminded herself of each night before she fell asleep. But when the day was over and she lay on her precious mattress, she revisited the hurricano. In the glaring light of day, she could see the beauty in the water, the clear blue liquid illuminating the shimmering sand beneath the waves. However, the presence of the *Sea Venture*, cradled between two rocks in the near distance, silently mocking them in its refusal to sink, refused to let her forget how she'd gotten here. Even now, with her planks being scavenged to make a new boat, she stood upright and proud. Defiant. Her Highness hated the *Sea Venture*, felt it had betrayed them. Her father blamed it for the misery he now endured, a life in which he was neither rich nor poor, and where neither made a difference. Alice was grateful the ship got them here safely, and could now save them further by donating her parts. They would never be without her, not even with a new pinnace. However, she hated its presence in her nighttime world.

Carrying her portion of kindling, Alice heard a commotion in the harbor. She could hear the distant shouts of men. A small boat was approaching. The men manning the bonfires yelled, first to one another, then to the men on the boat. The reply came in English! Then the men onshore and the men on board began conversing. They were…Could it be?

"God's teeth," Alice declared. Dropping the limbs, she took off like a shot toward the encampment.

Alice ran to her quarters, through the doorway, straight into her father. "He's back!" she yelled. "Ravens is back!"

"I bloody well know he's back!" her father screamed. "You know who's to blame, don't you? It's Somers. And his men. They did this! They're mad Gates is leading this expedition and he—not their precious Admiral—devised a plan for us to escape. Gates himself drew up the route! But they're back! And why? To prove Gates wrong, that's why. They never wanted to go to Jamestowne. They just want their money. And there's no money 'til they get back to England. Idiots! Why did Gates ever trust them?"

"Devils! We are surrounded by devils!" proclaimed her mother. "We're going to die here, upon this barren rock. No one will ever find us; no one will ever know what became of us. Why, Robert? Why did I let you talk us into this foolish venture?" She sobbed, flailing onto their bed. "It's because we're greedy. We're too greedy. We always have been. This is our punishment—banishment. I knew it, as soon as the hurricano came upon us. I heard God howling our faults, and I understood our lives were no longer ours to determine."

Alice stepped outside as her parents continued to rail at one another, at fate, at God. Mistress Horton approached. Standing together, they listened to the accusations being lobbed like cannonballs, each meant to destroy.

"It's your fault we're here. If you didn't indulge her—"

"Me? I was trying to pay off our debts! But you wouldn't let me marry her off to Mr. Cyrus."

Alice's ears pricked; her father wanted to marry her off to that old buffoon?

"So I guess they've heard Ravens returned," Mistress Horton said.

"Yes. I suppose it's not a good thing he's back?" inquired Alice.

"Me? Marry her off? Why? I didn't gamble my family into debt."

"No, 'tis not. Two days gone. Not good at all," she replied.

"I'm not the only one who wastes money in this family. Who must always have the latest fashion from London? How's your finery helping us now? Look at us!"

"She's not yours to trade, Robert. The dice for a daughter. What kind of a father—No. What kind of a man does that?"

"It's getting mightily contentious—perhaps I should help," Mistress Horton offered. "Hello? Hello? Anyone home?" Mistress Horton stepped into the fray, ignoring the reddened faces now staring at her intrusion. "There's to be a gathering with bibey in a short while. Fresh bottles too, so I heard. I thought perhaps the two of you could use"—she paused—"a distraction. What say you come with me and we get a head start before everyone else shows up? Claim a bottle for ourselves. It'll do us good; don't you think?" Her question didn't leave room for dissention, and her parents had no choice but to go along with the portly woman.

Winking as she passed, Mistress Horton said, "Don't pay their words any mind, my dear. They were merely spoken in anger."

Alice watched the three leave, glad to have quiet once again, but her mind returned to the revelation: the marriage to Mr. Cyrus had been her father's idea. Not her mother's. And what did she mean by *trade*?

Passing their quarters, Alice could hear her father snoring at mid-morning, a clear indication he would complain of a headache when he finally awoke. She'd seen this before and knew there'd be no joy for anyone this evening. With her arms full of kindling, she moved to the cooking area. Depositing her haul, she returned to the dining area, watching in amusement.

There were several people present, but none seemed to be eating. Or moving. All were resting their heads on their arms. Elizabeth, industrious as ever, placed bits of bread near each person, receiving a groaned acknowledgement.

"Thank you," said Elizabeth, stepping closer to Alice.

"It looks to have been quite the evening. Guess Father wasn't the only one to over-imbibe with bibey. Bibey imbibe," she giggled.

"Oh, I wouldn't laugh just yet. You need to get your mother. I can't handle her and the Mistress."

"My mother?"

"Wait until you see her." Elizabeth pulled Alice to the side of the dining area. A woman lay prostrate on the ground covered in mud. Moving closer, she realized the woman was Her Highness.

"Where's her cap?" Alice studied her from head to toe, the skirts pushed to her knees, her legs bare. "Elizabeth, where is her petticoat? Her shoes?"

"I suppose they're still where she was last," she chuckled.

Alice stepped closer and gagged on the odor. "That's not mud."

"Have you seen any mud since we arrived? No, I found her at the latrines. With the Mistress. They gleefully explained to me hose are a nuisance, then promptly flung them into the air. I managed to get the Mistress back to quarters. This is as far as I could coax your mother before she fell over. The Mistress is in a similar state, although not covered in, well, you know." Elizabeth left Alice to deal with her excrement-covered mother. Alice laughed too, at first, then realized she now had to touch her if she planned to get her back to their quarters.

"Serves you right." She nudged Her Highness with her foot, but received a moan for her effort. "Get up. It's mid-day." Her Highness moved, clutching her belly then her head, refusing to stand or help herself, unable to even move into a sitting position. "Yes, I know. Your head hurts, and well it should, you shite-covered hypocritical hobgoblin." Certainly her mother would stand now; certainly she should expect a beating of biblical proportion. Her mother moved to a sitting position. Then nothing; nothing but quiet tears oozing from liquor-reddened eyes.

"A hobgoblin? That's a bit harsh, but 'tis true I am a hypocrite." Her Highness sat motionless.

Alice stared at the figure on the ground in disbelief. Had she been told she was right? Alarmed, Alice briefly considered the woman to be in the throes of death. Where was the rage? Where were the slaps of admonishment? She stood in muted disbelief at the confession. Her father was always ill-tempered after a night of deep drinking. What was wrong with Her Highness?

"'Tis true though; I know better. I know the bibey-stuff makes us shit uncontrollably. I know that. But the drink is so good, and I'm so tired of thinking." Holding her head in her hands, she began to cry. "I have condemned others, your father in particular, for a lack of discipline, moral fiber, and self-control. For bending to the will of the drink. For over-indulging. Now look at me. I did the same damn thing."

"Where are your things?" Alice snapped.

"You're ashamed of me." She cried harder. "I'd be ashamed of me too. Just look at me. Look at me, Alice!"

"Where. Are. Your. Things?" asked Alice through clenched teeth.

"What things?" Her mother wiped the tears from her cheeks; taking in her bare feet, she ran her hand under her skirt to her knees. "Oh. Those things. I haven't a clue."

"You! Go home! I'll go look round the privies, where Elizabeth discovered you." Leaving her charge on the ground, Alice stepped away from her mother, uncomfortable to see Her Highness like this. The tears; the confession—Her Highness was an unwelcome sight. She'd grown accustomed to seeing her father drunk; she had no intention of tolerating her mother in this condition.

Alice handed each parent a mug of broth. Perched precariously on the side of their mattress, each reluctantly took the mug, then grimaced as the smell wafted into their nostrils. Her Highness closed her eyes and turned her head.

"Elizabeth says you need to drink the entire mug and eat the bread. It will settle your stomach. Or give you something to throw up. Either way, you'll feel better." Each took a sip, grimacing as the hot liquid passed over their tongue. Waiting before taking another small sip; waiting to see what would come up. When nothing did, they slowly repeated the process until the mugs were empty. Her father nibbled at the bread, but Her Highness wasn't so brave.

"You two owe Elizabeth a debt of gratitude. She not only procured this broth especially for you, but she has graciously offered to assist me with cleaning your clothes—a task requiring a heavy hand if all the *stains* are to be removed." She glared at Her Highness.

"I'm sorry," whispered Her Highness. "And I shall clean my own garments. This task is mine to bear."

"I've already started the soaking as it shan't be a one-day chore. And it certainly wasn't a task to be left. The stench was unbearable."

"Again, I'm sorry."

Her father, finished with his portion, laid the mug on the floor and turned to sleep.

"You should rest," said Alice. "It may help with the headache and queasiness." Moving toward the doorway, she grabbed the mugs.

"I am truly sorry."

"I know," said Alice, not bothering to look at her mother.

Chapter 12

Witness to Murder, 20 August 1609

"Who has so much food they must always be in search of firewood?" grumbled Alice. Turning, she found Elizabeth right behind her.

"I've never seen this much food in my life," exclaimed Elizabeth.

"How long have you been behind me?"

"Since you left camp. I didn't intend to follow you, but then you started talking. I thought you were talking to me. But you weren't. So who were you talking to?"

Alice shook her head, said, "No one," and continued walking. She had been talking to herself, a habit formed long ago to keep away the loneliness after her brother died, but she'd never been caught. She'd always been careful not to be overheard, lest someone think her mad. Realizing Elizabeth may come to the same conclusion, she shouted, "I talk to myself if you must know. And I'd appreciate you telling me when you're nearby, in the future. It's dreadfully sneaky and underhanded for you to secretly follow me, don't you think? Did my mother send you? Did she send you to spy on me?"

Elizabeth stopped walking. Not hearing any movement behind her, Alice turned.

"Didn't you hear me? Are you my mother's spy?" Alice barked. "Or shall I count you as a friend? Here voluntarily?"

"I didn't mean anything. Why are you so angry?"

"I'm not...angry, exactly. I need to know if you are my friend, someone I can trust, or someone who answers to my mother."

Looking her square in the eye, Elizabeth narrowed her eyes. "Why, on a deserted island, are we pretending we're still in England and I'm some servant without thoughts or feelings? I am a servant, as we are both well aware, and you are the daughter of a gentleman. But given what you did on the ship during the storm, your disregard for rules or personal safety, to care for all us women regardless of class? I thought perhaps you were different. I thought perhaps you, like me, simply wanted a friend. Someone to talk to. But perhaps I thought wrong." She averted her gaze to the ground as she bit her lip. Looking up again, she said, "I misjudged you, but make no mistake: I will not *spy* for your mother." She turned in the direction of camp.

It was the most Alice had heard Elizabeth speak, her speech usually fragmented, the words and sentences chopped into bite-sized portions. But this? This took concentration, effort. Effort she had afforded a friend.

Alice hurried behind Elizabeth, staring at her back, trying to determine the best way to apologize. Alice ran around her, forcing her to stop. Running her hands down her apron, she tried to control her breathing. *One breath; hold. Now another.* Susanna's words instructed her until she could speak without panting.

"I am used to people reporting to my mother, and I've only ever had one person I could fully trust—Susanna. She's older than me, wiser, and accepted my outbursts without question. Just waited my dark storms out. That's what she called them, my dark storms. And I have them a lot. I don't know where they come from; it's as though my anger comes and goes almost at will—its will, not mine."

Alice watched Elizabeth for a reaction, expecting to see indifference, or have her storm off never to speak to her again. It had happened before. Worse were the people who seemingly drifted away. But there was something else on Elizabeth's face: disappointment. She'd seen this look from Susanna, and it broke her. Her mind raced through how trusting someone new could hurt her, but Elizabeth seemed sincere. So what if everyone knew she was close to Susanna and her father the famous Bard? What secrets from her past could haunt her here on a deserted island? There was nothing left to lose, and it would be nice to have a friend, someone to chat with who wasn't her mother. Steeling her nerves, Alice decided to take a chance and trust Elizabeth, and she'd start by doing the one thing she loathed: apologizing.

"I'm sorry I accused you of working for my mother," said Alice. "I'm sorry for my outburst. I don't think my anger is actually meant for you."

"Then who?" asked Elizabeth.

Alice shrugged.

The two women returned to gathering firewood, working in silence until Alice could stand it no more.

"I really am sorry. I'll try to be a better friend."

"You speak of Susanna often. Tell me about her."

"She was our neighbor," said Alice. "Our families have known each other for decades; our mothers were friends. Their husbands, our fathers, both worked in London and were absent from home." How much should she tell her? It felt odd, sharing personal bits about her family. In spite of herself, perhaps because Elizabeth's quiet nature encouraged her to divulge long-held secrets, she started again. At the beginning.

"After my brother, Bertie, died, my mother took to her bed. For quite some time. Months, in fact. My grandmother moved in, to help, but she's old and, as I've been told many a time, I'm a handful. So Susanna started taking me to their house. I stayed with Susanna and her husband, Dr. Hall, for days at a time. Actually, for weeks. Away from Her Highness, as I…well, I was a handful and made her cry. Things became worse when Father started staying home and not traveling to London. He started imbibing more often and picking fights with everyone. Household staff. Neighbors. Business associates. He hated everything but his whisky. After Bertie left us." She stopped, blinking away tears. "Life was easier with Susanna. And her husband is the one who taught me how to make that salve I put on your hand. He taught me about medical remedies. I recorded the recipes, and they're still right here." She tapped her temple.

Dropping her firewood, Elizabeth embraced her, one hand rubbing her back in the process, just as Susanna had done. Alice cried as she embraced her new friend.

Returning to the task of collecting firewood, they strolled deeper into the trees. As they moved in companionable silence, their reverie was broken by shouts. They stopped and stood stock-still.

Alice dropped all her gathered limbs, moving toward the commotion. Elizabeth grabbed her arm, her nails digging into the flesh of her forearm.

"What are you doing?" Elizabeth whispered.

"I want to see what's happening," stated Alice.

"It sounds like the sailors."

Alice stared blankly.

"It sounds like a fight. You've no business being near a fight."

"I only wish to see what is happening; I'm not actually fighting," clarified Alice.

"Well, yes, but sailors," stammered Elizabeth, "with much of their lives spent at sea, we can't expect them to abide by the rules of land. They're not like us land-lubbers."

"Now you sound like Strachey," Alice sneered. "And what about your Thomas?"

"He's different. And he's the one who warned me to stay within our camp."

Alice scrunched her nose. "That makes no sense. They're still people, with morals. They saved us during a storm, so I doubt they're different than us. I'm going. Are you coming with me?"

Elizabeth shook her head, no. "I'll stay here. Wait for you."

Nodding, Alice moved toward the yelling, keeping close to the underbrush.

⚓

The men were in a circle. Alice could see a dust cloud emerging from the center of the ring. As she moved between the sailors, she could see the cause of the commotion. Two men, the focus of the action, were squaring off. Rounding each other like banty roosters, they carefully stepped around one another. If it weren't for the cursing, their slow movements could have been misinterpreted as the start of a dance. It appeared, to Alice at least, calculated and precise. But once Mr. Waters—Robert, to the few men shouting their support—reached across the divide and forcefully head-butted Mr. Samuel, it became clear this was not going to be a civilized affair.

One body was tossed to the ground as the other flung itself upon it, then reverse! They flip-flopped like fish out of water, the other men giving them a wide berth as they pummeled each other about the head and chest. The scene seemed to last hours. Later, Alice remembered every move as though time had slowed, allowing her to watch each swing, each punch. As the men grew sweatier, and bloodier, their fists merely thudded into the other's face then slid off into air.

Alice continued moving between the shifting sea of the men cheering on the fighting. She was jerked to-and-fro as she angled to catch a glimpse of the two men. The air became clouded as sand was kicked up, making her sightline less than optimal. They grabbed each other by the necks. The men were sweaty, bloody, and more often than not their hands slid from the neck of the other in a futile move to gain control. Forehead to forehead, each struggled to overcome their opponent. Just as one seemed to get the upper hand, there would be a quick jab to the ribs, a muted *thuck* as a fist made contact, then they'd fall back, and the scene would begin again. Mr. Samuel had gotten in more than his fair share of licks: to Mr. Waters' face; to his ribs; a sweep of the foot behind the knee and down went Mr. Waters. Pulling back, Mr. Samuel taunted him with curses. But then the scene would replay just as quickly, and the roles were reversed, both men bloodied and neither willing to concede a loss. Alice, growing bored with the shenanigans and looking to make her exit, sensed a change. The fighting became quieter, the men losing intensity. Perhaps this was how fights ended? The air tingled with anticipation on behalf of the spectators, the men more muted in their support of the fight.

Alice was growing tired of it all when Mr. Waters suddenly stood and backed away from the other man. Mr. Samuel lay in the sand, not moving, now gasping for breath.

"What say ye to finishing this now?" asked Mr. Waters. "I got ye where I want you, and there's no escape—no escape for any of us. We're stuck on the Devil's Isle now!" He flailed his arms at the crowd of men surrounding them as he stressed their location: *Devil's Isle.*

The men responded with shouts of *ayes* or raucous laughter, but to what they agreed Alice hadn't a clue.

"I don't know about any devils here except you, you son of a whore!" Mr. Samuel grinned as he steadied himself on one arm and rose to his feet. "And we all know what that makes you," he sneered.

"I don't think you do. I don't think you know me at all," taunted Mr. Waters as he lunged to the side of the fighting circle.

Then a glint of metal. Waters wielded a discarded shovel like a mace. The sun seemed to highlight the blade of the shovel as it traveled toward Samuel. Alice watched in horror, listening to a sound reminiscent of cracking twigs, as the iron shovel smashed into Samuel. Waters had struck Samuel in the face! His now flattened nose exacerbated his swelling lips. None of his features were proportionate to his face. Alice watched, shocked to stillness, as he fell to the ground, grunting, struggling to crawl away from Mr. Waters, but Waters was too fast. He lunged to the body, and with one swift movement brought the shovel down on the side of Samuel's head, pinning him to the ground with his face buried in the sand. He held his head still with the bloodied shovel blade. It seemed like time had stopped. Alice glanced to the other men. Wasn't anyone going to help him? Wasn't anyone going to take the shovel away from Mr. Waters? Suddenly she was afraid. Seeing a fight was one thing, but this?

Samuel, now barely moving, his hands weakly clutching at the sand, was struck again with the shovel—this time, the shovel met with the side of his head in a sickening thud and a ringing metallic buzz. Mr. Samuel's hands stopped moving, his fingers splayed lifeless in the sand. The crowd was quiet. No more laughter on the part of the sailors. In silence, they dispersed, as though nothing remarkable had happened.

Alice watched the blood ooze from the open gash on Mr. Samuel's head, running into the sand like water. Backing away to the grove of trees as the sailors dispersed, she looked around; Mr. Waters was nowhere to be seen. Suddenly realizing she too may be in danger, she turned and ran blindly toward the trees, and Elizabeth.

"Is he here? Did you see him?" asked Alice desperately.

"See who? No one has come here." Elizabeth smiled.

"We've got to go…We've got to hide."

"But we still need kindling, and the l-limbs," Elizabeth stammered.

"There's no time." Alice began to run.

"No! Alice, stop," screamed Elizabeth.

Expecting to find her friend with a shovel split to the skull, or a bloodied man standing above her, shovel in hand, she found instead a young woman resolutely collecting firewood.

"Good, now that I have your attention, may I remind you we are to collect firewood, or there will be no food this evening. I'm not going until I have collected my share, and I suggest you do the same." She began collecting limbs, filling her arms as though nothing had happened. "You left your pile there," she said pointing. "Now pick them up and place them back in your apron, or we'll be here all bloody day."

"I'm trying to save your life," insisted Alice.

"From sticks? Are you daft? Maybe the sun is getting to you," quipped Elizabeth.

"No—you don't understand. Over there. A man. Mr. Samuel was murdered. I saw it with my own eyes. And the murderer is here…with us," she whispered the last part, not wanting to tempt fate.

"There's no one here," assured Elizabeth, now scanning the vicinity. "We're on a deserted island, why would someone commit murder? There is nowhere to go."

"I don't know," said Alice, her lip trembling. "I want to go back. Now." Tears streamed down her face. "There was so much blood. It…it…made the sand red."

Elizabeth pulled Alice's apron out. "Here, hold the corners." She began filling the apron with the dumped firewood. "This way you look as though you've done your share."

"Elizabeth, he hit him with a shovel. Laid him out like the Admiral does the fish. He's dead, I'm sure of it." She paused. "Head wounds bleed a lot; I learned that from Dr. Hall. But this was more than an injury—he wasn't moving. I didn't see his chest rise and fall. I watched a man die…get murdered."

"Are you going to tell?" Elizabeth asked.

"Admit I've crossed Her Highness *and* broken camp rules? You've heard Father in the evenings. He's angry most days. If he finds out where I went, what I saw?" Alice shook her head, no. "Besides, who'd believe me? You don't, and you're my friend."

Elizabeth began gathering wood into her arms.

"I like being able to roam. I like my freedom. I like our walks, even if it is gathering wood." Desperately searching Elizabeth's face for understanding, she pleaded, "Promise me you won't say anything. Promise."

Elizabeth smiled. "What would I say? I personally saw nothing."

Alice nodded. Walking back to camp, limbs jostling in her arms, Alice found keeping her balance on the sandy path a welcome diversion from murder. She implored the bright sky to erase the image of dark, bloody sand. Approaching the cooking area, she almost felt herself again.

"Where are they now?" demanded Gates, followed by low murmurings. Never a good sign. Then Gates booming again.

"Gone? How can he be gone? We're on an island!"

More mumbled tones.

"Where's Somers? It was his men; he should answer for this." Gates was pacing, as was Strachey. And her father. Father!

Alice made sure to stay by Elizabeth's side as they nonchalantly moved through the area toward the cook fires.

"You, there—girl!" yapped Strachey, pointing at them. "What were you doing over there?"

"Collecting kindling, sir. As ordered," answered Elizabeth. "In those trees. You could see us from here."

"Take that to the cook," he ordered, then returned to the group, eagerly taking notes.

Alice tried to catch her father's eye, but he focused on Gates, the conversation now gone in another direction.

They walked to the cook site, disposing of their chores, searching the area for signs of Thomas, certain he would know why the men were arguing, and if they knew of the murder. As soon as she caught sight of him, Elizabeth's cheeks flushed as she called his name.

"Elizabeth." He smiled, coming to her side.

"Thomas, we need your help," she said.

Thomas nodded to Alice; his eyes, so like Alfred's, they pierced her soul. Oh, how she longed to feel his arms about her, especially in this moment. Her mouth dry, unable to speak, she returned the nod.

"While gathering wood," started Elizabeth, "Alice may have had a fright."

Thomas nodded, encouraging her to continue. Alice glared at her, willing her to keep quiet.

"She thinks she saw a murder."

Alice groaned and cut her eyes at Elizabeth, whispering, "We. Had. A. Deal. You promised to tell no one."

Nonplussed, Elizabeth continued talking to Thomas, oblivious to Alice's warning. "There was a commotion; we both heard it. Alice—she's so brave—she went to see what it was. She saw sailors wrestling. Maybe fighting. I didn't see this. But she told me a man was down on the ground by the end. Perhaps dead. Murdered."

Alice seethed as Elizabeth took a moment to reach for Thomas's hand.

"When we returned to camp, Gates was yelling. Then Strachey questioned us about where we'd been. They're searching for Admiral Somers. Saying it was his men. We couldn't hear everything. But I think, maybe, Alice did see something untoward. Can you help us?"

Alice's cheeks burned; how could she not believe her? Why would she lie about a murder? Now she was telling someone else, in spite of her promise. Alice tasted the blood on her tongue before she realized she'd bitten her lip. Elizabeth's gaze had never deviated from Thomas, nor his from hers.

Alice cleared her throat, startling both.

"I'll see what I can find out," he said. "I'm sure there'll be talk round the fire tonight."

"I could do that much," mumbled Alice.

"I would consider it a personal favor if you'd not mention our names."

Thomas bowed his head in assent.

"Thank you."

"Shall I come find you once I have details to report?" he asked.

"Yes," she whispered.

The young lovers stared at one another in a way that made Alice self-conscious. She'd discovered nothing from this man, and now he knew she'd witnessed a murder. And his help? To listen. The same thing she could have done! Why had she trusted Elizabeth? At the first opportunity, she'd betrayed her, told a secret to a man who clearly wasn't aware of anything. She didn't need them. She didn't need any of them. She could live here on her own and be entirely fine.

Chapter 13

Secrets, 21 August 1609

Finishing her chores, Alice went in search of Elizabeth. It was time to discuss betrayal and friendship. Strolling through the encampment, the skeletal beginnings of an English village, she spied Elizabeth at the edge of a cedar grove, laughing. How dare she laugh after what she did? Alice then heard the distinctive lower tenor of a man. Of course, Thomas. She listened as the two lovebirds fawned over each other. Was this how she and Alfred had sounded?

"We can see you," said Thomas.

"What are you doing?" asked Elizabeth.

"I'm not sneaking," explained Alice, defensively. "I was going to the privy and heard voices. And decided to listen, in case…" She trailed off because there was no more to her explanation. As usual, she blurted out whatever popped into her head, and this time it made no sense, not even to her. The privy was on the other side of the camp; if they'd been paying any mind, she would have been called out in the lie. Elizabeth and Thomas quickly, discreetly, slid their hands away from one another. After a few moments, Thomas nodded his head in her direction, and Elizabeth regained her composure.

"Thomas has new information regarding Mr. Waters." Elizabeth nudged Thomas playfully.

"You were right: Mr. Samuel was murdered, and a man has been arrested. Mr. Waters will be in custody until his sentencing tomorrow." Thomas smiled at her, and she was immediately transported to Stratford, to Alfred. She could almost understand why Elizabeth would tell him anything. She smiled back at him; then, catching herself, she scowled at Elizabeth.

"That is good news, I suppose, although not for Mr. Samuel, seeing as how he's dead, or for Mr. Waters because he soon may find himself in the same state. I'm cross with you, Elizabeth. You shared a private conversation. Never even consulted me before divulging my secret. That's why I'm here. Why I came looking for you." She jutted her chin a little at this.

"So you were sneaking, a bit," snickered Elizabeth.

Alice narrowed her eyes, then looked away.

Elizabeth patted the ground beside her. "I never meant to betray you—I didn't betray you. I never said I promised, only that I personally saw nothing. Which is true. Alice, I know Thomas. He's a good, honest man. And while I didn't completely believe you—"

Alice opened her lips to speak, but Elizabeth continued, shaking her head.

"—I knew he would be able to find more information than you or me. Yes, we are exceedingly good at listening—essential if we are to survive this place—but we're women. Smart and brave, but still just women. And I fear things are becoming much more dangerous for us. All of us."

Thomas nodded. Elizabeth briefly squeezed Thomas's hand.

"Alice, it's a fact the leaders will talk more freely amongst other men, regardless of social standing. That's why I told him. He moves between the camps. He hears the sailors and the Company. We need him, and he needed to know the truth. To see if your name is mentioned in either camp. To keep you safe. I didn't betray you; I was trying to protect you."

Alice deliberated on her words. Taking in Thomas's clothes and the fact he was a servant, albeit the Admiral's cook, she understood him to be exactly the type of person her mother told her not to trust. She assessed Elizabeth: her smile and apology sincere, she was also the sort her mother warned her not to befriend. But she had, and she wasn't sorry. Besides, at the moment, she trusted these two more than her mother. And what if the situation were reversed—would she have told Alfred without a moment's hesitation? Yes. She felt guilty for how quickly she'd been willing to dismiss Elizabeth.

Growing up, Susanna repeatedly cautioned her about purging people from her life for perceived injustices. *Someday, you'll need an ally, a confidant. If, for no other reason, than to save you from yourself. Not everyone is out to hurt you, Alice.* This sentiment was particularly poignant after today's events. She didn't think Elizabeth malicious, just in love. And there was wisdom in befriending Thomas. He too could be a useful ally moving forward. And again, she would have told Alfred without hesitation.

"I see your point, but I'm not stupid. I do understand more than I'm given credit for." She paused. "I do still worry someone will report my presence there. I know I was seen; someone even shoved me aside."

"Your testimony won't be needed. The tribunal already met, and all the necessary testimonies have been given. Your name was never mentioned. You're safe. I'm sure of it," Thomas soothed.

"What do you mean, the tribunal already met?" asked Alice.

Thomas swiped a hand over his forehead and through his hair, his wonderfully thick golden-brown hair. Alice had to struggle to focus on his words as images of Alfred in the barn made her cheeks burn bright. "At the tribunal, according to the sailors, the two men were wrestling and it got a tad out of hand. In the heat of the moment, Mr. Waters grabbed a shovel to defend himself. No one thought Mr. Samuel dead, simply knocked out. That is why, they claim, they all left and went back to camp without a word."

"You said 'claim' and 'according to.' What does that mean exactly?" asked Alice. "And does this whole process seem rushed to you?"

"All the testimony about the incident leading to the death was given by the sailors, who, understandably, operate under their own codes. So they were not taken as seriously as, say, Strachey. Who, by the way, knows nothing and witnessed nothing, but nonetheless drove the tribunal with his prompts to the Governor. The body was discovered on Mr. Strachey's morning stroll, I believe. Things moved rapidly after that. And of course, since Strachey *discovered* the body, the Governor was immediately involved. That's why I said *claimed* and *according to*. And yes, I agree it seems rushed. Again because of Strachey's insistence to the Governor that 'an atrocity such as this *must* be addressed immediately.'" They chuckled at Thomas's mimesis. "At noon day meal yesterday, Mr.

Waters, along with some of the sailors, appeared for dinner as though nothing had happened. While they were eating their victuals, Mr. Strachey came into the camp screeching there had been a murder." Thomas chuckled. "That man. He was screaming at least two octaves above his normal voice, *There's a murderer amongst us! There's a murderer amongst us!*" All three laughed as Strachey's antics had been a source of amusement since the first days on the *Sea Venture*. "No one knew what to do—we all thought him mad. But then he pointed to the sailors and accused them! But did the sailors get mad at the accusation? Did Mr. Waters jump up in a murderous rage at the accusation? No. They all returned to eating like nothing was wrong. Completely ignoring Strachey and his monstrous proclamation. Which served to enrage Strachey more. Then the sailors left. A few hours later, Mr. Waters returned and confessed to the murder, claiming it an accident. Gates immediately had him arrested, probably as much to shut Strachey up more than any sense of danger. A tribunal was called immediately, and sentencing is tomorrow. So, yes, while Strachey did place an immediacy on the event, Mr. Waters did confess."

Alice knitted her brow. "He's been arrested? Where is he to be kept? We have no jail."

"At the moment, I believe he is tied to a tree, with five men guarding him." Thomas shrugged. "Oh, don't look like that; it's one night."

"Who is to pronounce sentencing? Gates may be the governor of the settlement, but we aren't at a settlement. So maybe Somers? I mean, Waters *is* a sailor, and, like you said, they have their own codes of conduct. Shouldn't his commanding officer decide his fate?" Alice asked, repeating some of the leadership discussions she had heard between her father and mother when they thought her asleep.

Thomas nudged Elizabeth. "She is perceptive, isn't she?"

Elizabeth nodded.

"We shall find out tomorrow. The sentencing is to be pronounced with all in attendance. I think they'll make a show of it, like theatre. Instead of being a groundling at the Globe, we shall be groundlings on the isle. It provides Gates with an opportunity to demonstrate he is a decisive leader, not afraid to protect and punish. I also think he is trying to set an example of what happens when one of us strays too far from the law, even the sailors. Everyone, even you as a matter of fact, is expected to attend."

"But you said no one knew I was there," blurted Alice.

"No. I mean every castaway is to be present. Everyone, regardless of status. Men and women. Company men and sailors. We've all been ordered to attend." Elizabeth stroked his arm encouragingly. "I think after tomorrow we will all have a much clearer understanding of who is actually in charge. Tomorrow will be a sentencing for us all. Much more than one man's life shall be determined."

"I do find it all rather gruesome," confessed Elizabeth, "to think we were on a ship with a man who was murdered."

"I'm more concerned we were all on a ship with a man who committed murder," commented Alice. "Thomas, are you quite certain I won't be called up? For anything?"

"No—no one knows you were there. The facts were stated just as you told Elizabeth; even if they were to discover you were there, you have no new information to add," Thomas replied.

Alice nodded. "You two can never share that I was there. There is always my father. If he found out..."

"He won't. You have my word," Thomas assured her.

"Would you feel safer if we shared a secret with you?" enthused Elizabeth.

"I think this is known as quid pro quo, correct?" said Alice, smiling.

Elizabeth wrinkled her nose, but Thomas smiled back. "You are a curiosity," he said, shaking his head.

"Not as much as you think," Alice answered, standing to take her leave. "My father uses this term a lot; I stole it from him. All good writers steal. That's what my Uncle Willie says."

"Do you want to know or not?" implored Elizabeth.

"Yes, please. Tell me—what is your big secret?"

"We are betrothed!" At this, Elizabeth grabbed Thomas's hand as though he may slip away and deny it. But he beamed, clearly as enamored of her as she of him.

"I thought so," added Alice.

"How? We've been so careful. And just so you know, since we're all being so honest, I find your response incredibly rude. It's polite to say congratulations, not *I thought so*."

"It's the way you look at each other," answered Alice. "You can't control your face. You smile all the time. And I saw you holding hands when I first got here." Now it was her turn to smile.

"I told you: she notices much more than you think," laughed Thomas. "We need to keep an eye on this one."

"Will you help me? When the time comes to prepare?" asked Elizabeth. "It won't be for some months yet, but I would love to have you with me. Mistress Horton gave us her blessing straight away, and Reverend Buck and Mr. Hopkins have been counseling us on spiritual matters, so they are aware, but no one else knows. Except you."

"Of course I will help you. I'd be honored to," said Alice. "I will do whatever you need. You've only to say the words, and your wish is my command."

"Keep our secret—that's our command. At least for now. I'm sure as we get closer to the actual day of our marriage—our wedding day!—I will think of other things, but for now just wish us happiness. And keep our secret."

"I will. I promise."

Alice walked away, flooded with conflicting images: an elated Elizabeth beaming happiness about her upcoming nuptials, alongside Mr. Samuel's bloody face. And both a secret for her to keep. But her fear at being discovered in proximity of the mariners won out. Her father had warned her to stay away from them. Did he know they were capable of this level of violence? Why have this adventure with such a threat in the first place? And who *would* decide Mr. Waters' fate? Who *was* their leader? Gates or Somers? After weeks of indecision and bickering, they needed answers. And now there was a murderer amongst them. And her one friend? Now blissfully dismissive of the real danger.

Chapter 14

Proclamations and Problems, 22 August 1609

Mr. Waters stood on a makeshift dais before the entire encampment. Thomas was correct: they were all required to come, regardless of age, gender, or status. Observing Mr. Waters, his hands tightly roped behind his back, Alice sensed his fatigue. Gone was the bluster of a man filled with drink, incited by friends to have a bit of sport at another's expense. She'd heard her father and his friends enough to know men full of whisky seldom made good decisions, and, more often than not, whisky prompted aggressions from otherwise sensible, thoughtful men. So why should a sailor be any different? She was surprised to see blood on his shirt. Was it his or that of his victim? Certainly, someone could have washed it for him considering he was to be put on public display. Her father had spent numerous hours grooming before public events, insisting impressions are often made by appearance alone. So, shouldn't someone clean up a man accused of murder? Shouldn't he too look his best before sentencing was pronounced? But on the ship she had learned a few things about the sailors' way of life, one of which was their lack of clothing options. Most only had the clothes on their backs, the ones provided by their employer, so she didn't expect there to be a new shirt, but a washing wasn't out of the question.

Looking up, Alice watched the branches of the cedar sway in the breeze off the harbor. Without a cloud in sight, the sun shone so bright the earth seemed to be covered in gossamer. Looking to the people gathering, Alice noticed the high color in their cheeks. Being in bright sunlight daily accounted for some of it, but being fully sated at every meal was the real reason. For the first time in months, for some the first time in their life, all were well fed. It was true: there was much grumbling amongst the so-called elite that they had to work, most never having done a day's manual labor in their lives. If they wanted to eat, to have a roof over their heads, they all must toil, no exceptions. The beauty of this island: if one was willing to put in the time and energy, one wanted for nothing. Unlike her life back in Stratford, Alice had been allowed, encouraged even, to work too. She didn't mind, as it gave her something to do. She had adventures all by herself. But hadn't solitary adventuring gotten her into this mess in the first place? No. The fact remained she had not been involved in any mess. She was merely at the wrong place, at the wrong time. She would be more careful in the future. Not jump into things. She got lucky this time; next time…There wouldn't be a next time. She'd learned her lesson. *Listen more; think first; be patient.* Her new rules for life on the island. She repeated them, just as she had when writing them in her journal. Each morning, she'd reread, recommit. Acknowledge the struggle, then start the day anew.

As the crowd gathered, Alice noticed a visible divide in the groupings. On one side were the sailors, the Admiral standing at the forefront between them and the dais. To the other side were the Company men, the so-called elite, their wives and families to the rear. Off to the side were the artisans, servants, laborers, those who most vexed Strachey whenever he was forced to acknowledge them, but on whom they were all dependent for survival, even in a place with food as abundant as this.

Two men stood at the foot of the dais: Governor Gates and Strachey. *A study in contrasts*, Uncle Willie might say. Governor Gates, garbed in rich fabrics despite the heat, perched his hat carefully atop his head. The extra height insinuating he had more power than the observers. He exuded confidence. Strachey, on the other hand, donned a passé ensemble and sweated profusely. He strutted about like a preening, foppish caricature of a statesman with pen in hand. Trailing behind Gates, acknowledging his every utterance with reverential approval, Strachey revealed he was no more than a lackey. It made no sense as to why Strachey should be so public a figure. *He's nobody,* she'd heard her father say on more than one occasion. To Alice, he seemed like an errant child trying in vain to capture the attention of a dismissive parent, too eager to please to be fully trusted. Regarding poor Mr. Waters, Alice now understood his haggard appearance: to the Company, he presented like a murderer. Gates was using him to illustrate the differences between the groups. The message being no Company man would ever come to this.

Admiral Somers, standing in solidarity with the sailors, wore what he wore every day: an open muslin shirt meant for labor. Of the three men, he seemed the most at ease in their new environs. Fishing in the morning and hunting feral pigs in the afternoon, Somers appeared to be happy and at ease with this arrangement. Today no different than any other as he stood confidently with his men.

A fourth man stood neither with Gates nor Somers. The other naval officer, Christopher Newport, strolled to the middle of the crowd, his strides long and casual as he passed the dais. Strachey grimaced as he passed, as though he had caught a whiff of something repugnant. They all saw it, as did Newport. He annoyed Strachey and he enjoyed it. Just to needle the worm further, Newport wiggled the shoulder of his missing arm and winked at him as he passed. The crowd chuckled; Strachey bristled, amusing the crowd further. Noting the other observers, Alice realized no one really took Strachey seriously. Her father was right once again: Strachey was a nobody with no pedigree and no money. Her Highness worried he would take over, assume leadership for things that didn't concern him. Her father flippantly remarked the only way Strachey would ever be put in charge of anything was if all the members of the council, and possibly the entire fort, died. No, her father maintained, let him do this now. Ingratiating himself to a man not all agree was the rightful governor on a deserted island was as close to leadership as he would come. When they got to Jamestowne, he would undoubtedly be cast aside by men with more fortitude, more credibility. Her father had dismissed her mother's concern out of hand. Alice wanted to believe him, but she'd seen Strachey's machinations. Strachey was nothing if not tenacious, a trait that would serve him well in the long run. Take Mr. Waters, for example. This whole incident was because Strachey discovered a body while out for a stroll; he had been working to sow divide since they were in Plymouth, and now he had the perfect device.

"Hear ye, hear ye," began Strachey once the crowd had settled. "The Honorable—" Gates shook his head and Strachey abruptly stopped.

"As your governor, it falls to me to decide the fate of Mr. Waters," shouted Gates.

The sailors erupted, while some of the land-lubbers groaned.

"Silence!" bellowed Somers, turning on his men. "Hear him out."

"As some of you might now know, I have been in constant communication with Admiral Somers since we first learned of this unfortunate event. He was part of the tribunal that heard all eyewitness accounts of the untimely demise of Mr. Samuel, and while we may disagree on whether his death was merely an unfortunate accident, or something more sinister, it does not change the fact that a man is dead due entirely to the actions of another. Mr. Waters has confessed, as have countless others, that he did strike Mr. Samuel with a shovel. While he has professed profound guilt and regret for the consequence of his action, I have decided this grave matter will not go unpunished." He paused, watching the sailors closely. "As *your* governor, I intend to punish all infractions to the fullest extent of the law granted to me by the charter of the Virginia Company—a document you all signed when you agreed to come on this expedition." His gaze trained on the sailors. "I do not intend to allow a murderer to walk among us, however questionable the death. Mr. Robert Waters, come sun-up on the morrow, you shall be put to death for the murder of Edward Samuel."

The sailors lunged to the dais, Somers attempting to stay them with outstretched arms. Newport moved in to help quell them. The rest of the crowd broke into argument: some cheering Gates's decision; others calling it unfair as it was an accident. Alice felt herself being moved backward, an invisible arm pulling her away from the fracas. She struggled to free herself, but the hold was strong. She tried to step on the feet of her abductor, but ended up tripping herself. She continued to be swept backward. Once out of the crowd, she was spun around to face her mother, now gripping her forearm so tightly it felt she'd breach bone.

"Stop fighting me," seethed her mother as she half-dragged her to their quarters and thrust her onto her mattress. "Stay. There," she commanded.

"Do NOT move a muscle or I shall thrash you!"

Alice stared in disbelief, but shrugged her assent. As she sat waiting for Her Highness to return, she listened to the community become as vocal as when all thought they were near death in the storm. This was equally loud, but more menacing. As the light faded from the sky, her stomach reminding her there'd been no noon day meal, she wondered if she was the only one left alive. The village, now eerily quiet and still, showed no signs of preparing for night. Worse, the cook fire wasn't producing the nightly aromas of pork and fish. She didn't think Mr. Waters would massacre the village—he really had appeared contrite—but she wondered why Her Highness had yet to return. Peering outside, she checked to see if she was alone. Gingerly, she stepped onto the path, padding quietly to where she knew she could see the sailors.

The men sat round a fire as though they hadn't a care in the world, drinking and laughing with...Mr. Waters! He didn't seem to care he was to be hung on the morrow. But where were the rest of the survivors? Did the sailors kill them all? And now she was witnessing their celebration? Ensuring no one looked her way—for if she could see them, they could certainly see her—she retreated to her quarters.

"I brought you some food. It's not much and it's cold."

Alice tore into the bread, dabbing the end into the gelatinous fish, soaking up oil. Even cold fish here was more delicious than the fresh fish in England.

"I'm sorry I was so brisk with you earlier. I was worried; that's all." Her Highness watched as Alice ate. "It was such turmoil earlier, and we didn't know how the sailors were going to react. And then Newport changed sides, supporting the sailors' belief that hanging is too extreme a punishment. Then the laborers and the servants all took sides with the sailors. I know you think Elizabeth is a friend, but you don't know what they'll get a notion to do. And it seems like they're all against us now.

Everyone."

Alice continued to eat, never making eye contact. From the corner of her eye, she could see Her Highness fiddling with her skirts, her fingers pulling the fabric taut, straining it to the point of tearing. But Alice never moved, never acknowledged the anxiety now huddled in their room. She didn't take pleasure in watching Her Highness's torment, exactly, but it didn't seem like her problem. So she continued eating unabated.

"Well, it may all be for naught. He's escaped now—a murderer living in the woods! So, you see, it really would be best if you stayed here with me. We'll see what your father thinks about how to proceed."

Alice hesitated. "Escaped?"

"Don't talk with your mouth full," was the response she received. "And yes, escaped."

"You mean freed!" boomed her father as he entered their quarters. "That man has most certainly not escaped, my dear; he was let loose. No doubt by those rabble-rousers and low-lives."

Alice stared in disbelief.

"But never the two of you worry. Gates has it under control. As we speak, he is meeting with Somers, and they will hash out an arrangement for Waters' return. We know he is with the sailors, as those scoundrels have all disappeared too. Somers will do the right thing," he asserted as he leaned back on the bed.

"What is the right thing?" asked Her Highness.

"Well, abiding by our governor's ruling, of course!" Patting his wife's hand, he smiled. "You needn't worry about any of this, my dear; we have it under control. Besides, Ravens has left again in search of help. We've got everything under control."

"We?" asked her mother.

"But if it was an accident," insisted Alice, "surely you wouldn't condemn him to death. And he is a sailor; they should listen to the Admiral. He's one of his men, not Gates's."

Her father, smiling and shaking his head, responded, "Have you been listening to that little maid? Such nonsense. My dear child, you know nothing. You can't trust those people, not even her. No, you'd be wise to stay away from the likes of her." Taking off his shoes, he turned his back to the women. Mumbling, he added, "Somers helped Ravens clear the island's reefs. He's safely in the Atlantic and on his way to James Fort as we speak. With any luck, he'll be back within two moons and none of this will matter anymore." Within minutes he was snoring.

Alice watched her mother, her fingers clenching as she stared at her husband's back.

"I know you don't like me cavorting with the servants, but you know Elizabeth. She's my friend; she'd never do anything to hurt me. Or us. And she's trustworthy. Mistress Horton thinks so, at least. Why else would she have brought her along? Besides, we need her. We need her skills if we're to live. We need to stick together, as women, if we're to make it to Jamestowne. Don't you agree?"

Her mother nodded. "But only to a degree. Remember, my dear, she's not your friend. She's a domestic."

"Even though Mistress Horton trusts her? Even though she got you help after your bibey imbibement? You still consider her as only a domestic? You know what I think? I think we're all domestics here—all men, women, Company, laborers. We're all the same now." Alice watched her mother pick at her cuticles, her nails now rimmed with grime. Changing tactics, Alice asked, "You're worried too, aren't you?"

She nodded.

"About Father?"

Again, she nodded.

"That he's trusting the wrong people?"

"I love your father, truly I do, but sometimes I think he only sees what he wants. He believes things are just as they were at home. But we're not at home. It's dangerous here. Dangerous in a way we've never dealt with, not first-hand. Perhaps I have been too harsh in my assessment of Elizabeth, but I've no idea who to trust anymore. Even your father."

"It feels like the rules changed today."

"It does indeed," said her mother.

"What happens now?" whispered Alice.

Chapter 15

And Now a Mutiny, September 1609

Alice dropped the kindling near the cook fire, then proceeded to heap freshly shredded pork and boiled palm hearts onto her plate. She sat alone at a table, bringing the food to her nose and inhaling deeply. Elizabeth slid next to her.

"I dream of pork now. Dancing, feral pigs, gleefully flinging themselves into the flames for my feasting pleasure. I swear I can smell this in my sleep." Taking the first bite, Alice closed her eyes and thanked God for placing them on this island with its treasure trove of porcine delights.

"Our dreams differ greatly," said Elizabeth, shaking her head. "You best hurry and finish. Heaven knows what those two are planning now."

Gates and Strachey were once again inspecting the cooking area: Gates talking and gesticulating; Strachey lurking behind, nodding incessantly.

"Yes, Father says he's angry because Ravens has yet to return. He no longer believes Ravens should have been allowed to leave again. *Hell's balls, Maude! We were hoodwinked! That's six men we could use to build a boat. What the hell was he thinking?*" The two laughed at Alice's impersonation of her father. "Father doesn't think we'll ever see him again, in spite of the Admiral charting his way to open water. He thinks the boat's too small to make it to land on either side of the Atlantic. If we couldn't make it in a three-hundred-ton vessel, they have no chance of surviving. Oh, and he's beyond angry since Waters was let go. Doesn't matter they don't work together or that Waters lives with the sailors. He's furious we live with a confessed murderer who escaped punishment." Alice dragged a piece of bread through the fat pooling along the edges of the plate. Popping it into her mouth, she sighed. "This is so good. Tell Thomas he cooks the pork dreams are made of." She giggled as she filled her mouth with more meat, the juice running down her thumb, which she promptly licked clean.

"Oh, that's not why the Company and Somers are arguing now. No. Now there are much bigger problems," explained Elizabeth.

"Bigger than a murderer not being punished?" Alice eyed her friend suspiciously. "Or six men potentially absconding with a vessel that could have saved us?"

"You remember Gates assured us he would increase safety measures? So people wouldn't be so mad about Waters walking free?"

"Of course. I've seen more soldiers in the commons area than I knew existed on the ship," said Alice, "and mandatory daily prayer, with attendance. Another reason Father is furious."

"He's not the only one. Thomas said Somers is trying to keep the peace, views this as a compromise, but the sailors are angry as well, mainly because they despise Gates and are being forced to follow his orders."

"It's true. Some of the Company men are starting to question Gates too. They aren't used to being told what to do. Claim he's being disrespectful of their status. Father said every time he hears the bell for worship, he feels like a baited bear. Every morning it's the same thing: get up; hear bell; hear Father bellow, *Hell's balls, Maude!* He doesn't say good morning anymore. Just yells."

The two women watched as more Company men joined Gates and Strachey. As each man joined, Strachey scratched a note on his papers. It would be comical were he not so menacing.

"Father wouldn't answer me, and Maude didn't have the answer, but what about our morning chores? If we're all mandated to attend morning prayer, do I continue collecting before church, when it's still dark out, or am I to wait until after, when we risk the fires dying out? Did no one think of this? They can't make us do this; people still need to eat," Alice declared.

"Haven't you noticed Strachey is always writing?"
Alice nodded.

"He's writing about us! He's been recording attendance—at work, at mealtimes, at church. He's probably doing it right now!"

"So what?" snorted Alice. "Let him take our names. *Alice Drinkard and*

Elizabeth Persons were seen talking. Honestly, I don't think he knows our names. We're nothing in his life. The men? The Company men? Yes, I do think he knows all their names. And perhaps their middle initial." She laughed. "He's nothing."

"Do you recall Mr. Want refusing to follow orders? Refusing to go to prayer?" Elizabeth asked.

"He refuses church. His soul may be in peril, but that's hardly worth noting, even for Strachey."

Elizabeth stared at her friend. "Then you haven't heard. Oh, Alice, Strachey is not nothing. He's trying to get Mr. Want hung for mutiny. Something about defying direct orders."

Alice stopped eating. Mutiny was a hanging offense; even she knew that. "Mutiny? For refusing to attend daily prayer? That seems a bit extreme, especially since every man is now required to work on Gates's boat."

"That's what Mr. Want said! But it would appear there is more to it than a simple refusal to attend daily prayer. He's the leader of a group refusing to comply with any of Gates's orders, including working, since they claim the boat won't hold everyone. Rumor is Strachey is recording all comings and goings to determine who will travel on to Jamestowne."

"Strachey is tracking allegiance to Gates? And using that to determine who leaves?"

"Yes. Thomas said at least six men are in Want's group, maybe more. No one seems to know exactly how many are following his lead. They are planning to make a new community, away from Gates. They claim it's their right. They left last night, and Gates has had soldiers searching since first light."

"If the men don't answer to Gates, that means they aren't Company men. So how did Gates even hear of the plan?"

Elizabeth surveyed the men now gathered, their voices beginning to rise as each sought to have his voice heard.

"Strachey," Alice whispered.

Elizabeth nodded.

"That man will be the death of us all," Alice spit. "But, and consider this for a moment, doesn't hanging a man, or men, seem a little drastic? Father is incensed Ravens was allowed to leave because we needed those six men to work on Gates's ship. So why hang men able to work? That doesn't make sense. And on the word of Strachey? Even Gates can't be that gullible. He'd need proof."

"The attendance lists. That's the proof. If they won't follow Gates's orders for prayer or work, why should they travel on to Jamestowne?"

"Hell's balls, Elizabeth. That's scary. Strachey could have concocted all of this." Alice thought for a moment. "What about us? What if we don't attend? Certainly they don't believe us to be part of a mutiny if we miss prayer. They wouldn't hang us all. Would they?"

"There are to be fines."

"Fines!" Alice hooted. "We live on a deserted island. We have no need for money here. That is the most pointless rule I've heard so far. I guess if murderers can go free, then shipwreck survivors can be fined."

"Think, Alice, what is our currency? Food. The fine is to be food. The offender will be denied a meal; actually, the offender will not eat until they have apologized before the congregation. I guess, if the offender doesn't apologize, it could be more than one meal forfeited. At the very least, it will be an entire day of work with no food."

"There's no way these men can work on empty stomachs. Some are already at their physical limits." Alice thought of her father, of how he now cinched his trousers with Maude's belt; his shirts sliding from his shoulders; of his hands, once soft and pink, now blistered and cracked. While it was true they now had more food and ate better than they had in England, the constant back-breaking labor of felling trees and hauling rocks was taking its toll on his delicate nature. And he wasn't the only one suffering under the weight of constant toiling.

"Exactly! A fine that impacts every single person. Men and women. Laborers, gentlemen, and sailors. Brilliant, but heartless."

"The men won't stand for this," declared Alice. "Father may question Gates's decisions, but he told me he does believe him to be a decent man, with a fair sense of justice and mercy. Perhaps this will be Strachey's undoing. This is too far."

"Is it? Gates now has soldiers scouring the island for Want and his men. I heard other Company men crying for their pound of flesh, that an outright refusal to work demands swift and immediate action. The only acceptable action is hanging. That's the punishment for mutiny." Elizabeth eyed the men, now yelling over one another. "And your father's anger over Waters being allowed to live out his days as though he weren't a murderer? A lot of men agree with him. I'm afraid Mr. Want and his group will all hang because the men are still angry about Waters."

"And they're still upset about Ravens being allowed to leave when they desperately need more help."

"This is bad, Alice. For the first time since we landed, I'm actually afraid. What if Gates and the soldiers hang those men? Somers's men will retaliate. Thomas is with them! And me with Mistress Horton! We'll be in two different camps, unable to marry. Unable to see each other. Unable…" Her voice trailed off as her eyes filled with tears.

The sudden silence of the tent drew their attention. Looking to the path, they saw Gates's soldiers leading a group of men in manacles. As they approached, the first man in the group shouted at Gates.

"Is this really necessary? To put us in fetters when we are simply exercising our God-given right to live as we see fit?"

"Mr. Want," stated Gates, "you have no rights on this island. You will recall, you signed a contract before embarking on this journey, and by signing you agreed to follow the orders of Governor Gates. That is I. So, you see, you have no rights, and you are in breach of your contract."

"But you aren't *governor*," Mr. Want stated. "That's what you fail to realize. You are nothing until we reach Jamestowne. Until then, given our unusual predicament, I am my own man. As such, you cannot order me to worship or work. What I, what we, hope to create will be none of your concern. We merely wish to create a new community and will gladly live away from the rest of the survivors. We will take none of your food, none of your supplies. We only wish to take Mr. Bennett and a blacksmith." He stood, watching the Company men fidget, Strachey looking unusually gleeful as they outlined their mutinous plan for all to hear. "And furthermore, we firmly believe God in His divine providence landed us in this paradise. It seems unwise to contest His decision to follow the laws and edicts of man."

Gates turned to Strachey, who stopped scribbling. Gates's voice was stern, but his words inaudible. Strachey shook his head *no*, then, eyes cast down, he laid the sheath of papers on a table and walked silently to the path.

"He's been dismissed." Alice snickered. Elizabeth stayed her glee by firmly clutching her forearm.

Gates gathered the Company men in a circle, their words indistinguishable. Alice saw her father amongst them, arms crossed tight to his chest, jaw clenched and twitching. Mr. Want had created quite a conundrum: on the one hand, Gates, if he was in fact their leader, had the authority to hang the men for mutiny. But to kill seven able-bodied men jeopardized the goal of building a pinnace to save them. How ironic! On the other hand, Mr. Want's demands seemed fair, and his argument about divine intervention was becoming a common perception of all the survivors. They all felt blessed to be here with such an abundance of resources. As Alice watched her father, she determined the real problem: the Company men no longer fully trusted Gates after Waters was allowed to walk away.

Gates stepped away from the men; Alice's father aggressively pinched the bridge of his nose, closing his eyes.

"Mr. Want, you speak eloquently, a trait that no doubt led these men to trust you. After careful consideration, I have come to a decision: I will grant your *request* to be left alone, to build your own community, away from my *governance*. However, *I* will choose where this community is situated, and I will not allow the carpenter or blacksmith to accompany you. If, as you have declared, God has seen to lead you to establish a new community, then I trust He has also given you the wisdom to use your own God-given skills to build it."

The two groups erupted. Want and his men relieved to have been given exactly what they agitated for; Gates's men for exactly the same reason. Looking between the two groups, Alice spied the sheath of papers left by Strachey.

"Excuse me." Alice stood suddenly, patting Elizabeth on the shoulder.

"Don't forget to thank Thomas for me, please. For the pork."

Sensing an opportunity, Alice strolled to the table with the papers, edging closer as she kept an eye for Strachey's return. She glanced down and saw a chart, a chart with all their names. Lifting the page, she found another chart, this one with all the locations on the island carefully listed. Underneath each location were names and dates. The last page contained a new chart, one for attendance at worship, a big X marked by Want's name. Elizabeth had been right—Strachey was tracking their movements! Slowly, Alice slid the papers off the table; then, quietly tucking them into her apron, she left. She bolted to the quarters of Mistress Horton and Elizabeth. Checking to make sure she was alone, she stashed the papers under Elizabeth's mat, careful to slide them to the middle where they weren't likely to slide out and be discovered. Confident she'd concealed the evidence of her theft, she walked the camp for a few hours before returning home.

Alice casually walked through the door, unaware of her father. Her mother, pacing, paused for a moment to glance at her, but quickly turned away.

"Sit down," her father ordered.

Alice sat as instructed, looking to her mother for some hint as to why he was cross and home at this time. She only received a stony glare.

"I never thought I would have to ask you such a thing, but are you in possession of something you shouldn't be?"

Alice paused for a moment. Did he know what she had done? He couldn't. She resolved to answer honestly only what he asked, not volunteer anything. "No, sir, I am not."

"Are you quite sure? As you are accused of stealing."

"No, sir. I possess no one else's belongings." Sensing a challenge and the need for a bold move, Alice stood, motioning to her bed and trunk. "If you don't believe me, you are free to search my things."

"That won't be necessary." Her father cleared his throat. "I told William no one stole his damn papers, and certainly not a girl. But he swears you were there right before they went missing."

"Where, Papa? I've been in a lot of places today."

"In the cooking area."

"I was eating. You saw me."

"Aye, 'tis true. Did you see him with any papers? Perhaps where he may have laid them? He swears the last place he had them was in the cooking area. Laid them on a table. Right before...well, before he left."

"You mean before he was dismissed, don't you?"

Her father guffawed.

"Of course I saw him with papers—he always has papers. And a journal. If I didn't know better, I would think he was born with it permanently attached. He's always writing."

Her father chuckled. "He is that. I'll speak with Gates privately, let him know the papers are simply misplaced. That Strachey is unduly concerned, and they will turn up eventually. Somers already said as much. Defended you like you were his own daughter."

Alice smiled; she loved the old seadog. Of course he defended her honor. But did her father? Given his reaction here, she didn't think so.

"What do you think he's writing? I mean, he writes all the time."

"I have no idea, nor do I honestly care. I think that fool believes he is our secretary and he's making reports."

"Reports. That's interesting. Father, why is Strachey spying on us? Why is he taking attendance at breakfast? Or at the building bay? Is that why Want refuses to go to church? Because we're being monitored?"

"That's preposterous! Where have you heard such nonsense? That damn maid again?" Her father's anger returned unabated. "And why would attendance even be recorded? We're on a God-forsaken island, without another living soul. What purpose would it even serve? Gates would never permit such an intrusion."

"To determine allegiance to Gates would be my guess. I think Strachey is trying to make himself indispensable." Alice lobbed the information at him like a cannonball, forcing a reaction. Challenging his patience and temper, she hoped to show him the charts, make him understand what Strachey was doing, what he was capable of. Then, maybe, Strachey would be exiled and they could work together, like they had on the ship, toward a common goal. Maybe, without Strachey snitching on people, they could all get along and stop being suspicious of one another over minute infractions. Maybe, with Strachey gone, everyone would stop being so angry all the time.

"You stupid girl," he bellowed, springing to his feet, hand raised ready to strike.

"Robert—No!" screamed her mother, stepping in front of him with a deftness that surprised Alice.

"It's time she grew up. I've indulged her long enough." Reaching over his wife, he pushed a finger into Alice's nose. "This is not a game. This is not some wild adventure. This is about our survival, with potentially devastating consequences. Consequences you can't even begin to conceive of." He took a step back. "All you need to concern yourself with is staying in the good graces of Gates. And stay away from William Strachey. Do not, I repeat, *do not* give him any reason to take offense. Avoid him, at all costs. I will not die here." Walking out the door, he kicked the wall so hard the frame rattled.

Certain he was gone, and not returning, her mother sat next to her. "You father would never really hurt you. You know that, right?" Pulling Alice to her, she tenderly placed an arm round her shoulders. "He means well; he's merely protecting us. He's been worried of late, 'tis all. He's working to make sure we can make it to Jamestowne. To survive. Certainly you understand that?"

"He doesn't believe me about Strachey, about the attendance. He admitted it. Gates would never approve. And he's right. Why take attendance, or track compliance, unless Elizabeth and Thomas are correct, and it really will be used to determine who gets to leave? As determined by Strachey. I know you don't approve of my friendship with her, but she does know more than she's given credit for. And—"

"Oh, child, it doesn't matter who you befriend. Not here. Not anymore." Smiling, her mother continued, "It's alright; she's a lovely lass. I've been speaking with Mistress Horton, and she assures me Elizabeth is much more than a maid. She's a companion and a confidant. Quite a valuable asset as it turns out. She has an ear in all parts of the camp, handy for keeping abreast of plots. Including things your father didn't acknowledge, even to me."

"Such as?" prompted Alice.

"Such as the fact Want and his men aren't the only ones wanting to start a new community. They aren't the only ones wanting to stay here and avoid Jamestowne. This punishment isn't viewed as a strong enough deterrent to the others."

"What others?"

"Now that's the part no one knows. Or if they do know, they aren't telling. But others plan to mutiny." She relayed the information as fact, adding, "We are now surrounded by people no longer compelled to follow the rules."

Alice sat with the information for some time. Initially she had intended to share Strachey's papers with her father. She hoped he would see Strachey for what he was, or at least understand what a threat he was to Gates. When it was clear he didn't—or wouldn't—believe her, she considered giving the information to the Admiral. But why would he care? He already lived with the sailors, away from the landsmen. Who would want this information? Who needed this information? Alice could only identify one person who wanted, and needed, leverage: Strachey.

After her mother left, Alice sneaked back to Mistress Horton's quarters, confident Elizabeth and Thomas were together elsewhere. On the way, she concocted an excuse to be there, should Mistress Horton be present, but it wasn't necessary; the room was empty. Alice quickly moved to Elizabeth's mat and retrieved the papers. Carefully tucking them into the waistband of her skirt, she tied her apron overtop, securing them. Walking into the cooking area, she glanced at the fire. No one was tending it, and the flames were big and strong. She felt her waistband and decided the best way to ensure Strachey couldn't use the information was to destroy it. She placed the pages into the fire. She watched as the flames darkened first the corners, then the middle, finally igniting all in a burst of blue. She watched all three pages dissipate, their existence extinguished in the flames.

She felt someone step behind her.

"Impudent girl," he growled. "Do you think they were the only ones? Do you think there aren't copies?"

She calmly spoke to the flames. "I know there aren't. Otherwise why would you work so hard to discredit an impudent girl?"

"I'm going to tell your father."

"Go ahead. You have no proof. And if you do tell him, I'll tell him what was really on those pages, that you *are* tracking us. Without Gates's knowledge or consent. And then where will you be?"

Emitting a sound that started as a hiss and ended as a screech, Strachey took his leave of the girl and her fire.

Chapter 16

Deliverance and a Wedding, November 1609

Alice stole away to the rocks at the end of the harbor, a place she'd discovered and claimed as her own shortly after landing. She closed her eyes against the brisk ocean breeze, the threat of rain manifest by the gathering clouds. Unlike the welcoming fall breezes, the November gusts blew with the ferocity of a Highland squall. Gone was the warmth, replaced by a chill so vicious it made her eyes water. Pulling her shawl around her, she scanned the horizon for Ravens. They should have returned by now. The current rumor circulating round camp involved Ravens and his men intentionally leaving them and returning to England. Alice didn't believe this but wouldn't blame them if they had. If she had the chance to leave the bickering behind, she'd snatch it with both hands.

The castaways were at odds over every detail of daily life; in spite of the abundance of food and the agreeable weather, they chose to forgo the promise of a successful settlement and argue over who should be leading. And after the Want mutiny, there had been more men questioning why they were being forced to do Gates's bidding. The Company men, for the most part, stood by Gates, even though they no longer fully trusted him to make decisions. At the moment, they were united in the decision to finish the pinnace and continue on to Jamestowne. But it was a fragile truce, contingent on the tenuous relationship between Gates and Somers. If the two leaders couldn't communicate, how were the rest of them expected to get along? Without the help of Somers's men, they'd never finish the pinnace. Every moment of every day, Alice expected to learn of another murder or mutiny, but as the fall bled into winter, none had materialized. But she wasn't complacent enough to think all was well. No, she knew from experience when people stop talking, even yelling, something more troubling is brewing.

CCAAHHOOWW!

Alice jumped at the howl. *It's the Devil! Thomas warned me he inhabited the island.* Closing her eyes, she began whispering the Lord's Prayer, confident the Devil would disappear once he heard it. Cautiously, she listened. Then, afraid to move her head, she carefully opened her eyes, sweeping her surroundings for a demon. Nothing.

CCAAHHOOWW!

It was behind her! Alice focused her breathing and slowly grabbed the singular rock within reach. Clutching it in her fist, she turned and threw it at the demon! The demon fluttered up, four more taking its place. Looking about her, she noticed there were dozens. Leaning into the closest one, she discovered a bird, a bird unafraid of her presence. Its black eyes met hers, and it hopped into her lap.

CCAAHHOOWW!

It yelled, and a chorus of others joined in as dozens now began making their way toward her. She stroked the head of one perched in her lap, then another stuck its head out. They seemed to line up for attention. Alice giggled as she began petting the flock of birds now surrounding her, their deceptively demonic howls at odds with their trusting nature.

"Alice!" The disembodied voice was barely audible over the critters now scrambling for her lap.

Cooing to the birds, Alice failed to notice Elizabeth approach.

"Why didn't you answer me?" she asked, stepping into the ring of fowls, none of which were in the least bothered by another human.

"Aren't they adorable? And so tame. Why do you think that is?"

"They're birds—they're stupid," Elizabeth answered, trying to kick a few out of her path. "I don't care if they're tame. Get that filthy creature off your lap!" She bent down and shooed the bird out of Alice's lap, only for two more to take its place. Alice playfully swatted Elizabeth's hand away before she disturbed any more of the creatures.

"Do you need me? Have we been assigned more chores?" asked Alice. "I almost forgot—Sunday is the first reading of the banns."

"And the handfasting," blurted Elizabeth.

"You don't need that, not here."

"I don't care. I want everyone to hear us promise ourselves to one another."

"There is no one—literally no one—here to take him from you. I think you're safe."

"It's what we want, so stop trying to make me cross."

"But it's fun," snickered Alice. "Go on then, what can I help you with?"

"I only have one dress. It's nothing, really, but Mistress Horton said it's not good for a marriage. She suggested I add ribbon to it; she assured me the bride lace will brighten it. But it doesn't."

"I have a better idea," said Alice. "I brought a dress, a new one, that would be perfect with your complexion." Alice recalled how the yellow satin dress came to be with her, the fuss she made about bringing it, the glee she had taken in vexing her mother. "But it's yellow."

Elizabeth stared back.

"Dressed in yellow; ashamed of your fellow. It's bad luck, or so I've been told. I don't believe that, of course, but I wanted you to know. In case it's a problem."

"Oh," peeped Elizabeth, "that's what you consider a problem. No. I expect the problem to be length."

"Because I'm short," admitted Alice. "Let's try the dress first, then determine the problems."

Standing in front of the three women, Elizabeth twirled, the yellow satin skirt billowing out. While the skirt fell well above her ankle, from the waist up it was flawless.

"Simply divine," declared Mistress Horton. "But what to do about how short it is?"

"Hmmm. It's not so bad," said Maude, crouching next to Elizabeth. "Leave it with me."

"Thank you," said Elizabeth quietly, her hands gliding over the fabric.

"I'd like to make your headpiece," declared Alice. "With your permission, of course. It will be my gift to you."

"Alice, thank you." Elizabeth dabbed her eyes. "Thank you all so much. I never imagined I'd have anything as lovely as this. I don't know how I can ever repay you, any of you."

Alice helped Elizabeth out of the garment, carefully handing the dress to her mother. She'd never seen her mother do more than needlework, and while skeptical as to how she'd repair the dress to an acceptable length, she was curious to see what other skills the woman possessed.

"Oh, my dear, we don't expect repayment," declared Mistress Horton. "Your wedding is a welcome distraction for us all. Reminds us of happier times. When we were young and in love."

The women murmured assent as footsteps grew closer.

"I have another surprise for you," said Mistress Horton, stepping toward the doorway. "Come in, Thomas."

As Thomas stepped into the room, he smiled at Elizabeth.

"Elizabeth, I think of you as much more than my maidservant. I was quite fond of you before, but since landing here I now think of you as a confidant, even a daughter of sorts. Oh, let me just get to it." Reaching into her pocket, she produced a gold gimmal ring, the three interlocking spheres forming one ring. She separated the rings and held them in her hand. "In my family, these rings signify a betrothal. They are handed down mother to daughter as a reminder of familial bonds, of support in your new life as a wife and, hopefully, mother. As you have no mother, and I have no daughter, I'm giving you mine. There are three: one for each of us." She first placed one in Elizabeth's palm, then Thomas's, keeping the third for herself. "We each wear one on our ring finger until the wedding, at which time they will be rejoined into one wedding ring. Elizabeth, you shall wear that. You will have my ring on your wedding day as you will no longer belong to me, but to your husband."

"Mistress Horton, I can't. It's too much," whispered Elizabeth.

"I agree," said Thomas.

"Nonsense," replied Mistress Horton. "They're meant for people in love, to serve as a reminder of your bond. May you two find as much happiness as I once did." Mistress Horton's words hitched in her throat; then she took her leave. Each of the betrothed gazed at the gold band lying in their palm.

"I think it would hurt her deeply if you didn't accept them," said Maude.

"Shall we?" said Thomas. Taking the ring from Elizabeth, he placed it on her ring finger. "I love you."

"I love you too," she said, sliding the ring on his finger.

Alice and her mother stood watching the couple. "That will be you someday," assured Maude.

"Perhaps," said Alice, *but only if it's Alfred.*

Alice arose before dawn, with two thoughts on her mind: *26 November, Elizabeth's wedding day, and I need to hide.* They'd been preparing all week, every waking hour, for this day. In addition to her scheduled chores, which she'd performed alone, she'd also been tasked with knotting the ribbons for the tables—a tradition deemed necessary, especially here, as a sign of friendship, according to her mother. The woman had seized the wedding planning, demanding they follow all the traditions from home, much to everyone's chagrin as it meant additional days of preparation that neither the bride nor groom nor church official requested. But Maude had her mind set.

Alice agreed to knot ribbons because it sounded easy—who doesn't know how to make a knot? But the tediousness of working with the ribbon, combined with her mother's constant rebukes about her knotting skills, exhausted her. Thankfully, Goody Rolfe and Goody Eason volunteered to help, otherwise it would never have been finished in time.

Alice sat, allowing the little demon-sounding critters to fill her lap. She was excited for Elizabeth, but she reveled in the silence the harbor provided her. Perhaps that was the most draining part of this whole experience: having to constantly be polite. And sociable. She didn't always feel like talking; sometimes she merely desired her own thoughts. She shooed the birds off, having to return to quarters.

There was another reason Alice needed to be left alone: she had worked by candlelight for two weeks, secretly embroidering Elizabeth's wedding night chemise with Mistress Horton's coveted gold thread. She had placed the final stitch just last night, her mother marveling at how it shone in the dancing flame of the candle, the gold stitching resembling an embedded necklace at the edge of the neckline. She'd also created a headpiece of carefully woven ribbon decorated with berries and sprigs of cedar. Elizabeth's wedding was nothing if not thematically linked with miles of ribbon.

Alice could hear the women well before she saw their quarters. In spite of the hour, the women were raucously laughing as they shared stories of what Elizabeth could expect on her wedding night.

"Watch his toenails," chuckled Goody Rolfe. "They're sharper than they look. And when you turn over—"

"Or more likely he turns you over," snickered Maude.

"It'll stick you where you least expect it!" roared Goody Eason.

"It sure will!" added Mistress Horton.

"Ladies, I can hear you clear to the harbor," chastised Alice as she entered.

Pffft, was the collective response.

Alice retreated to her bed, the women still laughing hysterically at their wedding night revelations. Alice sat quietly as she didn't fully understand the humor. Once Goody Eason finished brushing her hair, Elizabeth began dressing, the women buzzing around her like bees at the hive. The rowdiness replaced by each woman's reflection of her own wedding day. As the last stay was secured on the wedding dress, the room fell silent.

"Oh, Elizabeth," breathed Mistress Horton.

Maude got on her hands and knees, pulling the skirt taut. Alice watched her mother as she smoothed the blue silk. The pale blue of the hem coupled with the yellow of the dress stopped Alice cold. Catching her eye, her mother smiled.

"Beautiful," said Elizabeth.

"I have something else for you," said Maude. Lifting the lid of the trunk, she retrieved a garter in the same blue silk, the ribbons edged with yellow thread to match the dress. "I can think of few things more traditional than this. May I?" Kneeling again, Maude lifted the skirt and tied it over Elizabeth's knee, making sure to knot it tight, a delight for a man to unravel when the time came.

"And my gift to you." Alice placed the headpiece atop her long hair, carefully brushed and scented with rose oil.

The women stepped back and admired their work, nodding approval.

"I have something for all of you," said Elizabeth. She produced four crimson ribbons, each knotted exactly twenty-six times. "I wanted to show you my appreciation. Goody Eason has been kind enough to give me this ribbon, as Goody Rolfe did for the table ribbon. Both precious gifts as we may never have more." She handed a ribbon to Maude and Mistress Horton, and the goodwives. But not Alice. She stood empty-handed. "Each strand has twenty-six knots, the date of my wedding, a date that serves as a reminder of what we accomplished together." She smiled through tears. "This is so much more than I expected."

"Ah, now, you mustn't cry, dear," prompted Mistress Horton. "The tears will stain the dress, and we don't want that now, do we?"

Elizabeth wiped her face and shook her head, forcing an uneasy smile.

After embraces and well-wishes, the women headed to the chapel, leaving Alice and Elizabeth alone for the first time in a week.

"You thought I'd forgotten to give you a gift, didn't you?" asked Elizabeth.

"I did, and the idea of the knots was mine."

"Our bond is special, different, like sisters. You deserve so much more than a knotted ribbon." She placed a small blue silk object into the palm of Alice's hand. Alice carefully unfurled the cloth.

"It's a cut-out hand." Alice laughed. "Are you lending me a hand?"

"Yes, but it's not just any hand; it's my hand. I traced my hand on the extra cloth your mother gave me."

"But the tips, they're all embroidered, with..." Alice looked closely. "It's our life here!"

"It is," said Elizabeth, beaming at her work. "It's my left hand, palm up. I can't afford to give you a friendship ring, but I can give you my left hand, my heart hand, like I will give Thomas in marriage. It's closest to the heart, like you have been. If you start with the thumb, you'll see a ship. I had trouble with the masts."

"It's exquisite," whispered Alice.

"Next, on the index finger, it's palmetto fronds, then berries, then a pig, and finally a cahow. All these things are reminders of you. Of our life here. From how we met to the hiding place only you and I know." Elizabeth smiled as Alice threw her arms around her neck.

"I will treasure it always," promised Alice. "But now, we best be on our way. Don't want to be late for your own wedding."

After eating more than her fair share, dancing with men that made her father's jaw flutter in frustration, and, reluctantly, helping to clean after the feast, Alice returned to their quarters exhausted. Since Elizabeth and Thomas were given the morrow off, as a wedding gift from both Gates and Somers, her workload would be doubled.

Sliding onto her mattress, she came face-to-face with the gaping maw of Mistress Horton. Jumping to her feet, Alice stared at the woman in her bed.

"You'll sleep with me," whispered her mother, lifting the blanket. "She gave the newlyweds her quarters for the night, and since your father saw it necessary to volunteer for guard duty, I said she could stay with us."

Perhaps it was the generosity shared throughout the day amongst the survivors, or perhaps it was listening to Mistress Horton snore and fart, precisely as her friend had described, or perhaps it was exhaustion, but Alice could think of nothing more comforting than crawling into bed with her mother and falling asleep.

"I love how you helped Elizabeth," said Alice. "Making the garter really surprised me, but the band of blue was truly inspired."

"Thank you," replied Maude. "She deserves a promising start. Especially here."

"I'm glad to hear that, as I gave her a gift. From both of us."

"Well, that was thoughtful. Would it please you to tell me what *we* gave her?"

"I have a confession," whispered Alice, "actually two confessions. The first is a considerable infraction, and understand I will never do anything like this again, but...I gave her your jewelry box. The carved one with the mother-of-pearl inlay. The one grandmother gave you. I took it from your room, before we left, and hid it in my trunk. Because I was mad at you, for some reason I can't even remember now. Then when Mistress Horton gave them the rings, I thought it would make the perfect gift for them. They'd appreciate it, and I'd never have to explain my childish prank to hurt you. But now? I am truly sorry. I should have told you before I gave it to them."

Alice's mother snickered. "Oh, my dear. I had no intention of bringing that with us. That's why it was still in my room. Didn't you notice it was empty? I've never been able to claim it for my own use because, well, I stole it from my mother, when I was angry. Mothers and daughters. We're so easy to anger, even when we're of a marriageable age. Obviously it only caused mischief in our houses. I think it's good it has a new home and was given for a good reason rather than stolen for nonsense. Good riddance! That's what I say."

"My second confession is a tad more serious. I wasn't angry when I did this, and I did it here. Recently. Mother, I know where the blue silk came from. You had another dress made for me. It was in your trunk. I saw the material from under the lid, so I opened it. It was the dress you wanted me to choose for our journey."

"Yes."

"But I fought for the yellow one."

"Yes."

"And you had both made, at great expense. Why did you do it?" She waited. "Did you think me false in my promise to let you choose my wedding dress when we returned to England? Did you think me a liar? Because—"

"Hush, child. I never paid any attention to your wants, not then. No, I didn't—still don't, in fact—believe we'll earn anything from this venture. And I certainly don't believe we will ever see England again. I've had my doubts all along: from the moment your father announced his intention to join the Virginia Company to the moment we were dashed onto the rocks."

"Then why did you agree to come?"

"Two reasons," she stated without hesitation. "To save Robert from himself and to save you from marrying that reprobate Cyrus."

Alice watched the wax pool, then slide down the candle. All these months, she had known the truth about that marriage but refused to believe her father would betroth her without her permission. Instead, she had found it so easy to blame her mother. Acknowledgement of the betrayal was unfathomable.

"Mother," she began, "why did Father agree to that marriage?"

Maude hesitated. Alice could hear the deep, measured breaths as her mother struggled against the words, then relented. "Your father incurred some debts...actually, substantial debts, from gambling. You have to understand: he wasn't always like this. Before..." She stopped.

"I know. Bertie's death changed everything. I remember the days before Papa was angry all the time. I remember laughter. But the marriage. How does this relate to the marriage?"

"Mr. Cyrus held the debt and offered your father a way out: if he could marry you, all debt would be forgiven. Furthermore, he would expect no dowry, just your hand. It was a good financial decision, not just for us, but also for you. You would stand to live in comfort for the rest of your years."

"So he traded me? Like a cow or a goat?" Alice felt the tears pricking her eyes, rage-filled globules threatening to betray her anger.

"He didn't want to, but what choice did he have? We stood to lose everything! The estate, the business. Your father was to lose his livelihood." She faltered. "He never meant to hurt you, merely to save his family."

"I am his family! You have no other children. Not anymore. I'm it!" Alice sputtered, the harsh reality now taking her breath. "He only stood to lose things that can be replaced; I stood to lose my womanhood, my virginity.

I hardly think that a small price to pay for a drunk who nearly lost it all gambling."

"There is more, if you'd care to hear," volunteered her mother. "It's how we ended up here. Mr. Cyrus gave your father another option: travel to Jamestowne. He would take the business, of course, and the estate, with the understanding your grandmother be allowed to live out her days there. In exchange, we agreed to represent his interest with the Company. He actually gave your father a chance to start over. This arrangement helps all of us, in the long run. Mr. Cyrus fulfilled his obligation to provide a man to help secure the settlement; your father now has no debt; and any money or property we make in the next seven years will be ours outright. We owe nothing to no one."

"But what about me? I promised Alfred I'd return. He promised to wait for me."

"Oh, my sweet girl," she said, smoothing Alice's hair. "Certainly you realize what a childish dream that is. I'm sorry. I'm genuinely sorry about Alfred. But you must know we would never have allowed such a relationship to continue. Not then."

"What if it were now?"

"Now," Maude exhaled. "Now I have no clue as to what your prospects will be. Here or in Jamestowne. Obviously I would prefer you to marry a Company man. He'll provide more security than a laborer. What I do want, above all else, is for you to be happy. I want you to find love, find someone you trust and respect. That much I've learned here. When you have nothing else, you'll still have each other. Best if you, at least, like one another."

"I love Alfred," whispered Alice.

"I know, and you will always have a soft spot for him as he was your first. But trust me, there will come a time when he won't be foremost in your mind or heart." She pulled the blanket tighter around them, the wind now threatening to blow in the cedar walls. "You asked about the dress. You must think me daft to place such hope into a blue silk dress, but last April it represented your future. From the color to the material, it was all I could control."

"Last April," Alice muttered, "our biggest argument was over the color of a dress. Now, we make sure we aren't murdered or hung for mutiny as we go through our daily routines. How different our lives have become."

"How different indeed," mumbled her mother. "By the way, the blue dress is still there for you. I only took a little off each sleeve should you ever change your mind and want to wear a blue dress your daft mother insisted you own."

Alice slid back into her mother, her warmth reassuring as the clouds let loose a barrage of icy pellets.

⚓

Alice felt his presence before opening her eyes. Her father sat splay-legged on the roughhewn cedar chair. Slipping from beneath the blanket, she wrapped her shawl tight round her shoulders, the pre-dawn chill felt through to her bones. As the emerging orange light slowly pushed the veil of violet from the sky, Alice watched her father. In spite of his betrayal, she still loved him. His greying beard and disheveled appearance softening her anger, she touched him gently on the shoulder, ushering him to the bed and the rest he so obviously needed.

"Papa, go to bed," she whispered.

Without opening his eyes, he shook his head. "Not yet. Not until I speak to your mother."

"I'm awake." Her mother sat up, groggy, then taking note of her husband, alarmed. "Robert, what's the matter?"

"Not in front of Alice," he said, waving her away.

"No, she stays," declared Maude. "As does she."

Mistress Horton sat up, greeting everyone with a nod of the head, then asked, "What is it, Robert? What has happened?"

"I don't know where to begin, but the gossip is true." He nodded to Maude.

"*The Deliverance* is too small for all of us," she stated.

"Yes, and worse, Strachey has been keeping records of all our movements, our compliance with orders."

"I told you!" shouted Alice.

Her father nodded. "But you didn't know why. I do. Gates is using the information to determine who goes and who stays."

"He approved this? This spying?" asked Mistress Horton.

"That part is less clear. I don't think it was his idea, not initially. But it doesn't matter. The fact is, he can only take half of us, that's what Frobisher said. And Somers confirmed." Her father stood and kicked the chair to its side. "After all this time. All this work. He knew he couldn't take us all. He knew!"

"It would appear he's deceived more than just you. What are other members of the Company saying?" asked Maude.

"We suspected. It was us who requested Somers take a look. It's why he's been at the building bay so often this month. Last night, he confirmed our suspicions. I have no idea what's to become of us now. I believed, as part of the Company, we would travel. Now I'm not so sure. And Strachey, heaven knows what ideas that sycophant has planted in Gates's mind."

"But you have his ear, have you not?" asked Mistress Horton.

"No, not really. Strachey is acting as his secretary. No one is allowed to speak with Gates without first getting permission from Strachey." Her father sank onto the bed, distraught in a way Alice hadn't seen since Bertie's death.

"I've heard talk Somers plans to build another boat," interjected Alice. "He's already secured another building site and now needs men."

Alice's father regarded her, as though she had materialized from thin air. "That's correct. He's making the proposal to Gates this morning. But how did you—"

"I know lots of things." Alice smiled. "Aren't you supposed to be there? I understood all Company men were to be present. Or has Strachey stopped that too?"

"I should be, if for no other reason than to enthusiastically support Gates so Strachey can document the occasion. It may give us a chance at being selected to go. On the other hand, it may not even matter. What if, despite months of work, of keeping my opinions to myself, of blindly supporting Gates in his skirmishes with Somers, he decides to only take his soldiers and a handful of others? What if, after all I have sacrificed, consented, acquiesced, to be a good, loyal member of the Company, we get left behind?"

"Robert, you're exhausted. Lie here for a few minutes, take a short nap." Placing a hand on his forehead, Maude declared him feverish and forbade him to get up. Within minutes, he was fast asleep.

The three women stepped from the door.

"I'm late tending to the kindling, but I'll make sure to time my return to the cooking area with the meeting. I'll be within earshot of the proceedings," said Alice.

"Very good," stated Mistress Horton. "I'm to work in the kitchen, so I'll stay sharp for any word."

"I promised the newlyweds breakfast, but I plan to keep Robert away from everyone today. He's too much of a liability when he's like this."

"And he does have a fever." Alice nodded. "Safer for him to stay away."

"He doesn't have a fever. I only told him that as it's the only way he'll give himself permission to rest. But it is an excellent, and plausible, excuse for his absence." Her mother smiled. "And no one will be willing to risk illness to check. Alice, if anyone asks, tell them your father is feeling poorly. Now run along. We don't need to incur Strachey's wrath because you're a tad behind in your chores."

Ah, Strachey, thought Alice as she left the women. *You sad little weasel of a man, you can't get rid of us that easily. I'll bet you never counted on Somers coming to our aid. He's the real leader, and once he announces his plan of another pinnace? You'll cease to hold sway over anything.*

Placing a tray on the chair, Alice woke her parents.

"You've been asleep all day," she remarked, handing each a boiled cahow egg.

"What did you learn?" asked her mother.

"Don't worry, we'll all be going to Jamestowne. Somers convinced Gates of the need for another vessel. Made sure he understood how the *Deliverance* was affecting morale. Gates had no choice but to agree."

"That was easy," declared her mother.

"Not really, but with witnesses and Frobisher's statement? If he had any hope of maintaining control and remaining a leader at all, he had to agree," Alice said.

"What about supplies?" asked her father. "Gates commandeered all salvageable wood from the *Sea Venture*. And the ropes. Actually, he may have taken every usable item."

"Except one iron bolt," quipped Alice. "Gates made a production of giving Admiral Somers one iron bolt. Nothing more. He did agree to allow Somers to use the tools, provided they weren't needed for the *Deliverance*. And twenty men, including Bennett, the carpenter. Remember him? The one from Want's mutiny?"

"Oh my," gasped Maude.

"Do we know yet which twenty men have been assigned to Somers?" asked her father.

"I didn't recognize the names, except Bennett, but I wasn't paying full attention. I was mainly listening for your name. It shan't be you with them."

"We need a plan," said Robert. "If we're to leave this island, we need to ingratiate ourselves with both Strachey and Gates."

Maude nodded; Alice remained still.

"Alice, keep your ears open. If you discover any more of Strachey's mischiefs, let me know immediately."

They all knew surviving the island would take a concerted effort moving forward. More importantly, there was only one way to safeguard passage to Jamestowne: don't land on Strachey's bad side. In spite of the danger, in spite of an uncertain future, knowing her parents were of a like mind made Alice feel calmer than she had since they'd landed.

Chapter 17

Christmas and New Year, 1609–10

Walking along the beach, Alice welcomed the solitude. Five months of walking the shore hadn't dulled her delight in the sharp bite of salty air on her cheeks and lips. Today, however, the bite felt more personal, as though the wind singled her out and stabbed her cheeks with its prickly fingers, reminding her nature is never to be ignored. Her eyes watered from the chill, but still she walked her route. She had missed her daily walks during November as she prepared for Elizabeth's wedding, but now with Christmas upon them, Maude had promised her a day to herself to wander as she liked. It was her Christmas gift.

CAHOW! CAHOW!

The familiar call of her fluffy fowl friends, once vaguely demonic, now beckoned her to the rocks. She hurried to join them. Moving a little here and there, they made a path, and she sat at the outcropping as she had when she first discovered them. There weren't as many now. The men had been killing upwards of three hundred per day since they were discovered, and yet the birds still trusted them. There was no hesitancy at all on their part, but it was Alice who hesitated as she was the one responsible for the slaughter of so many. Alice sat, her lap immediately brimming with chicks. She gazed into the soulful eyes of the trusting birds and felt the pang of guilt for being the executioner of so many of their friends and family, for it was she, after all, who had told the others about their existence. As she petted each within arm's reach, she apologized.

"I'm so sorry," Alice muttered over and over to each little chick dancing about her. Deeming she'd addressed enough of the flock to make penance, she submitted a collective, "Can you ever forgive me?" She smoothed back the crown feathers on a particularly large one. He blinked knowingly, nudging his head back into her palm.

"Whatever do you need forgiveness for?" came the low tenor of the Admiral, Chance at his heels.

Alice startled, but the birds were unperplexed, nestling further into her skirts.

"From them," she said, her hand sweeping over the crowd of birds now surrounding her.

"Ah, you beg forgiveness from birds." He nodded.

"I'm responsible for their deaths. Well, not these, but the deaths of their friends and family. I was the one who shared their location. I never imagined people would come and kill them. I thought..." She sighed. "I thought others would find them as curious as I did."

"Yes, well, when confronted on a deserted island with no salvation in sight, people do strange things. Things they would never have imagined doing were they back home and safe."

Alice nodded.

"People change in the most unexpected ways when confronted with their survival." The Admiral sat beside her as they both stared at the harbor.

"It's odd, isn't it," Alice started, "how this place has changed people. I mean, Elizabeth and Thomas found love; the Rolfes *and* the Easons will birth babies here. Such joy. But, at the same time, one man murdered another, while men quibble and quarrel daily about the most insignificant things when living in such an abundance." She shook her head.

"And you? What about you has changed?"

Alice watched as Chance dropped a stick at his master's feet. The Admiral threw it, and the beast lumbered after it.

"I quite like it here. It's peaceful. Something I never imagined I would like. And I've found I quite like to work." Smiling, Alice turned to face the Admiral. "Truthfully, I'd like to stay here. However, if, or when, the time comes to leave, I will have to do as Father orders."

"Give me your hand," directed the Admiral.

Tentatively, Alice extended her hand. Turning it over, he placed a small ball of something like wax into her palm. She gingerly tapped the slick mass, unsure what it was or what to do with it.

"It's called ambergris. It's from the whales that pass by, and it's tremendously valuable as the highly sought main ingredient in making perfumes."

Alice picked at the yellow wax, rolling it this way and that in her palm. Placing it between two fingers, she lifted it to her nose and sniffed. Nothing.

The Admiral chuckled. "Ingredients need to be added for it to have a scent. No, this is the main ingredient. Without this, there is no perfume."

"Wherever did you get it?" Alice asked.

"Why, here, of course," the Admiral answered, motioning to the beach. "It's quite common here, if you know what to look for. You have to train your eyes to spot it." He winked at her.

Alice smiled, still rolling the waxy substance in her hand. As it warmed, if felt lighter, and she could imagine perfume being coated onto the skin in such a way. She stared at the sheen of oil left by the warmed wax. She then handed it back to the Admiral.

"That's very interesting. I shall endeavor to find some while on my walks. Thank you."

"Oh no, this is for you," he said, his quiet voice a low rumble in his chest. "To start the new year with some luck. Keep it safe. You may need it one day."

"Thank you," Alice said, carefully placing the ambergris into her apron. "Thank you very much."

"Happy New Year." Rising, he whistled for Chance, then retreated between the birds as he headed to his encampment. Alice watched him with quiet fascination, feeling the lump in her apron as another cahow butted its head into her hand. Alice indulged the creature for a few minutes, then rose to leave.

"Happy New Year!" Alice shouted. A chorus of CAHOW, CAHOW followed her along the path.

Walking back to quarters, Alice took her time, nervously eyeing the ocean and sky, storm clouds already dark and menacing, threatening rain.

She knew she was safe, on dry land, but the feeling of impending death with storms never quite left her. It wasn't just her; the near constant rain and high winds of winter made for a particularly tense time around the camps, with one or more persons crying out in the night. Gone were the pleasantries of daily communion, replaced by sniping and cursing. Reverend Buck and Mr. Hopkins used prayers to remind them of God's anger and wrath for their uncharitable behavior. Declaring the skies would be clear were it not for them. But nothing could assuage the fear they all shared when the sky appeared threatening. If these clouds were any indication, God was furious with them.

Alice watched the ground carefully. If ambergris really were valuable, then it might be the treasure Uncle Willie assured her would come from her *grand adventure* to the New World. Her eyes swept from side to side as she walked. Nothing.

New Year's Eve and New Year's Day passed exactly as they had in Stratford: with worship services. While the prayers and the sacrament were the same, the setting made the mood ominous. Towering black clouds turned the day into night; droplets of rain, indiscernible at first, grew in intensity until the deluge made trekking to the cooking areas dangerous. Finally, the ferocious winds blew the roofs off living quarters.

The castaways gathered in the chapel. They huddled and prayed, promising to obey Gates and stop passing judgement on others. They voiced any promise necessary to assure their God they didn't deserve to perish after all they had endured, while silently accusing others' behavior for landing them in the path of His wrath. When the storm finally ended, the backbiting returned unabated. Alice wondered if living amongst vipers was God's wrath, not the storm.

By the end of January, Alice discovered she had been praying for something completely different than everyone she knew. Her prayer, her petition, became, "Let me stay. Don't make me go to Jamestowne." She whispered this to herself as she walked along the beach searching for ambergris. She whispered it to each and every cahow she petted. She whispered it to the palmettos as she picked berries. She whispered it on the wind as it blew over the camp. Perhaps, by putting this thought into the universe, she could will it into existence. Wasn't that how prayers worked?

Chapter 18

Another Mutiny, 24 January 1610

Staring at the sky, Alice tried to remember how many days had been filled with banks of dense black storm clouds. Staring at towering black clouds, her wrists tied round a palmetto tree, she wondered how long Strachey must have been out here waiting for her. She'd seen him step from a grove of trees as she was collecting kindling. She'd never seen him here before, but he was often spotted in odd places nowadays. She'd smiled, said *Good day*, but he'd remained steadfast, intentionally blocking her way. As she tried to pass, he grabbed her from behind and threw her to the ground. Not hard—he possessed little muscle—but purposefully. Placing a foot on her back, he'd tied a rope around her wrist, pulled her to this tree, and tied the other wrist. What he lacked in physical strength, he made up for in planning. Elizabeth and her mother had warned her about traipsing about alone, but she doubted they ever conceived of this type of danger.

"You're going to tell me truthfully or I'll have your father arrested," he sneered. "There is widespread gossip in the camp that Hopkins is trying to mutiny. And he has the support of most of the camp, including your father."

Alice stared at the man: his impressively straight nose ending in a sharp point, the extravagantly pointed goatee, cheekbones angled upward to a most distressing hairline. He was all angles. He kicked her foot.

"Answer me!"

Alice toyed with all the answers she could give, answers that would amuse her but anger him tremendously. *Behave. Behave. Don't antagonize him.*

"It's widespread gossip," she replied.

"A-ha! So he does know Mr. Hopkins."

"Everyone knows Hopkins; he does the Bible readings at worship every day."

"Don't play coy with me." Crouching next to her, nose to nose, she had no choice but to look him in the eye. "Of everyone in this camp, you have vexed me the greatest. I have it in my power to ensure your father never completes the journey to Jamestowne. That he never gets his land. That you and that termagant of a mother will be destitute. So, I'll ask again: is your father a personal friend of Hopkins?"

"I don't think so," Alice whimpered.

"Are you sure? Your father tends to imbibe quite a bit. Perhaps Hopkins has joined him. They, perhaps, shared a plan to overthrow Gates and stay here on their own."

"He hasn't been in the bibey for months, and Mr. Hopkins doesn't drink to excess. Part of his religion."

"Ah! You do know something of his religion." Strachey smiled. "I suspect, being the clever girl, you are also aware his religion, those wretched Brownists, disavow any authority except God. Which means what he has proposed is mutiny."

Alice sat quietly, wriggling her hands, loosening the inexpertly tied knots. The path wasn't visible, but certainly Elizabeth or her mother would come looking for her soon.

"Your friends, that maid and the ruffian who calls himself a cook, have acknowledged they welcomed Hopkins's plan. That you and your family have agreed to stay on the island and start a new community. Claim it for the Company. What say ye to that?"

Alice contemplated possible responses: if Elizabeth and Thomas had shared that information, wouldn't they be arrested? And it wasn't just them; everyone at some point had heard Hopkins talk about staying. Matter of fact, the longer they remained here, the more people had agreed with him: yes, there was an abundance of good food; yes, it could have been God's providence that led them to this island. Why did Strachey keep mentioning Hopkins now? And why was he concerned with her specifically?

"I can see your head swimming with possibilities of what to tell me, explain away the conversations," he began. "Tell him you're not a Puritan. Tell him you know nothing of the rumors. Tell him your father never tells you anything. Tell him you know nothing, that you're just a girl. An innocent girl. Well, Miss Drinkard, we both know better than that, don't we?"

Alice tried to stare him down, to be defiant, but found her resolve lacking. She felt one tear, then another slide down her cheek. *It's the wind,* she told herself, but she knew the truth: this man terrified her. He could dispense with her family like the berries she plucked off the bushes.

"Why cry now? You did take my papers and burn them, remember? And I've seen you cavorting with the maid and the cook—rather beneath your status, don't you think? Or do you have other designs for them?" He took her face in his hand, turning her head this way and that. "I dare say you're unblemished. It would be a pity to mar such exquisite skin with the whip. But unless you start talking, the whip on your alabaster back will be the next thing you feel."

Alice looked to his hands, to the ground around them. His hands were empty! For the first time, he was without any writing utensils. Without a way to document their conversation, Alice was willing to wager this wasn't sanctioned by Gates. She doubted Gates even knew he was here. Feeling her anger return, she took a chance.

"I told you—I know nothing of a mutiny. It's true: there have been conversations for months regarding why or how or when we should leave, but you were in those conversations too. There are plenty of witnesses who will claim you listened; hell, there are probably more than a few who will claim you participated. That makes you as culpable as anyone."

"Such language from a lady," Strachey mocked. "You father must be proud of the company you keep to have dispelled your breeding so quickly."

"Insults and innuendo, that's all you have. We both know you have no proof, otherwise you wouldn't tie me to a tree and try to scare me. It's the same way you gave yourself away with the attendance records." Alice smiled, feeling the knots loose, sliding her hands free.

"You think yourself so clever." Strachey smirked.

"I do," replied Alice, springing to her feet, pushing Strachey flat on his back. Running as though chased by the Devil himself, she was on the path and searching the camp for her father before Strachey even got to his feet.

Alice ran to the center of the encampment, searching the crowd for her father. Not finding him, she sought out her mother, tending the cooking fires with Mistress Horton. Trying to look nonchalant, Alice bit her lips to keep from panting after a hard run. Sidling up to her mother, she quietly asked, "Where's father?"

Maude looked to her daughter, red-cheeked and out of breath, her backside covered in dirt. "Alice, what—"

"Where. Is. Father?" asked Alice through gritted teeth.

"He's with Gates."

"So he's not been arrested?"

"Of course not. Why would you think he'd been arrested?"

"Strachey. He..." Alice thought for moment. Had he hurt her? No. Had he threatened her? More like her father. Honestly, he'd scared her badly; that was all.

"He what, Alice? What did Strachey tell you? Did he do something to you?"

"He detained me. Questioned me. In the trees."

"While you were out alone," finished her mother.

Alice nodded.

"I'll fetch your father; you stay here with Mistress Horton." Maude embraced Alice, whispering, "You're safe now. I'll find your father."

"Come, help me stir," said Mistress Horton.

Alice watched the cloudy brown water swirl, the occasional palm heart or pork rib surfacing briefly. It wasn't delicious, not like the seafoods they'd grown accustomed to in the summer, but it was comforting in this chill. Focusing on the broth, Alice neglected to see her parents scurrying toward her, careful not to draw attention.

"Alice, your mother informs me you have a matter of some urgency. Is this true?" Her father came into the cooking area, the rest of the Company men sitting with Gates. She looked carefully to the group; Strachey was not present.

"I had an encounter," Alice whispered. "I was stopped, questioned, by Strachey."

"You and everyone else," said her father.

Alice narrowed her eyes. "What do you mean, everyone else?"

"Strachey claims there is a mutinous plot afoot to unseat Gates. He's determined to get to the heart of the matter. It's laughable, really. Hopkins hasn't said anything we haven't thought, but to accuse the entire camp of a conspiracy? As a result of his delusions, he is now questioning everyone, hoping to find someone to support his view. I'm sorry if he scared you. He had no right to question you—or any of the women. We have made it exceedingly clear he is to leave you all to yourselves. I shall speak to Gates about it."

"He said he was going to have you arrested. That he would make sure we'd never arrive in Jamestowne, that we'd be destitute." Alice stirred the pot too fast, the broth sloshing to the ground beneath.

"He told everyone that. He'll have no one arrested; he hasn't the authority. Let me speak to Gates."

"Father. There's more." She'd tried so hard to stay on Strachey's good side. To do her chores, stay unnoticed, and he sought her out anyway. She wasn't safe from him, no matter what she did. Maybe this would be his undoing. Taking a deep breath, she blurted, "He tied me up."

"Where?"

"In the woods."

Flashing crimson, her father muttered, "Not my daughter."

Alice watched her father approach Gates, leading the Governor to a table where they could speak privately. Before they could finish, Strachey sprinted to the Governor, pushing aside her father as though he were a chair. Alice heard the words *two witnesses*, her stomach falling as he waved two men over to him. She fidgeted, hoping to gain her father's attention, his assurance Strachey would leave her alone, but he was straining to hear the private conversation Strachey was having with Gates.

"Arrest Stephen Hopkins," commanded Gates. "Immediately!"

Strachey smiled and nodded to all present.

Within minutes Mr. Hopkins was brought to Gates in manacles. Unlike his demeanor in the chapel, he was now confused and disheveled.

"You are hereby charged with mutiny!" declared Gates. "You have actively sought to overthrow my leadership and create your own community. You have sought to break your contract with the Virginia Company and remain here, rather than continuing on to the settlement of Jamestowne as previously agreed. You have abused your position as a religious leader to promote your own religious perversions." Turning to Strachey, he asked for the witnesses to give their statements. Every charge leveled against Hopkins was corroborated by the two men, although somewhat reluctantly. When they had finished speaking, Gates turned to Hopkins again. "What say ye to these charges?"

"I am innocent of mutiny. I merely meant to discuss what options we may have. It is common knowledge the *Deliverance* will not accommodate all of us, and we could determine who would stay now rather than when preparing for the voyage. To avoid any contempt. To aid in this decision, I was merely drawing attention to the fact God's providence has provided for us here. As a result of this bounty, perhaps staying here isn't so bad. This island could be claimed for the Company as the resources are plentiful. As for breaking my contract, well, that is already done, sir. The Company promised us safe passage to Jamestowne, in exchange for work. When the *Sea Venture* wrecked, that contract was nullified." Hopkins stood resolute in his declaration. "You can ask Mr. Strachey. He has been present at several of the discussions."

Gates turned to Strachey, eyes narrowed. Strachey feigned confusion and returned to his notes. Alice held her breath.

"I understand a fair amount of you—if not all of you—have been privy to such talk. May have even participated. Since I have no way of knowing who is actually involved, I will punish Hopkins on behalf of you all. As you are a man of God, Mr. Hopkins, you certainly can appreciate the reference."

Gates watched the crowd for a reaction. Alice watched to see who would stand up for Mr. Hopkins. It was unfair for him to be punished for them all, but every single soul present knew the price of subverting authority.

Next time it could be them. Alice wondered how many lashes of the whip he would receive, or how much the fine would cost. Perhaps they could help pay the fine.

"I sentence you to death by hanging," declared Gates.

A collective gasp erupted, the loudest from Strachey, whose face suddenly grew paler than usual. The Company men looked to one another in confusion. Death? That was not the Common Law punishment; that was Martial Law punishment. Strachey and Newport immediately began to petition on behalf of Mr. Hopkins, who broke down crying.

"Sir Thomas," began Strachey. "We'll be short a man for labor. If we're to finish the pinnace by summer, we'll need him."

"This is egregious," commented Newport.

"Sir, I beg of you. I left my wife and three children in England. If I am executed, they will be ruined. And I truly only wanted to help those who wish to leave by volunteering to stay behind. I only meant I would help to create a community for the Company. I was not seeking to usurp your authority." Hopkins crawled to Gates. "Sir, please. Spare my life. Whip me if you must, but please don't kill me. My family, sir, consider my family."

Gates considered the three men before him, the crowd gathered, his gaze settling on Hopkins, on his knees begging for his life.

"I'll reconsider punishment, but you are to remain in shackles, under armed guard, until I render my decision," replied Gates. Turning his back on the prisoner, he strode out the compound to his quarters.

The Company men did not immediately follow, unsure of what should happen now; the soldiers had no such qualms. They grabbed Hopkins roughly by the elbows and escorted him to the only place he could be locked away from the community. Strachey and Newport followed the soldiers, intent on keeping Hopkins alive until morning light.

"Why is Strachey trying to keep him alive? He had him arrested," said Alice.

"Men like Strachey don't think through their actions," said her father. "He never wanted Hopkins dead, only arrested on his word. He wants us afraid of him and what he might tell Gates. It was a power play, one he didn't think through. And now a man may die because of him. He's a toady, but unlikely to take responsibility for another man's death."

Gates commuted the death sentence, and no mention was made of the mutiny again, but life in the camp became much more unbearable. Mr. Hopkins now had Reverend Buck to answer to, his every move monitored, his every word scrutinized. He was no longer allowed to conduct services on his own, and when he read the Bible, gone was his enthusiasm for the Word. In addition to attendance at chapel, guards were placed at the door. No one was allowed to come and go freely from the compound. All movements were documented. There were guards assigned to all areas of the camp, listening. Waiting. When collecting kindling and firewood, Elizabeth and Alice were supervised. They could no longer speak freely, even when away from the camp. The general consensus was if poor little Stephen Hopkins, a religious zealot, could be accused of mutiny, then any of them could. And Gates was taking no chances.

Chapter 19

Women's Work, February–March 1610

Even though it was forbidden, and she was to be supervised at all times, Alice couldn't resist slipping away to the beach. No one really thought a young woman a threat, and after nearly causing an execution, Strachey had become more measured with his words and ceased roaming the area in search of infractions. The sound of the waves lapping at the shore and the excitement of finding another piece of ambergris made the risk worth it. She'd found three pieces today alone.

"Alice!"

"Yes, Mother. I hear you."

"You know you're not...Oh, never mind that. We have a child needing to be born. And yes, you do need to be present," her mother said, shaking her head, "in the room, not out here collecting bits and bobs."

"I helped plenty this week. I'm willing to take Goody Rolfe's chores for the next few weeks. I don't mind. But do I really need to see a baby enter the world?"

"Yes, you've been very helpful covering Goody Rolfe's duties, but that doesn't excuse you from being present at the actual event."

Alice continued looking for ambergris, ignoring her mother's sighs of impatience. Stomping to her daughter, Maude grabbed Alice by an ear and dragged her upright. The ambergris started slipping from her fingertips; Alice gripped it and stashed it in the waistband of her skirt.

"Ouch! You're hurting me," Alice yelped.

"Good!" Maude let go of Alice's ear, pushing her in front of her in the process.

Helping with a birth was something she wished to avoid. It held no fascination for her; but as a woman, she was required to be present and involved—whatever that meant. She had begged and pleaded with Maude and Elizabeth to let her run errands, be a porter to fetch water or berries or whatever potion women were given when they were to give birth. The two women had resolutely refused, and their solidarity in the matter had stifled all argument. The fact that even Elizabeth refused to indulge her ensured she would be present at the event, as Mistress Horton referred to the birth. As one of only six women on the island, she was officially considered a caregiver. Whether she wanted to be or not.

Alice heard the screams well before they approached the Rolfe quarters. She stopped mid-stride. The screams of the most pious woman in camp shattered her. She'd witnessed a murder more silent than this. Turning to Maude for guidance, she was thrust toward the horror.

Alice wished she were invisible. Trying to be as silent as possible, she pulled her hands to her chest involuntarily as she braced for the next scream. When it began, she could feel her hands moving toward her ears to cover them.

"Alice," whispered Maude, "put your hands down." Softening, Maude continued, "I know this is scary; it is for all women. But it is also a time for rejoicing. There's a babe wishing to join the world. A sweet little light from God is being given to the parents, to us, to the future. The mother's pain will pass in a week, maybe two. All this will be a distant memory." Maude chuckled. "Goody Rolfe won't remember any of this; we never do. That's just how life goes."

Alice stared at her mother. She seemed sincere this was normal, and for a moment Alice calmed. But then the screaming started again.

Mistress Horton was serving as the midwife, assisted by Elizabeth, of course. The two women were already perched on stools at the foot of the bed, herbs laid out beside them on a bedsheet. There was hot water and bibey. Alice had clear instructions: make Goody Rolfe as comfortable as possible by wiping her brow and helping her push. Alice looked to her charge. What was the point of wiping sweat from her brow when her entire body was drenched as though fresh from a bath? But she did as she was told, trusting these women knew much more than she and not wanting to be the one who caused Goody Rolfe any more discomfort.

Alice placed herself beside the woman, careful not to jostle her lest she add to the pain. Gently she dabbed the cloth across her brow, careful to catch a drop before it fell into her eyes. She took a fresh cloth from the stack. *Stack? How long would this last?* Needing clarification, she glanced for someone to ask. Maude, occupied with muddling herbs, stood too far away to ask without alarming Goody Rolfe, and Elizabeth, now stroking the woman's belly in a downward motion, seemed intent on silently coaxing the child out into the world.

Alice focused on Goody Rolfe's face; her eyes shut tight as she breathed in short exhalations. In spite of her fear, Alice found herself whispering to her as she did the cahows that gathered on her skirt each afternoon. Soft, soothing tones meant to calm and reassure that no harm was to come. But if she'd learned anything these past six months, it was that nothing was ever guaranteed. In her head she felt the lies pouring forth from her lips, but Goody Rolfe smiled with closed eyes, her energy drained, and gave a barely perceptible nod. Then, AAAAHHHHHH! She was sitting and screaming again.

Alice and Goody Rolfe did this dance until the island was shrouded in darkness. And thus it continued throughout the night; it continued until Goody Rolfe no longer had the strength to utter a sound, but with Alice's assistance managed to sit and push when ordered. Alice never left her side.

Then, at the break of day, Elizabeth announced what they had been hoping to hear for so long.

"One more and you'll soon meet your bairn," she pronounced.

Mistress Horton peeked from between Goody Rolfe's thighs to Alice and mouthed, *Help her.*

Alice assisted her to an upright position, muttering, "You can do this. Just one more and the child will be here."

Goody Rolfe, eyes barely open, nodded once.

"I'll help you," said Alice as she slid behind her and supported her weight with her body. When she was told to push, Alice leaned forward, forcing the goodwife into the push.

"Good! Good!" exclaimed Elizabeth. "We can see the head. Push her forward once more—hard!"

Alice did as instructed, excited to finally meet the infant whose pre-birth energy and stubbornness had exhausted six adult women.

"It's a girl!" announced Mistress Horton. Cutting the umbilical cord, Maude quickly took the infant, carefully tying a poultice of herbs and cedar sawdust over her cord. Elizabeth placed the infant on Goody Rolfe's chest as Alice slid from behind her, allowing the new mother to recline with her daughter.

Alice stared at the infant, purple and covered in white custard. *She shouldn't look this way; what's wrong?* As the baby lay on her mother's chest, Elizabeth and Maude rubbed the infant's limbs vigorously. Gradually, her complexion changed from purple, to dark red, to pink. And with the changing hues came tiny utterances, escalating into a deafening yowl. The women laughed, even Alice. Maude moved to her daughter's side. Alice welcomed her closeness, placing her head on her mother's shoulder as they watched the new mother welcome her first-born into the world.

Sometime later, Strachey made the announcement of the arrival to the camp, along with the new infant's name: Bermuda, his newest goddaughter. Alice stared at Mistress Horton.

"How can he do that?" exploded Alice.

"He keeps the records; of course he'd name himself a godparent. And choose the name. Did you expect anything different?" she asked.

"What about the parents?" asked Alice. "It's their first-born. Certainly they'd considered other names. Family names, perhaps."

"Goody Rolfe is too tired to care, and her husband will do whatever is necessary to stay in Strachey's good graces," stated Mistress Horton, forcing a smile to the crowd as her name was announced as one of the godparents, along with Newport. "It's none of our affair now. Leave it alone."

Alice now added a visit to baby Bermuda to her morning routine. Arriving early, she would hold the infant while Goody Rolfe straightened their quarters. It wasn't much, but the infant ignited ideas of what her own children might look like. She watched as a smile formed at the corners of the cherub's lips as she kissed first her nose then each eye. On the mornings the infant was fussy, she'd place the silver and coral teether between her lips, a gentle sucking her reward for the comfort. She held Bermuda until Mistress Horton or her mother would arrive, it being necessary for someone to help Goody Rolfe throughout the day; it was a task of love for them all, and handing the baby off to another was difficult.

On the morning of the nineteenth day of life for Bermuda, while collecting kindling, Alice developed a plan: she would ask the Rolfes if she could be their nurse. It was nothing as extravagant as what would have been available back home, but it would allow the Rolfes to have some help and her to safeguard the infant. No more sharing duties with other women; she'd become Bermuda's Susanna, and love her as Susanna had her.

Having deposited her quota of kindling, Alice ran down the path toward the housing area, eager to hear the Rolfes's response. Instead, she heard screaming.

"No! Oh God, no! Not my baby." It was Goody Rolfe, her pitiful howls audible throughout the housing area.

Joining her on the path were Elizabeth and Mistress Horton. The three women ran into the room as the mother fell to the floor, cradling the infant to her chest. The infant, now a pale shade of blue, appeared to be sleeping. Mistress Horton moved to Goody Rolfe's side, taking Bermuda from her arms. Placing her ear to the baby's mouth, she listened. Grabbing the blanket from the makeshift crib, she swaddled the infant, clutching her to her chest as she approached Alice and Elizabeth.

"Go fetch Mr. Rolfe," she whispered. "And the Reverend."

The burial was the worst Alice had ever attended. Goody Rolfe had been inconsolable, having never fully recovered from the delivery, and there were no herbs available to take away her pain or help her sleep. If they'd been in Stratford, Alice could have concocted an elixir to help, but she was helpless here without a full range of herbs.

Goody Eason, due to give birth any day, stood clear of Goody Rolfe, but cried as the tiny coffin was lowered into the Admiral's small flower garden, a place he cultivated, built to remind him of his wife's love and the daughter they'd lost. He'd suggested the infant be buried here. There weren't currently any blooms, the February winds proving much too harsh for that, but come spring the infant would be surrounded by the color and sweet fragrances reminiscent of an English garden. Alice found it comforting to know the child would be able to enjoy the fair winds and colors of the isle as she lingered in eternity. Unbeknownst to anyone, Alice had also placed the teether in the coffin with the infant. That too gave her a modicum of comfort to know the child had something to let her know she was loved.

As Strachey had recorded her christening, he also noted she was not English, the charter not providing any information for births occurring outside of Virginia. The fact her only daughter would not be recognized as English landed Goody Rolfe in bed. The trouble of the delivery, coupled with the death of her first child and lack of status rendered her hysterical. The women all took turns sitting with her, bringing her broth and cahow eggs to help her regain her strength, but to no avail. Alice's mother, as well as Mistress Horton and Elizabeth, assured her this wasn't uncommon. Some women had a hard time becoming mothers, and since Bermuda had died, there was nothing to move her on. They were convinced once she got pregnant again, all would be well. Alice had her doubts.

When Goody Eason prepared to deliver her child, Alice volunteered to stay with Goody Rolfe. The notion of meeting another child filled her with dread, a feeling made manifest by Goody Rolfe's deteriorating mental state. Not even Reverend Buck's scripture readings could relieve her malaise. She merely dozed as the word of God floated through the room.

Unlike Goody Rolfe, Goody Eason delivered a boy within hours and was walking about the quarters shortly thereafter. Tired, but intent on performing her motherly duties, she asked for no help and only took leave of her assignments for a few days.

With Goody Rolfe safely tended by her husband, Alice went to the cooking area. Strachey, once again, proclaimed himself the godfather of the new infant, along with Newport, and announced the infant's name: Bermudas. The group of women gasped.

"He named the baby the same as the Rolfes's child," hissed Elizabeth. "That's bad luck."

"He hath no shame," echoed Mistress Horton.

"He's a man; he hasn't the slightest understanding of how a loss like this will plague the rest of her life," remarked Maude. "How like a man to think naming one baby after a dead one will give a grieving mother any comfort. I realize the child has been dead near on three weeks, but she's not yet beyond her grief. I don't care if he claims the name a tribute; babies aren't monuments. Isn't it torment enough for Goody Rolfe to hear the constant mewing of the newborn? Does she need the additional reminder of the name? It's unconscionable."

"Should we tell her?" asked Alice. No one spoke. "I think we should warn her."

"She'll hear soon enough," said her mother. "At the christening, which I believe is to be Annunciation Day. That's a good sign, don't you think? Maybe an angel will tell her another child is to come her way. We should pray for that."

Annunciation Day began as all celebratory days had begun on this journey: with a storm. Massive towers of black clouds clung to the island as a shroud. Extra candles were lit for the service as noon was as dark as midnight. Regardless, the women tried to remain hopeful and encouraging as Goody Rolfe appeared in chapel, aided by her husband. As usual, Strachey proved himself the haughty buffoon they all took him for, his antics eliciting an ephemeral smile from Goody Rolfe. Afterwards, the community ate together, the quiet laughter and chatter a promise that life moves on. Goody Rolfe sat with them, pushing bits of egg, pork shreds, and palmetto heart around her plate.

"I'm glad you joined us today," said Alice.

The woman smiled, patted Alice's hand, and left to return home.

Two nights later, her parents returned to the quarters much later than usual. Alice listened as her mother began to cry.

"I understand her grief. A mother's grief." Her voice cracked. "To feel so utterly alone you think—you wish—you would perish with each passing moment, to be laid down in the ground with them. To want to trust God's plan, but not seeing beyond the darkness of your own mind. Every movement, every thought, every breath a weight tied to your soul. Thank God for Alice. Had it not been for her…Well, I understand how Goody Rolfe lost hope."

"I've never resolved what to say to others," admitted her father. "They're afraid to speak to me, for fear of reminding me, but there's no reminding—I never forget! I want to share my memories. That he was here. On earth. With us. He may be dead, but he'll always be my son." Her father began to cry as his wife pulled him to her. "If I can't mention him, it's like he never existed, and I miss our dear Bertie every single day."

Watching her parents care for one another, to share their grief about her brother, made her cry. Closing her eyes, she failed to notice her parents moving to her until the mattress shifted. The three huddled together in a tight embrace and cried together for the first time since Bertie's death three years ago.

"Alice," said her father, kissing her forehead. "We've some sad news to share."

"It's Goody Rolfe, isn't it?"

"Yes, my darling," replied her mother.

"She's died," added her father.

"She was a lovely woman, so kind to let me care for Bermuda. I wish we could have cheered her up. I wish I could have done more to help her," sniffed Alice. "At least now she'll be with her baby. For eternity. She can hold her, love her. I pray she finds peace."

"I too pray her soul is at peace. We should also pray for Goody Eason, that she finds solace in…" but her mother couldn't finish the words.

"Goody Eason? Why her?"

Alice's father took her hand. "It's baby Bermudas. He joined the Rolfes, just a short while ago."

"Joined? You mean he died too?"

Her parents nodded.

"No!" yelled Alice, snatching her hand from her father. "He's not…He couldn't have…He was healthy. He was growing. His cheeks were pink. Mother, you said so yourself."

"Sometimes that's not enough; nothing is enough. Babies die—they're present for a short while, then move on to heaven. That's how it is with children. You are so happy when they arrive, but when they leave, they take a piece of your heart and soul." She paused, dabbing her eyes. "Bermudas died in his mother's arms. He…stopped," said her mother. "He was with us, then he wasn't. He didn't make a sound, just floated away on the wings of the angels." She cried heavier. "That's how I am choosing to think of this. Oh, his poor mother." Maude's head fell to her husband's shoulder as he cradled her. Her body racked with sobs, he gently rocked her until she quieted.

Alice regarded her parents. She had never seen them express emotion so honestly before. She certainly had never heard them talk about her brother or the fact they missed him too. She wasn't sure what they needed, but for the first time she knew what she needed: to hold them both tightly. Reaching her arms round them both, Alice and her parents grieved for the boy who had made them so happy, whose absence had produced such a deep grief it sent them on a venture to rediscover what it meant to be a family. As each parent kissed her head, Alice realized how fortunate she actually was.

Chapter 20

Mutiny with a Twist, April 1610

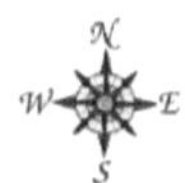

The crowd had already gathered. There had been talk of yet another mutiny, and while the thought of seeing someone's life hang in the balance had been entertaining in August, eight months later it felt like a minor distraction to a day's work. Entering the dining area, Alice noticed the table placed at the front of the room, a sheath of papers, quill and ink in front of one of the three chairs. Strachey's supplies, no doubt. But if he sat there, with Gates in the center, who would occupy the third?

The crowd parted as Gates moved through the room; Strachey placed himself at the table, quill in hand to record the proceedings. The other Company men shuffled behind the Governor. The castaways quieted, awaiting the proceedings, but Gates merely sat and stared. In the silence, Christopher Newport strode to the last chair. Taking his place, he made none of the pleasantries he was known for. His look inscrutable. Without turning around, Gates ordered the Company men to move into the room and away from him. In their stead moved two fully armored soldiers.

"I consider myself a patient man. One who has tolerated innumerable criticisms for my judgements. I have been accused of letting a murderer walk free; of letting a mutineer cry his way out of punishment, while allowing others to live in the woods as they wished. What you fail to appreciate when criticizing my judgements is the immense responsibility I assume in making those pronouncements, and the burden I must live with as a result. I made those decisions after careful consideration of the facts. I was not swayed by tears and sudden confessions; I considered what was best for the Company, for all of us. Some have accused me of being too soft, and to some it may look as though I'm not representative of a leader—I'm not trustworthy enough to be your governor." He stared at the Company men. "But I ask you this: have we not built a vessel to transport us to Jamestowne? Have any of you suffered starvation or deprivation of any resources? Haven't you each been afforded your own quarters? That's what leadership is: seeing a problem and creating a scheme to overcome it. Providing. Like a shepherd to his flock—he never leaves them to the wolves; he protects them. Wouldn't you all agree?"

The crowd nodded.

"As some of you may already know, we have another traitor in our midst. Mr. Henry Paine, a Company man, a gentleman, has agitated to have me killed. Not only me, but many of his so-called peers—men who have worked alongside him all these many months. In addition, last night he thought it wise to assault the captain of his watch, Captain Newport, and curse him with language too crude to repeat. And all with witnesses. As he ran away, much as any coward would, he dared me to arrest him."

Mr. Paine was brought to the front of the room, his hands and feet shackled, a soldier at each arm. Instead of the expected furtive expression seen on the other mutineers upon being caught, Paine held his head high.

Gates moved to the front of the table, Paine mere inches from him. "I have determined so egregious an action has no defense, so none will be allowed as there were witnesses. I have dispensed with a tribunal as is my prerogative as your governor. On the other occasions, three to be exact, the accused were both reticent and remorseful, and thus allowed mercy. But this attack, and the ensuing obscenities, were an attack not only on his superior officer, but also on me and the mission of this entire company. This man"—he pointed to Paine—"has, in essence, attacked each of us, and for this he has shown no remorse. He's offered no apology. Instead, he has remained resolute in his stance and obstinate in his attitude. As his reward, he shall receive a rope necklace."

The crowd stared in stunned silence. They'd heard this before, but never to a gentleman.

"Men, if you'll place the rope over yon limb," Gates ordered, pointing to a tree outside the door. The crowd followed the soldier with the rope and the prisoner. Once under the tree, the noose nearing his head, Mr. Paine finally spoke.

"Your honor," Paine boldly pronounced, despite facing imminent death, "I am not a common criminal; I am a gentleman—you said so yourself. I have paid my own passage; I owe the Company nothing but my labor. As you will not allow me to stay here, or return to England should the opportunity present itself, may I at least have the death afforded to one of my class?"

"A shooting?" quipped Strachey, his nasal voice scratching the ears of all.

Paine nodded.

"So be it," declared Gates.

Alice, looking around to see who would do the deed, unconsciously reached for Maude's hand. Anyone here could do it. After the Hopkins mess, Gates had ordered all the encampment to carry arms, as no one could be trusted anymore. Perhaps this was why she couldn't sleep at night, expecting to be shot at any moment. But this? He was to be shot on the spot? Without a tribunal? This was a complete change to their daily lives. Certainly her father or the Admiral...someone would speak up. But the men of the council remained silent.

"As I am your governor, and I pronounced the sentence, I shall do it." Gates, drawing his pistol, positioned his weapon at eye level, and placed the bullet squarely between Paine's eyes, his body hitting the ground before the ringing from the shot left the vicinity.

No one spoke. Gates stood with the smoking weapon still in his hand. Even Strachey had stopped writing as he stared at the former gentleman. Blood poured from Paine's forehead, and Alice felt her father slide to her and gently pull her away from the crowd. Maude was still holding her hand as the trio moved down the path toward their quarters.

Chapter 21

Leaving the Isle of Devils, 10 May 1610

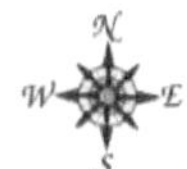

The Isle of Devils had been feared by mariners since time immemorial. No one could tell Alice exactly why. Perhaps this myth existed because the reefs ensnared any ship that dared get close; or perhaps those who made it ashore chose to stay as Carter and Waters now did and were presumed dead. Perhaps it was the sound of thousands of cahows that could be heard beyond the bay to ships passing. Perhaps it was yet another Company lie to vilify the Portuguese. Alice now believed the real devils were the humans. If there was one lesson she had learned while marooned, it was this: women die for family—men die from hubris.

After Paine's execution, every day had been filled with preparations to leave. Each day eerily quiet, as none wished to speak on the horror they'd all been forced to witness, the activities centered on securing enough food for the transport and increasing the larder at Jamestowne. Fishing; hunting; roasting; salting the hauls. Always salting. Salt: a huge concern when they arrived, all their supplies ruined in the hurricano. The Admiral tasked several of his men with creating a makeshift salt mine, which ultimately produced copious amounts of the precious spice. Since fresh food here, unlike home, was plentiful throughout their stay regardless of the season, they hadn't stockpiled preserved items. However, they never ceased salt production and now had more than enough to meet the demands of this next mission. At home, Alice never concerned herself with where things came from or the work involved to provide a meal. Now, she regretted not having thanked Cook for the incredible labor required to appease her and her family.

Three weeks to load the two small pinnaces, when it had taken an afternoon to unload the *Sea Venture*. Alice looked to the forecastle, to the overturned tortoise; it had stopped struggling but was still alive. They had been experimenting with how long the turtles could remain overturned and still be safe to eat. In two weeks, none had died. Even though she knew they provided a variety of benefits, it was still difficult to watch. Even more troublesome was the plight of the cahows. Her little friends were now scarce; they still weren't afraid of people, even though their numbers had been greatly thinned. She viewed the roasted carcasses now splayed across the deck. She winced, catching sight of the open, unblinking eyes hazy in death. It was necessary—of course it was—but it bothered her such trusting creatures could be slaughtered so callously.

Sitting on the deck, Alice watched their island paradise shrink into the distance. She had been so excited for this adventure, to see the New World, to help create a settlement at Jamestowne. Now? She was sad to leave behind her beloved cahows, their voices giving rise to the theory that devils inhabited the island but showing a trust so pure it made her want to weep. She would miss her walks along the shore, searching for ambergris; the smell of fresh fish and pork as it crackled on the fire; her private conversations with Elizabeth. Would she and Elizabeth remain friends once they arrived in Jamestowne? As she contemplated her own losses, she looked to Mr. Rolfe. He too stared at the horizon, his lips pressed so tightly together they no longer had color. Of all of them, he'd lost the most; he'd left his entire family on that scrape of dirt, a small makeshift cross the only mark of their existence.

Unlike the trip from England, this one was much quieter. No one to fete them as they left; no enthusiasm from the passengers at leaving, except one: Pearce, as he may finally be reunited with his family. Her father and the Admiral—Newport being commanded by Gates to captain the other pinnace—talking quietly from time to time. There was nothing much to do, this time, except sit and watch the gulls fly around the mast or watch the water pass beneath. There was nothing to look at: no coastline; no fleet to keep watch; no friends to greet when on deck. This time it was just the two pinnaces representing months of infighting; each aptly named and piloted by their leaders: Gates helmed the *Deliverance*, while Somers helmed the

Patience. Fitting tributes to how each leader viewed his role.

For two weeks, the castaways floated toward Jamestowne. Cautiously optimistic, yet aware they were equally likely to die at sea as ever see land again. Until, one morning, the announcement of leaves on the lead line, evidence they were near land. Within a day, the air became more earthy, woodsy. By the second day, they were at the mouth of the Chesapeake. It had taken nine months, three weeks, and one day to arrive, but now they were close to their final destination, Alice could feel the excitement building in her blood.

PART FOUR

"...To credit his own lie, he did believe..."
~ Prospero,
The Tempest, Act 1, Scene 2

Chapter 22

Jamestowne at Last, 21–23 May 1610

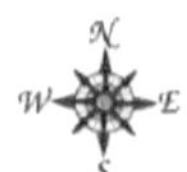

"Silence," bellowed Somers.

Alice slid behind the mast, trying to determine why the Admiral appeared concerned. The *Deliverance* slid alongside the *Patience* so Gates and Somers could converse. At the mouth of the James River sat a new fort, an edifice neither Somers nor Gates had any knowledge of. With no flag visible, they couldn't be certain who now controlled Jamestowne. Fear spread through the crew and passengers as they realized they may have sailed into Spanish territory. Sailing as close as they dared, they anchored offshore, hoping to determine which country held dominion.

They waited. They watched. No one dared utter a sound. The sun passed across the sky.

Before the gloaming, six men emerged from the fort and boarded a small boat docked at the river's edge. The castaways watched as the tiny vessel rowed toward them. The mariners and soldiers quietly shuffled into place, out of sight, muskets at the ready. These were men skilled at handling pirates—hell, even Newport himself had been one! Alice felt herself shrinking behind the mast, hiding should a fight break out, close enough to a hatch for an easy escape below deck. As the boat rowed closer, she heard the Admiral laugh.

"Ah—Percy! Is that you?" he asked, his voice booming across the water.

"Somers! You old dog! You're alive," yelled Percy. Once on board, the two men clasped hands heartily. "We assumed you were dead." Examining both pinnaces, he shook his head. "I should have known you'd find a way to succeed. Wreck one vessel; build two more." He stamped his feet on the deck. "Solid construction too." He waved a little acknowledgement to

Gates on the other pinnace, to which Strachey bowed. "I see that weasel survived too," he laughed. "Two new vessels." He whistled. "Impressive. But not as impressive as rising from the dead."

"Call me Lazarus! Actually, we didn't lose a single person. Well, not in the storm. And you—a new fort?"

"Just some fortifications to Point Comfort, but I gave it a name nonetheless: Algernon Fort."

"Am I to take it Jamestowne is gone?"

"Not exactly." Percy peered beyond the Admiral, to the ocean. "It's been a long...winter. We should leave it there, for now." He nodded to the listening passengers.

The Admiral narrowed his eyes. "How many people are left?"

"Not here," mumbled Percy. "Let me return to shore, inform the others of the news, of your miraculous appearance, and we will escort you to Jamestowne. Shouldn't take more than two days' travel with the tides."

"Thank you."

Before Percy disembarked, the familiar *ahem* of Strachey interrupted the departure. Everyone aboard both pinnaces watched as Strachey gestured to Percy, as though he were the new governor. Unlike the encounters on the island, Gates pushed him aside. They all saw it. Alice snickered, only to be sharply elbowed by both Elizabeth and Maude.

"Allow me to come with you; I am the governor after all." Gates pointed to the new structure. "What is this? I had no knowledge of this."

"No, sir, you did not. It was built—" Percy stopped, looking to the Admiral shaking his head. "You were a long time gone; in fact, we thought you dead. I'll explain all in due time. But now, I must go back ashore, inform the men of your return. We'll leave with the next tide for Jamestowne." He quickly climbed over the side into his skiff before Gates could detain him further.

Strachey leaned in to Gates and stated, loud enough for all to hear, "He must answer to you; you are the lawful governor after all. You can't allow him to dismiss you." Gates stayed the conversation with his hand.

"That's enough, Strachey. We're in Virginia now, back to civilization. Once we arrive in Jamestowne, you'd be wise to let the appointed council do their jobs. Stay out of our way." Hesitating, he added, "Take your notes, but simply as secretary; not my counsel. Just do your job, or I shall find another who can."

Alice smiled. It had been a long time coming, but witnessing Strachey get put in his place made leaving the isle worth it. Perhaps her father had been correct: Jamestowne was the right place for them all.

Traveling with the tides was the only way to reach Jamestowne, just as Percy told them. Alice rejoiced at hearing they would stay the night on Mulberry Island—an island of mulberries. How divine! But after Bermuda, this island failed in comparison: no friendly cahows; no ocean breeze. Presently a stifling heat with enough humidity to suck the breath from her lungs. Alice awoke feeling like someone had wrapped her head in a warm, wet blanket.

All were on deck for the approach to Jamestowne, eager to see their new home, be reunited with loved ones, catch up with friends, and continue with a life similar to the one they'd had in England. Excitement bristled through the group. Finally, after nearly a year, the homecoming they'd dreamed of; the reunion they'd been promised as they'd toiled, and bickered, *and killed,* thought Alice bitterly. As much as she'd dreaded leaving the isle, she was excited to see her friends.

As they turned a bend, they saw Percy pointing left, to an area on the shore. There appeared to be a clearing through the trees. She could see some palisades, though most were sheared and splintered. Sailing closer, one by one the passengers grew silent. Gone was the excitement of seeing loved ones. Gone was the glee of finally completing their journey. Unlike the new structure at the Point, this was less fort than stick village. The gates that opened to the river were hanging off hinges already rusty. No wonder they'd built a new fort; this one was in shambles. The castaways stood mute in disbelief. Their village on the isle, which none had ever referred to as a village, was palatial compared to what lay before them.

"Where are the people?" Alice asked. "Shouldn't there be five hundred or more?"

"Is this what we signed on for, Robert?" whispered Maude. "Did you know the settlement to be this destitute?"

"I understood it to be more challenging than what we're accustomed to," admitted her father. "But totally inhospitable? No. I never imagined they would knowingly send us into such dire circumstances. Not with our families."

Alice turned to look at her father; he knew? Or at least suspected? And still he forced them from paradise? How, after all they had endured, all they had survived, had he neglected—no, chosen—not to tell them?

"How many are left?" asked her mother cautiously.

"I overheard Percy say sixty."

Sixty plus the one hundred and forty they brought still only accounted for a third of the total people in their fleet from last summer. What had happened?

As the pinnaces glided through the brackish water of the James, Alice suddenly felt like an animal on display: too exposed and vulnerable. She couldn't distinguish faces, but she felt them watching her from the shore. Then, skeletons began to emerge from the fort. Looking to the beings, Alice gasped. Eyes sunken into dark sockets. Cheekbones so prominent skulls appeared misshapen. Bony fingers on bony arms pointing and waving. Mr. Pearce, whose wife and daughter were on the *Blessing*, scanned the crowd for his family, excitement and hope never leaving his countenance.

Alice shut her eyes, afraid she would see her friends amid the wretched souls before them.

Oh, merciful God, please send a sign you've brought my friends home and mitigated their suffering with the mercy of death. May they be at peace in your kingdom and not one of these tortured souls.

With the exception of Mr. Pearce, eager to be reunited with his family, the castaways hesitated to come ashore. Staying on board provided them protection from whatever curse had befallen these unfortunate creatures. Alice wondered how long it would take for her to transform into one of them. She desperately wanted to ask her father if sacrificing his family for the Virginia Company, a Company who so clearly had left these people to fend for themselves to disastrous consequences, was the better option than financial ruin. At the moment, begging for scraps in England seemed the wiser choice. Then it dawned on her: Mr. Cyrus had known, and used her father's circumstances, and a deal he couldn't refuse, to send them all to their deaths.

A woman moved away from the crowd on the shore. Her voice weakened, she called, "George? Is he here? Is my George here?" Her eyes implored those on the two pinnaces to action. Mr. Pearce, who had been scanning the crowd for his wife, failed to recognize her. Moving to the skeletal woman hesitatingly, he asked "Joan?" She nodded.

As they embraced, a young girl stepped forward. Joan brought her to them, and the little family held on to each other as the crowd watched. Alice felt her own family close in around her.

"Isn't that the girl you were speaking with in Plymouth? The one who talked fast and never took a breath?" asked her father.

Alice shook her head *no*.

"No, I think it is her," said Maude. "I think that is Joanne."

Alice scrutinized the figure. This entity showed no resemblance to the girl she befriended in Plymouth. This one didn't speak, wasn't a whirlwind of activity, a being of orchestrated chaos, incessant chatter, and hand gestures. This girl didn't move so fast as to be exhausting to watch. No, this girl displayed none of the characteristics of her friend. Alice continued to watch the little family in their unrestrained public reunion as others unloaded the boat. This girl didn't act like Joanne, and while she wore her straw-like hair in a braid as favored by her friend, Alice still wasn't convinced it was her. Then she saw it. Unlike the plain white of everyday wear, Joanne of Plymouth had taken great pride and made a production of showing off her apron: white muslin embroidered with red and yellow roses in a sea of purple pansies edging the entire garment. It was her! Alice clasped her hand to her mouth. She felt her parents slide in tighter; she felt protected.

"Robert, it's time to begin work." Gates beckoned from the shore.

"Come join me as we tour the fort." It was not a request.

"Aye," answered her father. "Alice. You need to stay with your mother. Every second. You two do not leave each other for a single moment." He took in the woods surrounding the fort, the dilapidated fort itself, and the two women at his side. "This place feels dangerous already. Until I am with you, you must promise to look after one another."

"Of course, Papa. I shan't leave Mother, not for a moment."

"It's alright, Robert," assured her mother. "We can take care of ourselves. We have before; we will again."

"I don't think this is anything like before. This feels dangerous, in a way I can't explain."

"It does to me too. But go—you have a job to do. We have our fortunes to claim. We'll be fine. Now, go!"

Kissing his wife on the cheek ever so lightly, he left them and took his place with the new council. In spite of the trials and tribulations of the past year, this place felt like death had patiently awaited their arrival and now intended to claim his prize.

Chapter 23

From Bad to Worse, June 1610

Alice swept the dirt surrounding the sleeping holes, the name she had given their new beds. Her father said they were actually soldier's pits, as the soldiers had dug them prior to any families arriving. But with every stroke of the broom, Alice cursed the Virginia Company. She eyed Joanne curled in her hole. Not for the first time, she realized how fortunate she was to have parents who concerned themselves with her comfort, as she still had her mattress. It fit perfectly in her sleeping hole. Joanne just had the hard dirt, not even a tarp to cover her.

"Uncle Willie would think this interesting," Alice said. Assuming Joanne wouldn't answer, she continued as though they were having a conversation like they had in Plymouth. "Why is that, Alice? Because who expects people to sleep in holes like rabbits in a warren? On Bermuda, we made our own homes. We had our own quarters, with walls and a roof. Here, a place that's been around longer, there's nothing. Just some poles stuck in the ground marking where a building should be and holes dug inside. There aren't even enough holes for everyone to sleep at the same time!" Missing her chores from the isle and the purpose they gave her days, she continued sweeping.

"Where is Jane?" she asked. "She was to marry, but I can't find her or her intended." Unlike on the isle, no one here talked. There was no hint as to what had happened to the other inhabitants, and no clue as to what had become of Jane. Odd, given there was no privacy; no private quarters nor even a chance for private conversations. Given the aggression of the insects, perhaps their secrets had been sucked out through their blood. Looking to Joanne, Alice reckoned her spirit had been sucked out in a similar fashion. "What happened, Joanne? To you? To her?" she asked quietly, her questioning cut short by the bell for daily prayer.

The young women ambled to the chapel, the only structure fully intact, albeit more a lean-to than a place where God would reside. As Alice listened to the Reverend drone on about God's promise and the need for obedience, she contemplated the meaninglessness of it all. What should they pray for? Food? There was none to be had. The food they had brought from Bermuda consumed in less than two weeks. All the cahows and tortoises; the pork and hearts of palm. Even the bibey. Gone. Should she pray for deliverance? Salvation? Death? When the service concluded, Alice pulled Joanne along with her to tend the fire. In another day, they'd be out of wood too. No matter—there was nothing left to cook.

At night, in addition to the sound of the owl's hoot and the constant hum of cicadas, growling stomachs added to the cacophony. As Alice lay in the dark, she wondered how long it took a person to die from starvation. How long had it taken their companions, who had numbered in the hundreds, to dwindle to sixty? She thought of the one hundred and forty who came from the island, well fed, healthier than most had been in their lives, now struggling to make it through each day. In her memory from a mere month ago, she could hear her father: *With the food we're bringing to supplement the crops already planted, Jamestowne will be a viable entity for the Company. Everyone will want to stake their claim, and we were here first! We'll have everything our hearts desire, and more.* On the island anything seemed possible as they'd done the impossible: survived the Isle of Devils. The reality? They wouldn't survive James Fort. *We were fools,* she thought. *We were all such dreamy-eyed fools.*

Each morning, Alice awoke with small hopes. Perhaps today would be the day they discovered a part of the river teeming with fish. Perhaps there would be a herd of deer standing at the gate. Perhaps Joanne would speak. Perhaps Jane would arrive to tell them about her new husband. Perhaps,

perhaps, perhaps. As the days wore on, she felt her spirits dwindling, and longed for Elizabeth's company, her jovial camaraderie. A return to life as she knew it on the Isle of Devils.

Her father exited the council meeting motioning for Alice to join him as he walked to her mother.

"It's been decided: we shall leave immediately," declared her father.

"Oh, Robert! Are we really going home?" Maude asked. "Or are we to return to the isle? Oh, never mind—I don't care. When?"

"We're returning to England, immediately. First, we shall sail to Newfoundland, establish contact with the English fleets there. Such an abundance of fish should provide enough for all our needs. We can restore our health and replenish our stores for the journey. By Christmas, we should be home. By the new year, we can put this behind us and start afresh."

"What about Mr. Cyrus? Our home, your business?" Her mother paused. "Alice? What's to become of her?"

"Aye, good questions. I'm hopeful once he hears of our ordeal, of thinking us dead for a year, he'll consider my debt forgiven. He's a gentleman, after all."

"Gentleman," harrumphed her mother. "Just because he's called a gentleman doesn't mean he'll do right by others. Did you learn nothing on the isle?"

"Well, it's not as though we have a choice, Maude. Gates is shutting down the entire enterprise. We're all to return to England. The entire Company is to leave, so I can't be faulted for not having tried. And if he takes everything, I'll start again. We'll start again."

"We've been through much worse. I'm sure we'll be fine. Just need to get our bearings, that's all." Maude bit her lip. "Alice was right: we should have stayed on Bermuda."

Alice smiled; she had been right. "So, am I still to marry Mr. Cyrus?" She thought of Alfred: Would he remember her? Would he have waited for her? How would she tell him she was to marry another? A man she didn't love...

"I don't know, but if I have to sacrifice every possession we own, then I will do it to see you happy." Placing his hand on her shoulder, he turned her to face him straight on. "Alice, I don't plan on giving my consent for you to marry that man, is what I'm trying to say."

"Thank you, Papa, but if it's what I must do to save the estate, your business, then I will do it. But you must promise me—swear to me, you will no longer gamble. No more wagers that jeopardize your livelihood or mother's well-being."

"I swear it is all behind me. After this past year, I have done my penance plus more. You have no need for concern. But please understand, I will try my utmost to stave off your marriage to Mr. Cyrus, or any man with whom you aren't entirely smitten."

"Papa, I am curious: What made Gates change his mind? What made him finally decide to leave?"

"Oh, that's a story for another time. On the voyage home, perhaps," he offered, smiling.

"No, I'd like to know. On Bermuda, he was so convinced of his own authority he put a man to death. He meted out justice as he saw fit, regardless of support. He used God and the good Reverend to coerce people to do his bidding. Then here? Here he finally listens to the council. He takes advice. Now he shows humanity, in a place where there is none. In a place where it is too late."

"I think he came here with an idea in his head, like we all did, of creating a new life, one with remarkable possibilities. Unlike the rest of us, he was also tasked with the impossible mission of making James Fort profitable for the Company. He assumed responsibility for its success or failure. Then he never made it here. On the isle, he planned; he never lost sight of his mission. The success of the Company ever foremost in his mind, he brought enough food to supplement the larder. How was he to know there'd be no larder to supplement? How could he ever imagine the waters would be fished out? That it wasn't safe to leave the fort to find food? But to see what remained of the people? That is what struck him. He refuses to have any more death. He's determined to save as many lives as possible, and that will not happen here. He's a smart man, a determined and well-disciplined leader, but even he knows when he's beaten. There is no winning here." Her father paused, shattered. "He did the best he could with what was available. We all did. Sometimes part of being a leader is admitting defeat. This place defeated us. This place defeated the Company. This place defeated England."

"This place did," Alice admitted, "but the entire journey hasn't been a loss. We did have our grand adventure, albeit not the one we imagined." Alice thought of Susanna and Willie. With any luck, she would see them in a few months.

Standing on the bank of the James, Alice patiently waited to board the Admiral's pinnace. She couldn't imagine sailing on the other vessel. With Gates. All her voyages had been with the Admiral, and she'd been fine, so why break protocol? However, unlike previous voyages, this departure lacked any sense of enthusiasm for the journey. Leaving England, they were feted as the conquering heroes saving an English settlement. Leaving Bermuda, castaways eagerly anticipated reunions with loved ones. Leaving here? Gates threatened the men who wanted to torch what remained of the fort.

Castaways and survivors alike, silent witnesses to the horrors of life in the New World, watched the fort fade from view. Their new focus: reaching the Chesapeake Bay. In a few weeks they'd be in Newfoundland, safely eating while awaiting ship assignments. But those luxuries didn't exist here; danger did.

Alice bore the resentment of Joanne and the Jamestowne survivors. Providence had seen fit to perch her on an isle graced with God's bounty, and Joanne in a hellhole where she'd eaten shoe leather and all manner of flesh. Birds. Snakes. Mice. And the unnamed meat rumored to have kept this group alive. Alice flinched. Could she have done that? Would she have become so desperate to live she'd have eaten...anything?

Alice considered Joanne, her feral desperation frightening. She hated to admit it, but Joanne had become one of the living dead: those who physically survived, but whose souls perished in the process.

Once again traveling by the tides, they arrived at the Point within two days. As they awaited the final tide before exiting the bay one final time, the mariners' shouts informed them of approaching ships.

"Ships?" bellowed Somers to the neighboring ship. "Gates! Why are there ships?"

Alice listened to the two men question one another; she watched Strachey write. What had he done? Did he know of the ships? His countenance indicated he did. Had he somehow contacted an outsider?

"I ordered Percy to inform those at the Point we were leaving—to be prepared to leave with us. It makes no sense they would allow ships in the river now," Gates countered.

The two vessels coasted silently toward the three ships, the heat and humidity adding to the passengers' unease. No one spoke; the eager scratching of Strachey's quill the solitary sound audible above the lapping of the waves against the ship's bow. As the three ships approached, the flags became distinguishable: England. Three ships from England. Laughter was the first thing heard, a low chortle that quickly grew into a chorus of laugher and cheers.

"We're saved!"

"They didn't forget us! They've come for us!"

Hugging; laughing; happiness. Then the flagship of the three-ship convoy pulled alongside.

"Governor De La Warr, it is an honor," Strachey said with a bow.

"Who are you?" asked the Governor. "Where is Lieutenant Governor Gates? Ah, there you are. What is the meaning of this? I was informed by the men at the fort you plan to leave on the morrow."

Gates, stepping forward, said, "Yes, a difficult decision, but given the circumstances..."

"I forbid it. You are to turn these vessels around at once and return to James Fort."

"But, sir, if you would allow me to explain..."

"Is there still a fort?"

"Well, yes, but—"

"Then that is where we shall have our next conversation." De La Warr gave the command for his ship to continue on its journey, expecting the two ships of survivors to follow in its wake. Gates reluctantly, but dutifully, gave the command to follow.

The return trip resembled a death march. No one spoke, not to question nor complain. The survivors of the winter spent at the fort were loath to return, their aspirations dying each moment they drew closer to the fort. The survivors of the isle hoped the new supplies would be enough to get the fort back on stable footing so they could, perhaps, make some money on this venture. On arrival at the gates it was made clear to everyone De La Warr was indeed the new governor, and as such, his was the final word.

Alice stood at the rail and watched the newly arrived council members line up by importance. The procession was headed by Governor De La Warr, then Lieutenant Governor Gates, and so on until the entire settlement of four hundred had its place. Once in the fort, they witnessed a brief ceremony wherein the new governor reiterated that he, and he alone, was in charge.

"Look around you; what do you see?" He paused as the people did, in fact, look around. "I'll tell you what I see: I see nothing. I see nothing that should allow me to congratulate you—any of you—on a job well done. What I see is shameful. The shameful waste of resources, English resources, on ones ill-equipped to care for this settlement or themselves. You are a wretched, shameful lot. You have no one to blame but yourselves for your lack of industry here. Sloth, as you well know, is a deadly sin, and a sin that will not be tolerated any longer. You have all been indulged for far too long. If you had worked harder, tried harder, I wouldn't have to come rescue you as you could provide for yourselves, this settlement, and England." He strolled around the congregation, straightening his back and strutting between the survivors, their eyes downcast. "But I will help you. I have come with a keen eye toward increasing your productivity, on helping you to better yourself. I think discipline has been lacking, an oversight that's easily remedied. From now on, I will guide you with the sword of justice, to cut out those of you who are unable, or unwilling, to carry your weight in this unique opportunity that you have been afforded. I should think in a month's time, we shall see the fruits of our labor; and within a season, you shall see what can transpire with the corrective attitude of strong leadership." The Governor moved to the front of the group once more. "I do understand you have had supply issues in the past. I can remedy that as well. With me"—he gestured to the ships—"I have brought enough food supplies for a year! I have brought enough medicine for a year! See, I don't come empty-handed. My promises are not in vain. I supply you. You follow my directives. A lucrative endeavor for all." He ended by striding back to the ships, and commanding the sailors to unload.

Father pinched the bridge of his nose; Maude sucked in her lips.

"We're not leaving, are we?" Alice asked quietly.

Her father shook his head. Maude closed her eyes, also shaking her head.

"Robert Drinkard!"

Her father raised his hand like an errant schoolboy. A stranger with a musket approached. "Your presence is required by the Governor. If you will follow me."

Her father, looking to Maude but speaking to Alice, said, "Do not leave each other's side. I will find you when I am done, and we will—"

The soldier stepped between them before her father could finish his thought.

"Sir? Now. I shan't ask again."

Alice watched her father's face blanch as he fell in behind the soldier as ordered. This New World was unlike any they'd expected, an exceedingly treacherous place with armed men they dared not cross.

Unloading the ships didn't take long. Alice and Maude watched as the sailors landed each container, a soldier then responsible for delivery of each item to its assigned location in the larder.

"He has food for a year?" asked Alice.

"So he says," replied Maude, focused on the food containers as they passed.

"I haven't seen any meat. Barely a few containers of meal and dried beans," commented Alice.

"I did see some cheese."

"That's it? That's not nearly enough for four hundred people. Look at how much we prepared and ate each day on the island, and none of us were starving then. What we brought from Bermuda should have lasted six months. Gone within two weeks! He didn't bring enough for a week, let alone a year."

"I know." Maude continued watching the supplies. "That's definitely not enough medicine for a year either. A month, perhaps. Barring any accidents."

"We need another plan," stated Alice, breaking Maude's concentration. She ran toward Thomas and Elizabeth.

"It's not enough, is it?" asked Alice quietly.

Thomas shook his head.

"We didn't think so," said Alice. "Me and Maude. We've been watching. There's not enough of anything to sustain those of us already here. With these added men? We'll all be dead within the year."

"Well," Elizabeth whispered, "if we can get some planting in...maybe if we try harder."

"Are you daft?" Alice nearly screamed. "There are no seeds for planting! There is no drinkable water! Look at them." She pointed to the fort survivors, winded and fatigued from the little work they could be implored to do, no strength to carry even the lightest bundle to the new governor's quarters, a solitary tent pitched just for his use. "They're dying! They have no strength and, I'd reckon with today's pronouncement, little will to live."

Thomas nodded; Elizabeth eyed the neighboring soldiers as though she expected to be shot on sight.

"I need to talk to the Admiral," Alice whispered to Thomas.

"I don't know."

"Tell me plain: where will he be staying now?"

"On the boat. But, Alice, you can't."

"I can't what, Thomas?" she snapped.

"You can't simply prattle off as you wish. Not like you did on Bermuda.

Please, for me, for Elizabeth, don't do anything rash. You're putting us all in danger."

"Never you mind. His location is all I need."

"Alice, this isn't like on the island. This is dangerous, dreadfully dangerous." Thomas inclined his head to her. "This new governor, you heard him."

"I need to speak with the Admiral; that's all. If anyone comes looking for me, say I'm with you."

"Oh no, Alice," stammered Elizabeth. "You can't go to the boat."

"I can. And I must." She turned and left the two to wonder why she would put her life at risk to seek out the Admiral.

Alice crept along the shore, the water lapping at her ankles as she took in her surroundings. The moonlight reflected on the water, made the landscape appear brighter than the midnight hour. She spied a dinghy tied to a tree. She walked slowly toward it, the water rippling with the steps. It didn't look too far; certainly she could manage to row a dinghy. She slipped the rope from the trunk, pushing the tiny vessel into the water as she'd seen the men do. She tried to crawl over the side, almost losing an oar in the process. She turned the vessel to its side, clinging to an oar, and managed to get inside. Gaining her bearings, she tentatively placed the oar in the water and began to row toward the ship. Impressed with her ability, she began to pick up speed; but lost her balance and flipped to the side, tumbling into the water in the process. She flailed the oar overhead, catching it on the side of the dinghy to give her a moment of respite before going under again as it slipped from the boat. This time, she didn't flail, but purposefully tried to gain purchase on the tiny craft. She kept hitting it, but could not make full contact. Up. Down below the surface. Grab a breath. Go down. Breath. Down. Breath. Down. Then swoosh! She was lifted from the water, a strong arm around her waist, placed into the floor of a skiff. Her eyes closed, she drew in a few hesitating breaths to make sure she wasn't dreaming and hadn't actually drowned.

"Child!" the voice boomed. "What are you doing?"

"Coming to talk to you," Alice stated matter-of-factly, regaining her composure.

"Let's get you aboard," he said, eyeing the shore. Then, turning to three lanky sailors flanking him: "We shan't speak of this again. If anyone asks, you never saw her, am I clear?"

"Aye, aye."

Draped in a blanket, safely delivered to his quarters, Alice sat across from the one man she trusted to save them.

"Child," the Admiral chuckled. "I shouldn't laugh: you nearly drowned, but—"

"But I didn't," Alice affirmed. "You saved me."

"You are a tenacious one, for sure. But you took a dangerous risk just to talk to me. You could have waited until the morn."

Alice shook her head. "I don't believe that, sir, not anymore. I don't think any of us will be free to talk anymore. Which is why I'm here. I have something to tell you. Something so important I couldn't risk anyone hearing."

"You mean you didn't want anyone to eavesdrop." He chuckled. "As I recall, that's your special skill. You'd make an excellent spy."

"This is serious." She knitted her eyebrows.

"Oh, well then. Let's get to it, shall we?"

"I think the new governor is lying," she whispered. "I saw what he brought on the ships. He doesn't have nearly enough supplies for a year." Alice's cheeks blazed red, her eyes alight with the excitement of sharing her information.

"I see. And what would you have me do? I know you." He winked. "I feel you must have a plan; otherwise, why would you be here?"

"I do, I do indeed." Smiling, she leaned forward. "I think you should go back to Bermuda for supplies. This week." She sat back, clearly proud of herself. When he didn't acknowledge the brilliance of her plan, merely stared uncomprehendingly, she leaned forward again. "Don't you understand? It makes sense. It took us a little over a week to get here, so no more than two weeks' travel time, to-and-fro, a week to load supplies. The fish and hogs are so plentiful, it's really a matter of catching them. It would be so easy. You could be back within a month, six weeks at the longest. And we'd have plenty."

The Admiral continued to stare.

"Sir? Admiral? Did you hear what I said?"

"I'm sorry, my dear. Sometimes, when you're animated and sharing some scheme, I see my Sarah so clearly. Yes, I heard every word you said. I always do. And you're right; it would be easy." He thought for a moment, rubbing his chin. "And you came up with this plan on your own?"

"Yes, sir."

"No help from your father?"

"No, sir. It's all my idea."

"Have you told anyone else of your plan?"

"No, sir."

The Admiral grinned, then laughed, a loud, full-belly laugh. Standing, he continued to laugh as he paced the floor behind his chair.

"Does my idea amuse you? I assure you; it is sound. I have done the calculations, estimated the days. I may be off by a day or two depending on the weather, but otherwise I think this plan is entirely practical and reasonable," stated Alice resolutely.

"Oh, my dear, you are a delight. It is a marvelous plan, which is why I made an identical proposal to the council this evening. They are taking it under advisement. And you are correct—it is a good plan. A feasible way to save everyone here. I should have known you would think of it."

"What does *under advisement* mean?" she asked.

"Usually, it means nothing will come of it. Here, things are bleaker. I think patience is what is needed with our new governor. Give him time to realize people aren't lazy. We don't actually possess any means with which to plant a crop, nor the implements to harvest anything should this ground ever receive rain. Let his men deal with the natives. Help them understand all sides have taken advantage of the other, with none prospering. No, I think given some time, he will be humbled."

"We—well, the survivors, don't really have time though, do they?"

"No." He returned to his chair, the wood rubbed smooth from years of making life-and-death decisions. Draping his hands across his midsection in contemplation, he continued, "The new council, of which your father is a member, held a meeting tonight. The Governor"—he paused, a slight furrow to his brow—"he needs empirical evidence. Proof the fort and area are no longer viable."

"What kind of proof?"

"He needs to experience daily life in the fort to see the error of his thinking. He's arrogant at the moment, in the way people who haven't actually experienced life here can be. I can't fault him for his misperception. We've all had our misgivings and doubts, but the experience is what determines our character, our way forward. He'll learn; he'll see. And when he does, I am certain I will be dispatched to the isle."

"We don't really have time for him to have an epiphany."

The Admiral smiled. "No, dear, we don't. But I don't think it will take him long to have his *epiphany*."

Chapter 24

Goodbye, Somers, 19 June 1610

Alice watched the sailors load the meager supplies aboard the *Patience*. The Admiral was heading back to Bermuda, his prediction correct: De La Warr had changed his estimation of the inhabitants within days as he succumbed to the flux. After calling them names, withholding food for laziness, and insisting the water was safe to drink, he succumbed to the same physical ailments as the settlers. It had happened with such speed Alice wondered if God himself wasn't punishing him for judging them by teaching him a pointedly personal lesson about humility. There may have been four hundred in the fort, but word traveled fast as to his daily vexations, which the little family of three recited each evening. But even the thought of De La Warr's gaseous exertions couldn't lighten Alice's mood as she watched the Admiral prepare to leave.

"I thought I espied you," he said, walking to her.

"I shall miss you."

"Ah, the intrepid Alice." He sighed. "You said it yourself: I shan't be gone long. Inside two months, I'll be back. With food enough to carry us through the winter."

Alice nodded. "Just, please, come back safely."

"But of course," exclaimed the old seadog.

"Is there any way you could take my father?" she asked. "Or my family? We're hard workers—you've seen us. We'll do whatever you request. And my mother and I can preserve the food as fast as your men can bring it."

"Alice, you are more than capable, and I've no doubt your family would be tremendous help. But I'm sorry. I have a skeletal crew as it is; we need the room for provisions. This isn't like last time; we know what we're up against here. This time it's a mission, no time for strolls on the shore to collect ambergris." He motioned to Chance. "He'll be the only one free to enjoy the isle. Free to run the shore, chase those cahows."

"I understand." Alice tried not to cry—not here, not now—but she couldn't help herself. Unable to stop the tears, she turned her head toward the river, hoping he wouldn't see her cry, but to no avail. She felt the familiar wet lap on her hand as Chance nudged her. The Admiral wiped a tear from her cheek and pulled her to him. As he embraced her, Alice heard him whisper, "Thank you. You have no idea how much you've helped me."

Alice whispered back, "You're welcome."

As the Admiral took his leave, he turned and waved to Alice, now joined by her father and Maude. The trio waved back.

"God speed," yelled her father.

They stood on the shore and watched the *Patience* fade from view.

Chapter 25

Strachey Strikes Again, 6–9 July 1610

Alice sat with Joanne, their crewelwork untouched in their laps. The heat and humidity, combined with the constant buzz of cicadas, drained them of any vitality. It was easier to endure the oppressiveness of mid-day by dozing.

Distant yells broke the spell, as people ran past them. Alice watched the commotion as some grabbed weapons, while others attempted to hide in their sleep holes. No one mentioned a word to them: no warning, no cautionary explanations—nothing. Joanne immediately pulled her knees tightly to her chest, burying her head between them like a child making themself invisible.

"Joanne." Alice shook her friend, who was now rocking back and forth. "Joanne, look at me."

She raised her head slightly. Her eyes wide as saucers, Alice realized her friend was truly terrified. For the first time, she noticed how much her friend had transformed in their time apart. The crusted blood on Joanne's lips, from her swollen, ulcerated gums; the yellowing whites of her eyes; and the deep blue of the iris, so beguiling when they'd first met in Plymouth, now faded and dull. There was no light in her anymore, and the current situation rendered her a petrified shell of a human.

"It's alright," Alice soothed. "I'll stay with you. There's nothing to be frightened of. We'll have a little adventure, just the two of us. Now come, let's see what's afoot."

Joanne was stone; she wouldn't budge. For someone so fragile and thin, she was surprisingly difficult to move. She started shaking her head vigorously, with more animation and energy than Alice had seen from her since their return. Her lips, moving in earnest, reminded Alice of the nuns at prayer. She had seen them once in Scotland, when visiting her father's family; rosaries in hand, they mumbled words meant solely for the Virgin's ears. Oddly fascinated by her friend, Alice failed to realize Joanne was speaking to her. Leaning in, she could barely make out, "No. No. No."

"No, what?" asked Alice. She put her ear to Joanne's mouth, grateful her friend was finally speaking.

"Too dangerous. Kill us."

"Who will kill us?" Alice glanced around, expecting to be pounced upon immediately. Joanne began frantically shaking her head again, her extreme terror palpable. Alice placed an arm around her, trying to comfort her, when she saw Maude running along the path to her.

"There you are," she panted. "You need to come with me now. Joanne, go to your mother."

Joanne didn't respond.

"I can't get her to move. I've tried," Alice explained. "She said they're going to kill us. Who are they? Mother, what's going on?"

Maude, moving to the other side of Joanne, slid an arm around her waist, and began ushering them toward the church. "The natives."

Immediately upon entering the structure, Joanne's mother snatched her from them like a morsel of meat. Alice and her mother continued to the center of the room and crouched behind a pew, Maude holding Alice's forearm in a grip that pinched bone.

"You're scaring me," Alice whined.

"Good. You need to be scared; it might keep you safe."

Maude released her arm. "There's been an attack. One of Gates's men was slain."

"Gates's men," repeated Alice. "You mean Strachey. What was he doing?"

"Trying to find us food. The nets aren't yielding anything, so Gates sent some men to try and find us crabs, or fish down river, set the nets there. But while they were casting about, they were attacked, and one of the men killed."

"Is Strachey dead?"

"No. Strachey wasn't killed. It was some other man. I forget his name."

They sat quietly, listening for sounds of approaching danger. The fort, eerily quiet, was as unsettling as the chaos was before. The air, stagnant and hot, added to the sense of impending doom. They sat. Waiting. Only the occasional raised voice, overheard from the council's chambers, along with those infernal cicadas, making any sound.

"Of course it wasn't Strachey," mumbled Alice. "Why do they keep sending him? Everyone knows he won't actually work."

Maude chuckled, "Oh, Alice. I do love your sauciness."

That night, her father insisted they take a walk with him, the only way they could speak privately.

"We don't have enough food—" He stopped. "We don't have enough food to make it until Somers returns. There're no fish here. There's nothing left to hunt here. We have no crops. So we've decided to take the drastic measure of severely rationing what little food there is, or none of us will make it. I think De La Warr finally sees this. He finally sees what we were trying to tell him when he arrived: we aren't lazy, we're out of options."

"But, Father, the survivors of the winter—"

"They'll likely starve to death now. But we have no choice. We can't save everyone; so the council, through necessity alone, determined to preserve the ones that still have health enough to work. And the incident today?" He blew air through his mouth heartily. "We were hoping there would be more fish, or crabs, or something down river. There is not. And apparently the man killed was merely trying to trade for corn. Or so I heard." He shook his head dismissively.

"You don't believe that?" asked Maude, her lips tightening to a line.

"I don't know what, or who, to believe anymore."

Alice watched her father: his face revealed weary exhaustion in deep crevices lining his forehead; dark circles beneath puffy eyes, made more pronounced by darkening freckles and ruddy cheeks; his weathered skin now constantly awash in perspiration. The mosquito bites were now angry red whelps that seemed to grow larger with each passing day, one encrusted with pus from his relentless picking. For the first time, she felt her father's anguish.

Alice slid her hand into her father's. "It will be fine, Papa. The Admiral will return in less than two months, and we shall have plenty of food. Ignore Strachey, he's a..." She struggled to find the word he'd used so often when describing the weasel. "...a sycophant!"

But there was no response. Instead, her father murmured, "Two months is a long time."

"Not really. We were on Bermuda for ten, and—" Alice enthused.

"It wasn't like this. There was plenty of food. There was clean water. No one was ill. No one was starving. We were blessed with plenty of natural resources. And we didn't have this infernal heat!" he practically shouted. He pulled away and began pacing, raking his hand through his hair. "And now? Strachey will get us all killed! Or worse!"

Maude calmly asked, "What do you mean Strachey will get us all killed? What has he done?"

"The altercation from earlier isn't over. In fact, it's far from over," he mumbled.

"Meaning?" asked Maude.

"Strachey has persuaded Gates to retaliate, to send a message to the savages we aren't to be touched. To make it clear we are here and we aren't leaving. Nor will we be intimidated."

"Oh, no," whispered her mother.

Her father dragged both hands over his face, reddening his cheeks further. He explained the proceedings from the council meeting. Some of Gates's men, along with Strachey, were going to sack Kecoughtan, the closest native village, in reprisal for the soldier's death.

"Certainly there was some dissent?" said Maude, shaking her head in disbelief. "You didn't vote to allow this. Did you, Robert?"

"Me? No, of course not! But hotter heads prevailed, and it will be our next *official* action."

"Oh, Robert." Maude crossed to him and wrapped her arms about his shoulders.

"What do we need to do, Papa? A siege requires preparations. How shall we prepare?"

Her father shrugged. "I have no idea. That's the problem. We'll be lambs to the slaughter. We can't go into the forest because we'll be shot. Take those men who went out with Gates. You saw what those arrows did to that William fellow. And he was the lucky one. We could end up like Humphrey Blunt; that poor bastard's head was skinned with a shell, and returned! We can't go into the river. Hell! We can't even get everyone safely to the Point. I guess Strachey will be doing us a favor by getting us all killed at once, long before we slowly starve to death or are overrun within the fort."

Alice remained unconvinced they were defenseless. In her mind, she could hear Uncle Willie: *With a little imagination, anything is possible.* She just needed to get creative.

Alice had never actually been in a siege, but she had read about them. As best she could recall, they would need food and weapons. Weapons would be easy enough: she would sharpen several sticks to points and use them as spears. If the sticks were small enough, she could hide them on her body and use them as she had the paring knives Thomas had trained her to use in the kitchen, but in a pokey way, not a stabby way.

After she'd witnessed the death of Mr. Samuel, Elizabeth taught her how to defend herself should she ever be seized by a man. Alice could still hear Elizabeth's emphatic instructions: *Always aim for the soft parts.* Then she'd kick toward the trousers. Alice thought about what other body parts might be soft. *Eyes are soft*, she whispered as she whittled twigs into long needles. Certainly stabbing someone in the eye would slow an attack as effectively as kicking them in the soft parts. Once she had amassed two dozen needles, she began collecting rocks. They were easy to throw and would hurt wherever they landed, no matter her terrible aim.

Maude watched as Alice brought all manner of forest detritus into her sleeping hole. Never uttering a word, she allowed her daughter this last act of freedom as they were facing certain, imminent death. But Alice's attitude surprised Maude. In spite of hearing her father's dire predictions, Alice hummed as she made her preparations. Maude watched, silently impressed with her fortitude.

Chapter 26

The End Is Nigh, 15 July 1610

Both to her chagrin and relief, Alice never had the opportunity to use her makeshift arsenal. She never got to prove to her father that preparedness is always possible, and no matter the odds, giving up is never the answer.

The Strachey-led attack on the village of Kecoughtan was a massacre. Her father did not rejoice in the victory; he did not see the honor in revenge; and, unlike others in the fort, did not see this as a de-escalation of hostilities between groups. Even Gates and Newport saw the futility in the event, and convinced De La Warr to allow them to return to England under the auspice of getting help for the fort. If relations between the two groups continued to disintegrate, they would need many more men for defense. As a result, within six days there was transport back to England, Gates and Newport chief amongst those departing, Alice and her family amongst the civilian passengers.

Alice stored her small retinue of tiny spears and rocks into a satchel. If nothing else, she had learned two valuable lessons over the past year: plan for the unexpected and plan to fight for your life. Spying her mattress, she decided it should stay. She'd gift Joanne this small mercy. Feeling the pangs of hunger fresh with the new day, she placed a hand over her abdomen.

"We'll be home soon enough," soothed Maude. "We'll eat well by summer's end."

"Such luxury—it's hard to imagine." Alice smiled, thinking of what she would eat first. A roast chicken, a plate of bacon. Bacon. Pork. Pigs. Ah, Bermuda, but her smile faded as she thought of the friends she was leaving behind. "I do, however, feel guilty. About Joanne, and the others. Does any of this bother you?"

"Bother me we have the chance to go while they have to stay? Aye, it does. But I don't feel guilty," her mother replied. "Life is a game of chance. Why, just look at how fate changed the women in this fleet, the women on our own ship. Some thrived; others perished. In the end, it all unfolds according to God's plan, and for that I shan't feel guilty. Pity, perhaps, but not guilt. No, if I am given the opportunity to save my family, then I shall count my blessings and take it." Maude finished folding the last of their belongings into the one trunk permitted.

"Wait! You forgot Father's things."

"He can pack his own things," she answered.

As they shuffled through the fort one last time, saying their goodbyes to the few women remaining, Alice noted with horror the desperation of those they were leaving. These women, Goody Eason, Mistress Horton, Joanne and her mother, wished them well, but their eyes told a different story. Gone was the kindness, replaced by sorrow, the sorrow of having no choice, of having to remain in a place shrouded in death, a death equally likely to come from within as without. Their spirits were as broken as the palisades around the fort.

Stepping forward, Joanne stood patiently before Alice. Still not speaking, she hugged Alice. Alice accepted her friend's embrace, afraid to hold her tightly lest she crack her ribs. Holding her, the image of cahow bones came to mind, the featherlight bones that snapped like twigs now littering the well outside the cooking area. Shuddering, Alice whispered, "I've left you my mattress," then moved to her mother's side.

As they moved further down the path, Alice saw Elizabeth and Thomas waiting by the gates.

"I brought you this," said Thomas, handing her a ball of ambergris the size of his hand.

"Oh, Thomas, this is too much. I can't take this."

"I insist. It's what the Admiral would want."

"He's here? He's back? Already?"

"Unfortunately, no. He said you collected this on the isle. He gave it to us as a wedding gift, claimed it was valuable, but we can't see how this will help us here. You, on the other hand...It's much more valuable to you now than it will ever be for us."

"Thank you."

"Keep safe. And try to stay out of trouble." He hugged her, then stepped away to return to his duties.

"I will truly miss you," cried Elizabeth. "I will always treasure our adventures, and I will always be grateful for your help making my wedding so special." She began crying again.

Alice hugged her tighter. "I will miss you too. I'll treasure our memories forever."

"Stay safe," said Elizabeth, pulling away.

"Always go for the soft parts, right?"

"Always," said Elizabeth. "But I think this may serve you better." Wrapped in an ornately embroidered handkerchief lay the small paring knife from the kitchen, the one she had coveted in Bermuda. "Between the potential cash from the ambergris and this, I'm confident you'll be fine."

Touching her arm, Maude whispered, "It's time."

Alice hugged Elizabeth one last time, unsure if she'd ever see her again, and lost her composure, tears falling unabated. "Thank you."

Alice followed her parents down the path to the shore. Finding it harder than expected to say goodbye, she turned her attention to the skiff that would take them to their ship, the *Blessing*. She regarded the ship suspiciously; to her mind, the *Blessing* had failed to live up to its name. Alice thought of the shrouded bodies tossed overboard, early in their voyage, and the fate to which the *Blessing* had delivered her friends—one a starved survivor; the other a mysterious disappearance no one spoke of. For her friends, the *Blessing* had proved a curse. What fate did it have in store for her?

"Send word as soon as you arrive. I may not get your letter for some months, but I do wish to know you made it back safely," her father instructed.

Maude was crying. *Why is my mother crying?*

"And write to me every day. Tell me every detail of your life. Of Alice's life," he continued.

Maude nodded, tears cascading down her face.

"I love you. I have loved you fiercely from the moment we met." Tilting her face toward him, he kissed her fully on the mouth. Alice had never seen them kiss, and the action made her feel awkward in their presence; she averted her gaze.

"I love you more than you will ever know," whispered Maude. "I will miss you every minute of every day until we're united again." She placed her head in the curve of his neck.

"There's to be none of that," cracked Newport as he passed them. "I've got a ship to sail; I don't have time for this nonsense. Hurry along now." He continued walking to the skiff, chuckling good-humoredly along the way.

Alice turned to her father. "You're not coming with us?"

He shook his head.

"Why, Papa? I thought you were going to reason with Mr. Cyrus, explain what we've been through, and him being a gentleman he'd see reason," implored Alice.

"I'm sorry. My scheme could work only if the Company failed. The moment De La Warr ordered us back into the fort, it all changed." Pulling his daughter into his chest, he whispered, "I love you. It's not safe here, and above all else, I need to know you and your mother are safe. Take care of her until I see you again."

"That's seven years. Seven dangerous years for you," Alice pleaded, pulling away. "Even Gates is leaving, and he was Lieutenant Governor! If he can leave, so can you."

"No. I can't. If I don't meet my obligation..." He paused. "Well, the terms of our arrangement haven't changed. You deserve to make your own choices, your own marriage. I meant what I said: I'll never consent to you marrying someone you don't love."

"It won't be worth anything if you're dead!" Alice cried.

Her father and Maude together brought her into their embrace, and with more strength than she could fight, held her tight betwixt them. Once she stopped struggling, the reality swept into her chest and quickened her heart.

"Father, if you let me stay, I'll be the most obedient daughter in the fort.

I promise I won't be quarrelsome; I'll behave. I'll make you proud, I'll..."
But she didn't know what else to promise to change his mind.

"Ah, Alice. My adventurer. You always make me proud. It's nothing you
have or haven't done. Things change; circumstances change. This"—he
gestured with his free hand—"changed. This isn't what we were promised;
this is dangerous. Deadly. Especially now. And I'd prefer if my first-born
didn't perish here." He winked at Maude.

"Didn't you once say, we don't always get what we're promised?" Alice
asked, certain she had found a new argument.

"I'm not debating with you; this isn't negotiable." He smiled at her, then
pulled her close as he kissed the top of her head.

Alice and Maude stepped into the skiff, their eyes never leaving Robert.
Once on the *Blessing*, they didn't speak as they waved to the shore until
Jamestowne was no longer visible. They didn't speak as they watched the
Point, with its new fort, recede into the horizon as they hit open water.
They didn't speak until the gulls no longer circled the mast.

⚓

"I don't understand," Alice said. "Why was Father so insistent we return
home?"

"Your father believes the attack on Kecoughtan will incite new fighting.
The prospect of war coupled with insufficient supplies for the remaining
population..." She shook her head. "The situation is calamitous. We never
imagined this scenario when we agreed to this scheme."

"But he's there alone, without us."

Maude nodded, her cheeks blanched and nose reddened from crying.

"Mother, what is it? What aren't you telling me?"

Maude shook her head. "It's too soon," she whispered, her hands
moving to her belly.

"Too soon for—" Alice stopped. Nodding toward her mother's hands,
she quietly asked, "Are you?"

"Yes."

Alice clapped her hands and yelped. "This is wonderful!" The response was involuntary; ever since the death of her brother, she had imagined having another brother. It wouldn't be the same, but at least she wouldn't be alone in old age. There would always be someone to call family, someone with whom she had shared memories. But then she remembered the babies on Bermuda, and how Goody Rolfe hadn't survived the ordeal. She tried to keep smiling, not wanting to alarm her mother, but the older woman's tears let Alice know she too was concerned.

Alice wanted to reassure her they were safe—there was nothing to fear; but she couldn't make her mouth form the platitudes. They were both keenly aware that death came often, and swift, for women and infants.

"Eight weeks. We'll be home in eight weeks. That's not a long time. Do you think you will give birth on the ship?" Alice asked. While she had assisted with one birth, she had avoided another, cognizant she lacked the skills of a midwife. As there were no other women on the ship, she would be on her own, and she had no idea how to care for her mother—for her pregnant mother.

"No, not that soon. I think it will arrive shortly after the new year."

"Then we've plenty of time to prepare." Relieved her mother felt it too early to be concerned about the baby, Alice fell into her old habit of sitting forward of the forecastle, watching the day pass with few interruptions.

This trip was vaguely reminiscent of that on the *Sea Venture*. She missed Chance, of course, but her time was now spent caring for her mother rather than ruffling the canine's fur. As before, her mother was proving a bad fit for sea travel, and while food on board lacked the heartiness of the voyage over, it was more regularly served than at the fort, as fresh fish was caught daily. At least their stomachs didn't complain as loudly, and it provided her mother something other than bile to retch. They didn't have the privilege of a private cabin, but Captain Newport did hang a tarpaulin around their shared bed so they could have a modicum of privacy when resting.

Rising at daybreak, she watched the sun rise over the bow. It was the one time of day her mother seemed to rest easier. Taking advantage, Alice sat in contemplative quiet. Breathing in the salty air, the wind tousling her hair, made her feel more alive than she had since leaving the isle. Even with the dangers of a hurricano, Alice loved being on board, no land in sight with only the stars and sun as guides.

"Sorry, miss, but the Cap'n needs ye," said Archie, Newport's cabin boy. "He's with yer mother." His accent thick, it took Alice a moment to translate his instructions.

"My mother?"

Archie nodded; Alice tried to reason why Newport would be with her mother. She moved across the deck toward the Captain's quarters, but Archie stopped her.

"With her," he restated. "Below."

Alice nodded. Taking in one last deep inhalation of ocean air before descending the ladder, she was more confused than ever. It was highly irregular for Newport to be with her mother below deck. She could hear the quiet whispers of men stop as she walked by. No one was speaking; the 'tween deck was eerily silent as she approached their bed.

An unknown man stood over her mother. Newport quickly stepped into her line of sight.

"I'm sorry, Alice."

Alice took in the countenance of the captain, the one-armed former pirate now cowed by emotion. Here was a man used to being in control, and Alice understood his reticence; if her behavior of the past year was any indication, she had proven herself to be anything but controllable.

"Sorry for what?" Alice looked about the room. It was then she noticed the man pulling a blanket over Maude's head. "What is he doing? She's asleep; she hates the blanket over her head. It makes her too hot. She'll start retching again!" Lunging forward, she reiterated, "Stop! I said stop!"

Newport again blocked her path as she tried to side-step him.

"Alice," he started. "She won't mind. Not now."

"Of course she'll mind. You don't know her; you don't—" She stopped, her blood running cold. She stared at the bed, at Maude's covered face. Swallowing hard, she needed to know; she needed for one of them to say it out loud. "Is she...dead?"

The two men nodded.

"Then tell me. Tell me as you would my father," Alice demanded, suddenly furious at the men before her. "Tell me how she died." She forced herself to focus, to calm down. Men didn't speak the truth when confronted by weepy women. She'd have to do better if she was to learn the truth. She tried again, the words measured and even. "I assure you, she's had no fever. As no one else is ill, I doubt there is pestilence aboard. Please, tell me your suspicions."

"She appears to have died in her sleep," Newport said.

Alice eyed the bed. "In her sleep? How?" When he didn't answer her right away, she knew he was keeping something from her. "The Admiral told me you were a decent man, a man he trusted. A man who would speak the truth, even if others refused to hear. I understand I am not my father, and you may be hesitant to divulge your suspicions to a young woman, but I assure you, after the events of the past year, I am more than capable of handling the truth about my mother's death. I deserve no less."

"He told me you were clever, the second most intrepid girl he ever did meet. After his Sarah." Newport dropped his gaze to the floor.

"Then you know I'm not to be trifled with."

Newport chuckled. "Yes, miss, I was warned."

"How did she die?" Alice's hands were now trembling; in spite of her bravado, she was actually quite afraid of what he might say.

Newport pulled back the blanket, exposing the entire bed, the ticking stained with blood, her mother's blood, from her hips to her knees.

Alice fell to her knees as she held her mother's hand. She stroked her hair, as though she were a child who needed comforting. She could hear Newport talking, but couldn't make out the words. She could hear someone saying prayers, but didn't know who. All her attention was on her mother, her pale skin, still warm to the touch. She noticed the locket around her mother's neck; the locket that contained a lock of Bertie's hair. Unhooking the golden trinket, she apologized for being disrespectful and addressing her as Her Highness. She whispered the Lord's Prayer to her mother, the words flowing from her lips as natural as breath as she felt herself floating above the scene.

⚓

Sitting bolt upright, Alice felt the soft mattress underneath her. It was dark, the room lit by a single lantern. She felt the locket around her neck. Like a tidal wave, her mother's death crept from the edges of her vision, crashing into clear focus.

"Ah, miss! Ye're awake! I was worried—ye gave us quite a scare."

"Archie? Where am I?"

"Ye're in the Captain's quarters, ye are. He brought ye here after ye fainted. Wait here; I'll fetch him."

"This is his room?" asked Alice, still confused.

"Aye. He's down below with us. He said ye're to have his room 'til we dock." At the doorway, he stopped. "I'll find ye some supper too. I'm glad ye're alright, miss."

Alice squinted in the darkness, the flame of a solitary candle the only movement. For the first time in her life, she was truly alone. She gasped, remembering what happened before she woke here. It hadn't been a dream; her mother really had died. Alice fell back as the tears came, this time with a searing pain that spread from her heart to her soul. Fingering the locket once more, she prayed. She prayed for her mother and the unborn sibling; for her father, may he survive the fort; and for her dead brother, may he welcome their mother in the hereafter and care for her as a son should. Lastly, she prayed for herself. She prayed for answers. She prayed for guidance. She prayed because she was angry. She prayed because she didn't know what else to do. Because she'd gotten exactly what she wanted: freedom to do as she liked and a grand adventure. She just never imagined everyone would be dead at the end.

PART FIVE

"She will outstrip all praise and make it halt behind her"
~ Prospero,
The Tempest, Act 4, Scene 1

Chapter 27

Stratford, England, November 1610

A death at sea may be the loneliest endeavor one ever experiences, for both the dying and the family forced to watch. Mother's burial at sea haunts me. With no grave to mark her life, nor ceremony to memorialize her passing, I'm left with nothing but the image of her encased in the deep, wide ocean. An ocean that a mere year ago mercifully delivered her to paradise, but this time swallowed her whole.

Alice stared at the entry, unable to halt the flood of images that haunted her days and nights. It was always the same. Her mother, wrapped in tarpaulin, perched prostrate on the ship's gunwale. Captain Newport reciting a prayer over the lifeless body. Her mother calling to her for help. But she could never reach her. The ship always pitched, throwing her to the deck and her mother into the ocean below. Sucked below the surface in one gulp, still calling, *Alice, help me. Alice, please, I need you.*

"Alice," Susanna soothed, gently wiping the tears from Alice's cheeks, her head slumped on the desk asleep. "You're safe. You're home."

Picking up the journal, Susanna read the entry. Alice snatched the journal from her, shutting the cover and fastening the clasps before she could read more.

"You ask a good question: Why not you? Why do you believe you were spared, in any of this?"

"I have no idea," mumbled Alice. "And how have I been spared? I've lost everything—my family, our home, even my grandmother. Mr. Cyrus laid claim to it all. I have nothing. And after all this, I think I'm still to marry that paunchy, beetle-headed barnacle."

"You've been playing word games with Father, I can tell. And need I remind you? You haven't lost everything; you still have us. While you are welcome to wallow in self-pity, I should think it wise to acknowledge what you do have left." Susanna pointed out the window. "He's still there. Been here every day since you returned. Eight weeks now. The epitome of devotion."

Standing at the edge of the garden was Alfred. Seeing Alice at the window, he waved and motioned for her to come down. She returned to the desk, slammed her fist on the top, mumbling, "Tidy your mess."

"He loves you, you know. And I believe you love him still. Go, talk to him; let him know how you feel."

"Not yet," said Alice. "There's something I must do first."

Alice approached the entrance of her former home, black iron knockers punctuating ancient oak doors. The last time she'd seen them, her grandmother had cursed them all, slamming the wooden doors shut on their very existence. At the time, Alice had been amused; in hindsight, her grandmother's words had proven to be horridly prophetic. *If I never hear from any of you again, it will be too soon!* Alice shuddered. *I wonder how she felt when she realized her wish had been granted.*

Reaching for a knocker, the door suddenly swung open as a handsome, well-dressed man rushed through, knocking her off-balance. "Oh, dear. I am so sorry. I didn't hear a knock."

"I hadn't yet," stammered Alice. She looked past the man, into the familiar front hall. Catching a glimpse of her grandparents' faces, their painting still hanging on the wall to the right of the stairs, she collected herself and proceeded with her mission. "My name is Alice Drinkard, and I—"

"Used to live here!" finished the man. "Do come in."

Alice locked eyes with her grandmother, the immutable gaze eerily as frightening as the woman herself. The same furniture as before, but not in the places her mother preferred. At once familiar, yet strangely disorienting. *It's not your house, not anymore*, Alice reminded herself.

"Well, as I said, my name is Alice Drinkard, and this used to be my home. I have returned and now wish to speak with a Mr. Cyrus. I believe he had dealings with my father."

"I am Mr. Cyrus, Mr. Harrison Cyrus."

"Are you sure?"

"Am I sure? Of what, my name or who I am?"

"Well, I understood Mr. Cyrus to be an older gentleman. Not your kind of old, but much older. No matter. Mr. Cyrus, you are the reason I'm here. I've come to fulfill my father's obligations, to settle his debt. I will agree to marry you in exchange for you clearing my father's accounts." She stood to her full height, making eye contact as Thomas had instructed her to when she needed to be particularly aggressive.

Mr. Cyrus chuckled. "What an enticing proposition, extremely appealing indeed." He slowly eyed her, as if she were a meal he wished to devour. "But, alas, I don't think my wife would be pleased if I accepted your offer."

"Your...wife?" Alice had never considered he may already be married. She plopped onto the nearest chair, the ancient wooden legs groaning in protest. Clutching the armrests, Alice stroked the familiar wood, summoning any residual strength her mother may have left behind. With each stroke came new tears.

"Oh, please don't cry. I'm sure you're a lovely lady. You'll find someone. I'm definitely not worthy of weeping. You need simply ask my wife; she'll gladly tell you I'm not the best husband. You can certainly do much better."

"I'm not weeping over you," Alice hiccupped. "It's my father."

"He's still alive?"

"Yes." Thus began a recounting of all the Drinkard family travails, from the moment they left England to her sitting here right now. Thanks to Uncle Willie's goading her to write—and relive—her adventure, Alice enunciated in stark detail precisely what had happened. Once she finished, she asked, "Excuse me for being forthright, but did you ever intend to marry me?"

"Honestly? No, and I was never your intended. I merely wanted someone to represent me, my interests, at James Fort. They required a body, someone to physically be there. I had no intention of going, so I approached your father with a scheme: either marry you to my father or go to Jamestowne. He needed a way out of his debt. I needed a body for James Fort. I thought if given the right incentive, he'd go in my stead. Between marrying you to my father, a man old enough to be your grandfather, who was, quite honestly, a most disagreeable sort of fellow or going to a frontier settlement? Well, you know the choice he made. I'd say things have worked out quite well, for all of us. I have this wonderful home; you're now free to marry whomever you choose as my father is dead; and yours is still alive." He smiled, as only the indulged and spoilt do, with too many teeth and lips pulled tight.

"So I was just a pawn? In a game where only you have prospered? Like my father, you gambled with all our lives. My mother is dead because of this scheme."

"Oh, Harrison, what have you done?" The voice came from the door, a voice both gentle and stern. She walked to the man, then shoved him into a chair. "I'm Daphne, his wife. I've been listening, as my husband doesn't always make sound financial decisions. I assumed you were another of his...but clearly you are not. This scheme, as he called it, is distasteful. After what you have lived through, what your father has lived through, well, it's more than erased his debt. Wouldn't you agree, Harrison?" She kicked his foot as a prompt.

"Yes, dear."

"I suppose you want your house back. We can be out within a month's time."

"No! Absolutely not. I never agreed to let them have this back. I like it here. It's mine. A deal's a deal."

Alice stared at Harrison as he pouted, slouched in the chair like a petulant child.

"Ours, I think you mean. But no, it's not yours or ours. Not now. Not under these circumstances. Besides: my money, my rules," hissed his wife. "I'll not live in an ill-gotten house. We can move back to London, with my father." She smiled for Alice's benefit. "Is a month manageable for you? Do you have somewhere to stay until then?"

Alice regarded the room: the hearth that had kept her warm as she played with dolls; the couch where her mother had read to her; the vase her grandfather brought back from Spain. All items from her past—now merely objects from a bygone time. She no longer needed the objects, no matter the sentimental value; she needed the people that went with them. And living here wouldn't bring any of them back. With the exception of Susanna and Uncle Willie, nothing remained here for her now. No, she understood exactly what she needed to do.

"No. I don't want the house. You can keep it."

Eyeing her suspiciously, Harrison leaned forward. "Then what do you want?"

"I want our shares in the Virginia Company, all of the shares, in my father's name, my name. And I'd like those designated for my mother to be relinquished to my father as well. I think with all we've endured, all we've lost, we've more than earned this as recompense."

Harrison walked to the window, pulling his chin hairs taut. "This request, it's impossible. You see, after I learned the *Sea Venture* had been lost, never completed its mission to Jamestowne, I let my subscription with the Company lapse. There was no point to it. I'd lost my investment. I had no further obligations to fulfill. So, you see, there are no shares, not anymore."

"You lost your investment? You had no *further obligations?*" Alice's voice rose. "We're your obligations! Are you telling me there's nothing? That my father is toiling away in Virginia for naught? That my mother died for nothing?"

"You can't collect anyway. It hasn't been seven years. You aren't entitled to anything."

"Harrison!" snapped Daphne. She turned to Alice, her lips drawn into a tight line, her jaw tight. "I'm sure we can reach some agreement. Certainly there must be something I can do."

"Not you, although I do appreciate your understanding. No, this offer is for your husband, and your husband only. Here's *my* scheme," began

Alice, "go to the Company and pay for our shares; pay what we are owed. Resubscribe. I hear they need money now more than ever; I'm sure they'll overlook your neglected *obligation*—for the right price. Place all the shares in my father's name with the caveat that upon his death, his shares revert to me. Or, you have a month to move out of my house. And you'll need to pay me a year's back rent."

Alice watched as he continued pulling chin hairs, one coming loose in his fingers.

Daphne smiled. "It's a fair deal, Harrison. I'd take it if I were you. Otherwise, you'll have my father to keep you company in the evenings. And you know how he hates...Oh, how shall I put this? Everything about you."

"Fine! You shall have your shares," conceded Harrison.

"He'll go to London tomorrow to take care of this. You have my word." Daphne moved to her husband; placing a hand on his shoulder, she added, "And if you'd like to select some pieces of furniture, I'd be more than happy to ship them to Jamestowne for you. Perhaps this chair?"

Alice had hated that chair since childhood; but now, with her mother gone, it served as a reminder of all she had taken for granted. Alice pictured the last time she saw her mother in the chair, her bracelets clinking as they met its wooden arms. Thinking of the fort, the lack of privacy, the lack of anything to call their own, Alice replied, "Perhaps at a later date, but for now the shares will do." Alice stood to leave, having accomplished her mission of erasing her father's debts, when it occurred to her Mr. Cyrus may be useful for one last thing. "May I share a ride to London with you? I need to sell some ambergris."

Alice walked away from the house, the house she couldn't wait to escape two years ago, the house she held close in her memory like a priceless heirloom while in James Fort, the house she traded for Company shares. While still packed to the rafters with reminders of her once opulent lifestyle, without her parents they lost all meaning. The objects she once believed important were of no value to her now; this house was no longer her home.

The figure once again appeared. Stepping from a grove of oaks, he blocked her path. His pale blue eyes the color of the Bermuda sky; his smile, his playful, lopsided smile, the fresh breeze her soul craved. Running into his arms, she embraced him. She wanted to melt into his skin, pull him to her so tightly they'd meld into a new being. He stroked her hair as he kissed her cheeks.

"I love you, Alfred." Kissing him full on the mouth, Alice poured all her love, grief, and hopes into this one moment, this one gesture she had dreamed of for the duration of her absence.

He smiled as their lips parted. "I love you too. I always have. But why wouldn't you see me? Talk to me? I thought I'd never see you again. I thought you were killed in the shipwreck. Then here you are! But you didn't even acknowledge me. I thought perhaps you'd married another. That's why you wouldn't speak to me. You haven't, have you? Married another?"

"I just kissed you and told you I loved you, you idiot! What kind of woman marries one man and tells another she loves him? No. It's nothing like that."

"Then tell me what it is like," he cooed, his hands circling her waist.

"It's much more complicated than I can explain just now. But—" She stopped, her lips curling into a smile. "But what if I told you I could explain it over a lifetime? Would you be willing to listen? To an explanation lasting a lifetime?"

Alfred narrowed his eyes.

"What say ye to a lifetime of talking? What say ye, Alfred Marshall, to marrying me?"

Scooping her off the ground, Alfred swung Alice around in a circle, whooping so loud a flock of birds flew from a nearby tree. Setting her down, he kissed her.

"It would be my honor to marry you," he said, beaming.

"Then let it be known, that on the twenty-sixth of November, in the year of our Lord 1610, Miss Alice Drinkard and Mr. Alfred Marshall did betroth themselves to one another." Laughing, Alice remembered Elizabeth and Thomas, their ease and happiness with one another. She hoped they were still as in love as they were when they married exactly one year ago.

While she couldn't share her joyous news with her friend, she could share a special day nonetheless. Remembering the blue dress her mother had made for her, the blue satin gown still tucked away in the trunk at the foot of her bed, she took Alfred's hand. "I already have my dress. And Uncle Willie knows a man who can marry us. Tonight, then?"

Chapter 28
Returning to Jamestowne, March 1611

Alice took one last look around the room: the room she'd spent so much time in as a young girl, hiding from her mother with dear Susanna; the room where she'd found her voice as a young woman, as she traversed the minefield of grief and guilt; and, ultimately, the room where she'd rediscovered her resolve and set a course for her future, sharing a bed with her husband. A lifetime ago, a young girl had wantonly thrown a fit over a yellow dress, as if that was all that mattered in the world. *You were such a selfish, stupid girl*, she admonished her former self. Looking to her hands, at the manicured cuticles, the clean white nails, she saw her mother's hands.

"Oh, Mother," she whispered to the empty room. "I miss you so much—so much more than I ever imagined possible." Her fingers moved along the chain around her neck; finding the smooth, cool metal of the locket her mother had kept safe, she delicately placed the locket between her thumb and forefinger, stroking it like a talisman. Her cheeks burned as she reflected on her former self. Angry. Selfish. Unfair. "I have a lot to apologize for, as you well know. I was a querulous child. An irksome being who tried your patience at every turn. I am grateful you never saw fit to thrash me as I deserved, and I mean to make amends with my actions as a woman. I will take care of Father—for you. No. For us. I promise. And, if you can hear me, I never meant to hurt you. And I am so, so dreadfully sorry I left you to die alone. For that I will pay penance all my life."

Standing motionless in the doorway, hand on the door latch, Alice trained her eyes on capturing the essence of the room. The gleaming wood panels of the walls; the smell of fresh-cut lavender; the desk where she'd finally compiled her memories of her time on the Isle of Devils and the journey to Jamestowne. On the desktop, she left the journal for Uncle Willie in the hopes it would help him complete his play, *The Tempest*. With the words purged from her soul, she didn't care what became of them.

Alice took in the finality of it all. She would never again see this place; she sensed it in every fiber of her being. She would never again sit for hours talking with Susanna. She would never again discuss another of Uncle Willie's plays as he paced the floors talking himself through lines. But this time, leaving felt like the right thing to do; there was no more unfinished business here. It was her choice, and her choice alone.

Choice. The word echoed through her brain. She was her own person now; she owed no one anything. She had Alfred, and now it was her turn to do what her father could not: save the family.

Choice. A concept she'd clung to as they had boarded the *Sea Venture*; the elusive idea she would be able to do as she pleased, when she pleased, without any restrictions once she was an adult. Or free from her parents. But as she'd learned over the past two years, choice doesn't always present itself as choosing a desirable thing over a not-so-desirable thing. What she understood now, that she hadn't then, was that choice had a flip-side, that of responsibility and consequence.

Unlike the first time, when her father believed the Company had their best interest at heart, and instructed his family to pack according to their directions, she would arrive in Jamestowne equipped with more than a new gown and kid-skin gloves. This time, she packed her trunk with practical items: seeds for a vegetable garden, dried meat, and two pistols—items to ensure their survival, hers and her father's. *And Alfred's*, she reminded herself. *Her family*. She would return to her father's side in Jamestowne with Alfred, and she would have to be the strong one now. Alfred had no idea of what they were facing when they arrived in Jamestowne. But she did. And what of her father? Assuming he was still alive, which she had to believe until proven otherwise, he would need two things: help navigating his grief over losing Maude and strong arms to work. She could provide both.

Returning to Jamestowne was no longer an adventure; it was a choice and an opportunity. And it was hers.

⚓

Alice stood on the deck of the *Hercules* as it slipped its moorings and escaped Plymouth. She inhaled the salty air and tilted her face to the sun.

"It's very hot, is it not?" asked Alfred. "Don't you worry your nose will overly pink?"

"No, not anymore," said Alice. "The sun is a luxury I won't waste while we're on board. And if you think this is hot, then Jamestowne will be a most unpleasant surprise. Even when it's not hot, the humidity will make you sweat in places you didn't even know you had."

"So you have said." Taking her hand, Alfred looked to the stern. After several minutes of trying to find his words, with the false starts and stops of one afraid of feelings, he finally spoke. "I think it's very brave you came and got me. I thought you didn't want me, especially after I proposed, and your father..." he hesitated "...explained why I'm not the right sort of husband for someone like you."

"You were foolish for only asking my father. Had I known you'd asked, I would have eloped that same night."

"But I wanted your father's permission; I thought it necessary, the proper thing to do. I truly believed if he saw me asking for his blessing, he wouldn't care if I was just the blacksmith's son."

"I don't think he'll see things that way anymore. And if he does, he won't mind once he realizes I've managed to secure all the shares he is owed—doubled, in fact, thanks to Daphne. We're free now, no need to toil for seven years to pay back the debt. We own our lives outright! Besides, we're married, and I'm alive." She paused, reflecting on how her views of her father had also changed over the last two years. "I have told you some of my story in the New World, but not all. My father learned a lot about how power corrupts even good men, and how one little untruth can ruin a person's life. I think he made you feel bad about your status because he was uncomfortable with his. For a variety of reasons. I think in the time we had together, he learned to love again. After my brother's death, he tried to stop feeling because it hurt too much. As a result, he fell into some less than desirable habits, made some bad decisions, decisions that ultimately changed our lives forever. But that was a lifetime ago; we have all changed, and the man you will meet—God willing he's still alive—no longer has much in common with the one you encountered previously. I think the man you will meet is one with whom you will have much in common. He's humble. Practical. Thoughtful. He learned to be his own man, in the end. At least that was the father I left. I pray he is still there. And alive."

Alive. The word danced in her mind. How was she to tell him his wife and unborn child weren't? Three of them left, and she was the only one returning.

"But you haven't changed. Not really."

"I have; at least, I feel like I have. I understand people more. I understand things are never as they seem, even when things are going well. I feel more mature now. More...something. I'm not sure how to define it."

"Determined," Alfred finished. "Before, when you were younger, I loved your carefree nature. You refused to be told what to do, even when it was something you wanted. Now, I love your determination. I love your forthrightness. You are one high-spirited woman. That has never changed, and I hope it never does. It scares me a little—I shan't lie—but I do love it when you're forceful." He pinched her waist. "And you know what I love most of all? You. I love you, Alice Drinkard Marshall." As he leaned his head down to kiss her, Alice closed her eyes, anticipating the warmth of his lips on hers.

"You there!" yelled a man to the rear. "Stop that this instant! I don't allow such behavior on my ship. Have you no shame, woman?"

Alice jumped away from Alfred. The man approached, his stride all too familiar. Could it be?

"Ah, what would the Admiral say about his girl messing about with a man?" he laughed.

"Captain Newport!" Alice embraced the captain, his presence a welcome sight. "Well, Alfred, I feel safer already. This is the finest navigator to ever cross the Atlantic. I've sailed with him on every voyage I've ever taken, and I'm not dead yet! Please allow me to introduce Captain

Christopher Newport. Captain Newport, this is my husband, Alfred."

Alfred took in the man with one arm. His height. His smile. His booming voice. The man who oozed mischief and confidence. Alfred bowed his acknowledgement, unsure of how to proceed as shaking hands seemed inappropriate.

"Ah, the Admiral would be so happy to see ye on the ship again. Proof he was right. Ye aren't one easily scared off." He laughed.

"Are the rumors true?" asked Alice. "Did he really die on Bermuda?"

"Aye, I'm afraid so. His nephew brought his body back." He shrugged. "For the most part."

"For the most part?"

"Yes. Seems the old sea dog wished to remain on the island, but his nephew needed to prove he was dead. Some business about inheritance or what not. So, there was a compromise to appease both men. The Admiral's heart is buried on the island, and his nephew pickled his body and returned with it to England."

Alice laughed.

"Alice, a man is dead, with a most gruesome deed inflicted upon his corpse," chided Alfred.

"No. He was my friend for decades," said Newport. "I think he would have appreciated the practicality of the...situation. Quite ingenious, albeit a tad unsavory."

Thinking of her friend made Alice smile. "I miss him," she said.

"Aye, we all do," replied Newport. "But I do take comfort in knowing he is, for all eternity, in the one place he was happiest. Now, if I may take my leave. I have a ship to sail." Hugging Alice once more, he squeezed her shoulders as the Admiral had done. "Please, feel free to join me for meals. And Alfred, take good care of our girl. She's a special one." He winked and strode to the officers' quarters.

"She certainly is," said Alfred, leaning in to kiss Alice's cheek. "And she's my wife."

Author's Notes

"Hey, Bermuda Hundred has GPS coordinates…it's about 30 miles from here."

"Let's do it!"

A road trip with a dear friend. An unplanned excursion. A family origin story. Thus began my wild ride to writing this story.

I knew my father's family was, supposedly, at Bermuda Hundred in 1613. But rather than tracking down records to see if this were true, I spent my time looking into why there was a place with Bermuda in the name…in Virginia…in the early 1600s. I learned why on the day I followed those online GPS coordinates.

I learned, from the two historical markers placed at the site where Bermuda Hundred once existed, that a ship named the *Sea Venture* had wrecked on Bermuda en route to a frontier settlement we know as Jamestowne. According to the signage, this shipwreck inspired William Shakespeare (yes, that guy) to write *The Tempest*. I was hooked.

I began researching the *Sea Venture*, studied the layout of the ship (or rather, what marine archeologists think it looked like, as no definitive schematic of it exists). I read why the James Company sent this one last fleet to save an embattled English settlement. I became enchanted with the castaways' adventures on Bermuda, known then as the Isle of Devils. I read and re-read William Strachey's account on the island. What I discovered was a story only half told.

Using William Strachey's book, *The True Repertory of the Wreck and Redemption of Sir Thomas Gates, Knight*, as a guide, as biased as it is (his goal is stated clearly in the title), it's the most comprehensive primary source we have for life on the island in 1609-1610. In the end, it was his omission of the women present that prompted me to write their story. How do I know they were present, you may ask? Because according to Strachey's own account, of the four women mentioned: one got married and two gave birth. He named himself the godfather for crying out loud! But both infants died there, as well as one woman. No exact dates are given and only one woman is named with her given first name. They needed closure, so I gave it to them. Although Alice, her parents, and the Cyruses are complete fabrications, all other characters were real. As for other pieces of research I altered:

I left out one incident and two indigenous men because of the callous way the only two persons of color were portrayed. They deserve their own story, not relegation to a subplot.

I changed a few names for clarity. As someone who comes from a family filled with people with the same name, I wasn't doing that to my readers.

I tweaked a few dates and added a few more for specificity.

I altered the location of the camps and cook fires for narrative flow.

While my story is grounded in historical evidence, this is, after all, a fictional account of life on the island as told from the perspective of a sixteen-year-old young woman. I attempted to keep this perspective, as well as maintain the understanding that these castaways were unaware of what was happening in Jamestowne at the time (the Starving Time). For ten months, they were completely cut-off from the world. That's what I had to keep foremost in my mind as I was writing. It's hard for us in 2024 to imagine a world where there is no communication, no updates, no cell phones, but that's the world I shared with Alice while writing this novel. They knew nothing about what was happening in Jamestowne, and were genuinely surprised when they arrived...as was the rest of the planet when it was discovered they had survived.

This is a work of fiction. If you happen to learn something, excellent. If you're looking for history and wish to know what books or websites I referenced, please visit my website. I share my research there.

Acknowledgements

This novel wouldn't have seen the light of day were it not for the support of family and friends. This is my weak attempt to publicly acknowledge them, as words can never express how much I love and appreciate them in my life. Life with a writer is not for the faint of heart. I have conversations with imaginary people, even as I'm in the midst of conversations with real people. I often suddenly stop an activity to write out an idea before it gets away. I may not seem to be in the moment with the people I love, but I am. Here is to the people who understand this...and still invite me into their lives.

To Tammy Smith for patience and a willingness to play my lame made-up games of "What If" and "How Would You React." And then recognizing what I really need is to walk and get ice cream.

To Betti Kreye, the best aunt anyone could have. Without her insights, humor, and endless stash of Skinny Pop and Klondike bars, I'd still be staring at the words on the screen, afraid to put them into the ether. Trust me when I say she's magic in human form.

To my dad, for making me explain, "What were you thinking?" continuously as a child and teen. I didn't come from a family that believed in spanking. Instead, I had to explain, and later write, why I behaved as did. (By the way, saying *I don't know* is not an appropriate response.) At the time of the incidents (yes, plural), I would have preferred any punishment over having to figure out why I did what I did. It was grueling; however, it forced me to examine motivation and a host of other psychological processes that have benefitted me in life. As a writer, it provided the framework for evaluating character motivation. Thanks, dad! You've created a monster. Love you!

To Regina Phillips, my sister from another mister, and the preferred child of my mother. I knew you understood me when you gave me a journal, decades ago, with the inscription, "...it's time we got out into the world and set it on its ear. Then you can write it all down for us to read when we're too old to remember it." And just like that: we took off to parts unknown. Thank you for creating space for me to write when we travel, for agreeing to participate in my shenanigans, and helping me extract just the right word. Mellifluous!

To my partner Carl. You've lived with my stories for decades, seeing their worth even before I did. You willingly and selflessly listen to my ideas, then respectfully retreat when I'm in the zone and need to be left alone. You've helped me embrace my process; never rushing or assuming, just calmly waiting for me to find my own way, regardless of where we are. (Thanks for the pictures! I honestly never realized how often I sit and write.) Your encouragement to just go for it, to take the leap from education to full-time writer was spot-on, and I'm glad you're on this adventure with me. Love you 11!

To the two women who transitioned to the other side before this book was written, yet are still an inspiration: my mother for insisting I could be anything I wanted; and my grandmother Matt for pushing me to write letters so vivid she could see what I saw on my travels.

And finally, a special thanks to: the historical interpreters at Jamestown Settlement and Historic Jamestowne; my Beta Readers, especially Scarlett Alcorn; editors, Sarah Dronfield and Rachael Mortimer; book designers Joanne Morgante and Roberto Magini at Maxtudio; author assistant Stephanie Caruso at Paste Creative; Elaine Schroller and Karen Chase, indie-pub gurus who are the embodiment of women supporting women. Thank you. Thank you. Thank you.

And you—the reader. Out of thousands of books, you chose mine. Thank you.

About the Author

Inspired by her students, and her fervent love of travel, Elisabeth Carson-Williams thrives on meeting new people and hearing their stories. This, coupled with her own desire to understand her family's history, led her to write historical fiction, to capture the themes and voices of those not found in a textbook. "Ricochet," her short story in *Feisty Deeds: Historical Fictions of Daring Women* anthology, is about the quiet battles women fight in order to survive, and how one person's actions can ricochet through multiple generations. *Castaway on the Isle of Devils* is her first young adult novel.

To learn more about Elisabeth's publishing journey, writing process, and research trips, or sign up for her newsletter, visit: www.ecarsonwilliams.com.